PRAISE FOR LIZZIE SHANE AND THE PINE HOLLOW SERIES

PRIDE & PUPPIES

"Entertaining subplots add zest to this sweet tale. Thoroughly saturated with Austen allusions, this cute contemporary is sure to charm."　　—*Publishers Weekly*

TO ALL THE DOGS I'VE LOVED BEFORE

"Adorable second chance romance."　　—*Publishers Weekly*

ONCE UPON A PUPPY

"The endearing characters will capture readers' hearts from the first page…It's hard not to fall in love with this spirited tale."
　　　　　　　　　　　　　　　—*Publishers Weekly*

"Could not put it down…Beautifully written."
　　　　　　　　　　　　　　　—Harlequin Junkie

THE TWELVE DOGS OF CHRISTMAS

"Just right for animal lovers seeking a seasonal happily ever after." —*Publishers Weekly*

FOUR
WEDDINGS
AND A
PUPPY

FOUR WEDDINGS

AND A PUPPY

PUPPY

Lizzie Shane

FOREVER

New York Boston

Copyright © 2023 by Lizzie Shane

Cover art and design by Sarah Congdon. Cover copyright © 2023 by Hachette Book Group, Inc.

Forever
Hachette Book Group
1290 Avenue of the Americas, New York, NY 10104
read-forever.com
twitter.com/readforeverpub

First Edition: November 2023

Forever is an imprint of Grand Central Publishing. The Forever name and logo are trademarks of Hachette Book Group, Inc.

The publisher is not responsible for websites (or their content) that are not owned by the publisher.

The Hachette Speakers Bureau provides a wide range of authors for speaking events. To find out more, go to hachettespeakersbureau.com or email HachetteSpeakers@hbgusa.com.

Forever books may be purchased in bulk for business, educational, or promotional use. For information, please contact your local bookseller or the Hachette Book Group Special Markets Department at special.markets@hbgusa.com.

Print book interior design by Marie Mundaca

Library of Congress Cataloging-in-Publication Data
Names: Shane, Lizzie, author.
Title: Four weddings and a puppy / Lizzie Shane.
Description: First edition. | New York : Forever, 2023. | Series: Pine Hollow
Identifiers: LCCN 2023026144 | ISBN 9781538710340 (trade paperback) |
    ISBN 9781538710364 (ebook)
Subjects: LCGFT: Romance fiction. | Novels.
Classification: LCC PS3619.H35457 F68 2023 |
    DDC 813/.6—dc23/eng/20230609
LC record available at https://lccn.loc.gov/2023026144

ISBNs: 978-1-5387-1034-0 (trade paperback), 978-1-5387-1036-4 (ebook)

Printed in the United States of America

LSC-C

Printing 1, 2023

For my folks, who put me on my first pair of skis when I was still in preschool. Thank you for all the mountain memories, and for always encouraging me to chase my dreams.

CONTENT WARNING

This book contains references to a suicide that occurred prior to the events of the story. If you or someone you know is in crisis, call 988 to reach the Suicide and Crisis Lifeline.

Amanda Bailey Jenner,

daughter of Dr. Rupert & Mrs. Emilia Jenner

and Mr. Frederick & Mrs. Kathleen Kennedy,

and

Anne Elizabeth Rodriguez,

daughter of Mr. Matias Rodriguez and the late
Emily Laughlin Rodriguez,

request the honor of your presence

at their wedding

on the sixth of January,

at four o'clock in the afternoon

Pine Hollow Mountain Resort

Pine Hollow, Vermont

Dinner & dancing to follow

Black tie optional.

Chapter One

There comes a point in every wedding planner's life when she finds herself chasing an escaped golden retriever across a ballroom, futilely trying to reach him before he takes a swan dive into the five-tier wedding cake.

Or maybe that was only Kendall's life.

It was like some scene from a wedding movie designed to make the audience cringe—but it was a lot less entertaining when it was *her* disaster.

As the golden menace launched himself at the cake, his tongue flapping gleefully out of the side of his mouth, Kendall lunged forward—along with half a dozen guests with outstretched hands, as if they were trying to stop time or freeze the dog with telekinesis.

She saw her wedding planning career flashing before her eyes—which admittedly was a short replay. The ski resort had never been much of a wedding venue. But she'd been so sure she could do this.

Five minutes ago, she'd been standing at the back of the

ballroom in a sleeveless black pantsuit and a French twist, hold-ing a tablet and trying to be invisible and approachable at the same time. On a dais forty feet away, the father of one of the two brides had been crying his way through his toast.

It really had been a sweet moment. There hadn't been a dry eye in the house. Except Kendall's.

Even if she'd been the type to feel all sappy at weddings—which she absolutely wasn't—she'd been too busy scanning the ballroom for potential mishaps and making sure the staff whisk-ing away the dinner plates were doing so in a suitably unobtru-sive manner.

Everything needed to be perfect.

This wasn't just a wedding. It was an audition. Her chance to get out of conference purgatory. To show her father that the resort should be courting more wedding business.

Kendall didn't have a romantic bone in her body. Which made her quite possibly the least likely wedding planner on the face of the planet, but she'd learned long ago that sometimes life took an unexpected turn and all you could do was hang on and ride it out.

Destination weddings were a big business in Vermont. The resort's massive ballroom with its two-story curved windows and attached veranda provided jaw-dropping views of the sur-rounding snow-covered mountains. It appealed to conference organizers for its sheer size, but it could be a gold mine as a reception venue. Maybe even a way to get the resort far enough into the black that they could hire more help and she could finally take some time off.

All she'd needed was perfection.

So she'd been scanning the room, on guard for anything that might develop into a problem if left unchecked.

Orchestrating a flawlessly timed meal for 275 guests had felt a bit like trying to turn water into wine, but they'd done it. Dinner plates were being cleared. Champagne flutes were being deftly topped up. The toasts would be wrapping up soon. The brides would open the dancing, and then it would just be cake cutting and keeping the smiles on everyone's faces for the rest of the night. As far as her staff were concerned, the hard part would be over.

But then she'd seen him.

Furry, golden chaos in canine form.

Banner.

Kendall adored dogs. She *wanted* a dog. She just didn't have time to commit to one long term. So fostering Banner until he found his new home had seemed like a nice compromise between her wants and the realities of her life.

Unfortunately, her best friend Charlotte had left out one or two things when she'd suckered Kendall into fostering the demon dog.

Like the fact that the eleven-month-old golden retriever had been returned to the shelter by two different families after chewing through three cellphones, five pairs of designer shoes, and one couch in the last six months. Or that he was a canine pinball, constantly in motion, and a giant klutz who hadn't gotten used to the length of his gangly legs and ran into things constantly—when he wasn't chewing the furniture.

He'd seemed so sweet and harmless when Charlotte brought him to Kendall's doorstep—but he'd also been three-quarters asleep after playing with Charlotte's dog all afternoon. Kendall's heart had gone out to the little guy with his big black puppy dog eyes. She'd hated that the people who'd promised to love him had given up on him the second things got hard.

But after only eight days of fostering, she was now certain

the only reason he was called Banner was because naming him Hulk Smash would have been too on the nose.

He was an adorable furry wrecking ball.

And someone had left one of the double doors to the lobby open wide enough for him to get in.

Spotting him, Kendall had jerked to attention so fast that her back twinged.

One of the ski instructors was supposed to be distracting the energetic puppy and keeping him far away from the wedding guests, but she should have known if there was an opportunity for trouble somewhere on the resort property, Banner would find it.

As the golden puppy had made a beeline for the nearest table, Kendall moved quickly to intercept, trying to keep her movements calm and restrained—both to avoid spooking the dog and so no one at the head table had reason to wonder why the resort's wedding planner was chasing a golden tail through the distant-cousins-and-work-acquaintances tables.

He'd moved through the back tables, leaving a ripple of murmurs in his wake—though thankfully the reactions had seemed to be more "Oh look! A dog!" than alarm. He'd wagged his tail eagerly as he veered from mark to mark, looking for someone to beg food off of.

The dog was extremely food motivated, but Kendall didn't have his treat bag to shake as she edged along the side of the ballroom, so she'd paused long enough to set down her tablet and grab a dinner roll off a bus tray.

"Banner!" Kendall shout-whispered as Bailey's brother took the microphone to begin his best man toast.

The dog had glanced in her direction—and then performed evasive maneuvers around table eighteen.

"Banner!" Kendall tried again, a little louder, wagging the roll in his direction. At that point, the brides hadn't yet noticed the kamikaze golden retriever on a mission to destroy all of Kendall's hard work from the past several months, but it was only a matter of time.

"Is that Bingley? Here, Bingley!" one of the aunties at table nine cooed, mistaking the troublemaker for his littermate, Charlotte's perfectly behaved angel puppy. Charlotte's aunt extended her hand—which Banner mistook as an invitation to play, crouching and wagging his tail before romping away.

Kendall smiled at Charlotte's aunt as she tried to give chase without looking like she was giving chase. With the toasts directing everyone's attention toward the bridal table, so far only a handful of the guests seem to have noticed the furry wedding crasher, and she'd been trying to keep it that way.

"Banner!" Kendall hissed, creeping closer, but the best man's toast ended in that moment and everyone in the room rose to toast the brides, sending the dog into spins of excitement. "Come here!"

He leapt in little circles, zigging and zagging. She could almost grab him—

And then a cellphone rang. Banner's siren song. Someone had left their phone out on the dessert table, and it had called the food-obsessed dog's attention toward the magnificent wedding cake on display there.

His head had perked up, ears twitching forward—and Kendall's heart had dropped to the bottom of her chest.

"No no no no no." She'd given up on stealth as Banner suddenly bolted across the open dance floor, straight for the glorious five-tiered lemon raspberry masterpiece from Magda's Bakery.

Kendall needed everything to be perfect. Which did *not*

include a dog she was responsible for demolishing that tower of buttercream perfection.

She'd sprinted after him—but he was fast and he had a head start.

Gasps and shouts rippled through the room as the wedding guests caught on to the imminent destruction of the cake.

She could see it all happening in slow motion—the dog building up speed, the cake looming ahead.

Back when she'd been a professional athlete, her brain would click into a different mode: race mode. Everything would slow down and get a little sharper, a little brighter. She didn't often find herself in that mode anymore, when everything was instinct and reaction and it all felt so clear—but she clicked into it now.

At the head table, the brides rose, clasping one another's hands, and Kendall caught sight of Charlotte, seated next to her sister as part of the bridal party, her face twisted into an almost comical mask of horror. More guests were surging to their feet—the entirety of table two making it nearly impossible for Kendall to see Banner, let alone reach him in time.

She'd *needed* this.

And she certainly didn't want to ruin the lovely wedding of two lovely people by splattering them with buttercream shrapnel after a puppy grenade landed in the middle of their cake.

Kendall shouted a pointless *"Noooo!"* along with two-thirds of the occupants of the ballroom.

Banner soared through the air—

And slammed into a solid chest in a fitted gray vest.

Kendall hadn't seen him move, but somehow the tall man in the charcoal vest caught the squirming puppy in the nick of time.

A cheer echoed through the ballroom, but Kendall didn't

join in. She was too mortified—and too busy rushing to help the man in the charcoal vest before Banner could wriggle free.

She grabbed Banner's collar, fully focused on the dog and trying to figure out what she could fashion into a leash to get him out of here—though it was hard not to notice the arms holding the dog.

The man was *fit*. Not surprising, since he was the only one who'd managed to move faster than a speeding golden retriever. The event was black tie, but he'd taken off his suit jacket and rolled up his sleeves. Tanned forearms flexed as he hefted Banner's wiggly weight, getting little white-gold hairs all over his perfectly fitted vest.

"Thank you," Kendall said, still looking around for something leash-like. "You just saved my life."

"And here I thought I just saved dessert."

At the laughter rumbling in his voice—that familiar sound—Kendall looked up at his face, actually *looked* at him for the first time.

Recognition kicked her hard in the chest, forcing out a gasp.

He had a beard now. His trademark sun-streaked curls were gone, his sandy brown hair seeming darker when it was short like this and gelled up in some fancy style that probably took hours to complete, but damn if it wasn't worth every second. Sophisticated. Like a box of luxury chocolates. The man was pure eye candy.

But then he'd always been.

And the laughing blue eyes were exactly the same.

His name floated out on a breath. *"Brody."*

He grinned, those straight white teeth that had actually been on a toothpaste commercial flashing out of his neatly trimmed beard. "Hey, Speed Demon. Been a while."

Brody James. Pride of Vermont. Two-time Winter Olympian. Four-time medalist.

Her childhood best friend. Her brother's *current* best friend. Her first crush.

And the man who was the walking example of what her life could have been, if one awful fraction of a second hadn't changed everything.

"What are you doing here?" She shook her head, dismissing the question before he had a chance to answer. "Never mind. Here. Give him to me."

She had no idea what to feel when she looked at Brody anymore—but she didn't have time to feel any of it. She needed to get Banner out of here before he got any more white-golden fur all over Brody's perfectly fitted charcoal vest.

And then hopefully she'd find some way to erase the last five minutes from the memories of everyone in the room.

Kendall thrust out her arms for the dog, only realizing she was still holding the dinner roll when Banner lunged for it.

"Whoa," Brody chuckled, catching Banner when the dog would have tumbled out of his oh-so-capable arms.

Other wedding guests were gathering around, patting Brody on the back and gushing about his heroism. It was about to become even more of a spectacle.

The absolute last thing Kendall needed when the guests left was everyone talking about how the Pine Hollow Mountain Resort weddings featured rowdy dogs who nearly ruined everything. This wedding was supposed to be their freaking calling card.

And Brody was just *standing* there, holding the squirming dog in his stupidly gorgeous arms in the middle of the dance floor.

"Do you have a leash?" he asked, and Kendall badly wanted to snap, *If I had a leash, don't you think I would have used it?*

Instead, she kept her voice calm and wedding-planner smooth. "I don't. I'll just carry him. Here."

She gave Banner the roll and tried to take him, but Brody hitched him up higher—and he was enough taller than she was that it made it impossible for her to get the gangly puppy from him without making an even bigger scene. "I can carry him," he insisted. "Where do you want him?"

Kendall rapidly weighed the satisfaction of arguing with him against the virtue of getting Banner away from the other guests—and the cake—as quickly as humanly possible.

"Way to use those quick Olympic reflexes, Brody!" one of Bailey's uncles called out—and Kendall officially tipped in favor of *get the hell out of here.*

"Fine," she said briskly. "Let's go."

She started toward the closest service door, but Charlotte was suddenly there in her powder-blue Regency-style brides-maid dress, blocking their path. "Is that Banner? Bingley's supposed to be at George's—"

"It's Banner," Kendall confirmed, proud of herself that she refrained from adding, *The demon dog you conned me into fostering.* "And the sooner everyone forgets he exists, the better. Do you have some magical distraction that can erase the last five minutes from everyone's brains while we get him out of here?"

At the *we* Charlotte's curious gaze moved to Brody, still holding the dog, and her eyes flared wide with recognition. "Brody. Hi."

She was staring—but then Charlotte knew *all* about Kendall's inappropriate teenage crush, and all the other emotions she'd pinned on an oblivious Brody over the years.

"Charlotte. Distraction?" Kendall prompted.

Charlotte snapped to attention. "Right. On it. I'll shove a microphone in Elinor's face and make her sing a song for the happy couple. No one will remember anything about a dog."

That might actually work. Charlotte's oldest sister, Elinor, had one of those voices that could have been on the radio, if she hadn't been happier as a small-town librarian. Her karaoke performances were legendary.

"Thank you." Kendall squeezed Charlotte's hand, jerked her chin at Brody for him to follow her, and beelined toward the nearest exit.

Thankfully, no one else tried to intercept them. She pushed through into the bright white service hallway—and her anxiety level dropped fifty percent as soon as the door closed between them and the wedding.

Everything's fine.

She was just going to keep telling herself that until it was true.

"Do I know Charlotte?" Brody asked as Banner wriggled more frantically to be let down. Brody shifted him in his arms, cradling him with one big hand rubbing his belly. The dog instantly settled down, going limp in his arms and gazing adoringly up at the source of the pets.

"One of my best friends, Charlotte Rodriguez," Kendall explained, eyeing a couple napkins on a rack to see if she could MacGyver them into a leash. "Also, sister of Anne, one of the brides." She grabbed the napkins and looked back at him, frowning as she began to knot them together. "Why are you here?"

"The other bride. Bailey's my stepcousin."

"No, why are you *here*? Aren't you supposed to be in Switzerland or the Italian Alps? Isn't there a World Cup competition this weekend?"

Her attention was on the napkins she was tying, but she looked up when he didn't immediately respond. He opened his mouth, something complicated shifting across his face, before his high-wattage movie-star smile flashed back on his face so brightly she almost convinced herself she must have been imagining his hesitation.

"I'm just taking a little time off," he said, still absently rubbing Banner's tummy. "Rehabbing the knee."

"You okay?" Kendall glanced automatically down at his leg, but none of the old injury was visible beneath his perfectly fitted trousers.

"Yeah. You know how it is." He shifted his leg back, almost like he didn't want her looking at it.

She had the strangest sense that he was lying—but that didn't make any sense. And she didn't need to be staring at his legs. She pulled her attention back to adding another napkin to the chain before she got caught ogling her old crush. "You should put him down," she said. "Carting Banner around can't be good for it."

"I'm fine," he insisted.

"Don't play macho and make your recovery worse." She yanked a knot tight. "You should get back anyway. My office is close. I'll take him in a sec," she said, nearly done jury-rigging a leash out of stray linen.

"You have an office here?"

Her face heated. "Didn't Kev say? I work at the resort. Staffing and events."

"Oh…" His brow furrowed, something distinctly pitying in his eyes.

Yes, she'd run home with her tail between her legs and never left, but did he have to look at her like that? Brody, whose life had always been so freaking perfect. "You can set down the dog."

"I can help you find the owner—"

"I'm the owner. At least this week. I'm fostering. Look, just—" Kendall broke off, gathering herself with a deep breath. Had Brody always been this aggravating, or was it just the fact that she hated the idea of him seeing what her life was like right now that made it so excruciating for him to keep *standing* there, petting the dog and asking her questions?

"I really need this wedding to go well," she explained with forced calm. "So I would appreciate it if you would just brush the dog hair off your two-thousand-dollar suit, go back out there, and pretend none of this happened. Consider it a personal favor to your friendly neighborhood wedding planner."

"I can't wrap my head around you as a wedding planner."

"Yeah, well, life's full of surprises."

She'd never been the hearts-and-flowers type—the Kendall Walsh who'd tried to jump her bike across the Woodland quarry when she was eight and eloped on a dare at twenty-three had been more of a risk-taker than a romantic. But she wasn't that girl anymore.

Banner tried to do a backflip out of Brody's arms, and Brody set him down before he could hurt himself, keeping a firm hand on his collar. Kendall quickly took her own grip, attempting to tie on her leash.

"I've got him," she insisted, refusing to look at Brody's face so close to hers. His aftershave smelled freaking *incredible*—which was frankly irritating. Did he have to be so damn perfect?

"I can help—"

"I've *got* him," she snapped.

"Okay." Brody straightened and she gave her napkin-leash a firm tug to make sure it was going to hold before following suit. The man was ridiculously tall, so her gaze hit two inches below his collarbone—where his vest was *covered* in white-gold hair.

"Oh God, you're a mess." She automatically swiped at the hair—and his rock-hard muscles tightened beneath her hand. Kendall jerked her hand back, reminding herself that she did *not* need to be petting Brody James. "Sorry."

"It's fine. It's just a little hair."

Her face was hot enough to roast marshmallows, but Brody, in typical Brody fashion, was utterly oblivious to the fact that touching him might give her feels. He'd never seen her that way, and it didn't look like he was about to start now.

"I guess I'll see you out there, Speed Demon," he said with that same easy, carefree smile he'd always had—and Kendall nearly flinched as he repeated the old nickname.

She wasn't that person anymore. She hadn't been that person in a long time. Right now, she was just the one who needed to find a place to stash the dog and get back to the wedding before anything else went wrong.

And the absolute last thing she needed was to spend any more time being reminded of who she might have been in another life.

She jerked her chin in farewell. "See you around, Brody. Enjoy the wedding."

Chapter Two

Kendall Walsh hadn't changed a bit.

Her blond hair still looked like sunshine—and she still had that ever-present grumpy frown line between her eyebrows to warn the world that they should assume she was sunny at their own risk.

And Brody still couldn't resist grinning in the face of that semipermanent glower.

God, it was good to see her.

He'd wanted to talk to her longer. He could easily have spent the entire night in that service hallway with her, but he'd gotten the distinct impression that she couldn't wait to get rid of him.

Kendall had never been subtle.

Brody returned to the ballroom in time to join the standing ovation for Anne's sister, who had brought both brides to tears with her rendition of "Time After Time." Which did seem to have helped distract people somewhat from the surprise guest appearance of one overgrown puppy.

He made his way back to table eight but had to pause several times to accept handshakes and pats on the back on the way—so maybe the puppy incident wasn't completely forgotten. But he did his best to downplay it, since Kendall very clearly didn't want it to be a thing. Though he didn't know why. People loved stories like that. They'd be telling their friends they saw Brody James save a cake from a runaway puppy for months.

"Hail, the conquering hero," his sister, Steph, drawled as he reclaimed his seat, raising her champagne glass in a toast.

"I've never seen anyone move that fast!" gasped one of his cousins, whom Brody hadn't seen since he was seventeen. His voice a little too loud, his eyes carrying the awestruck glimmer of a superfan. "Must be those Olympic reflexes!"

"Must be," Steph confirmed, meeting his eyes with a glint of humor in hers—as if she knew that he'd already heard that phrase three times in the last ten minutes.

Steph always seemed to find it hysterical when people were in awe of him, and he hadn't realized how much he'd missed that reality check. He'd been away from home a lot these last few years. Hell, the last decade.

No wonder members of his own family were treating him like a visiting celebrity. None of them really knew him anymore.

He hadn't planned to be back for this wedding. Nothing about this trip had been planned or thought out. It had all been impulse. Reaction. He'd arrived back in the States four days ago and scored a last-minute invite to Bailey's massive spectacle of a wedding, grateful for the distraction.

He'd thought he could come to the wedding, see some family, do the chicken dance, and soak up some normalcy. Maybe get his head on straight. Figure out his next steps.

But his plan to fly beneath the radar hadn't exactly panned out. Even before the puppy incident, people had been buzzing around him. Asking for his autograph. Asking him how long he was back for this time. Where he kept his Olympic medals. What it was like dating an Italian runway model.

He'd had to play the part. Be *the* Brody James. And that hadn't exactly helped his quest for a little peace and hometown clarity.

Not that anyone knew what he was doing here. He hadn't even told his parents or his sister why he was back. If they asked, he wasn't sure he'd even be able to put into words *why* he'd walked off the training course and left his entire life behind. His chest still felt tight whenever he thought about it. So he pushed the thoughts away. Introspection had never really been his thing anyway.

The knee was a good excuse. Every professional skier was always managing various injuries, especially at his age. So he'd let people think that was why he was here, skipping a pivotal World Cup event right as the season was kicking into high gear. Pretending everything was fine.

A hand clapped him suddenly on the shoulder, and he flinched. "Back to grace the mortals with your presence, eh, Brodster?" his uncle Pat slurred, squeezing a little too hard. "Show us all up with your perfect life?"

At his side, Steph stiffened, going into protective big-sister mode. "We're all here for Bailey and Anne," Steph corrected, glaring down their mother's most obnoxious brother.

"Yeah, but not all of us left a freaking lingerie model behind to come. Unless she dumped your ass already. I see you didn't bring her with you."

Steph smiled her sweetest smile, somehow pairing it with a steely glare. "Maybe he was afraid she'd run for the hills if she met you, Uncle Pat."

Uncle Pat snorted, saluting Steph with his drink. "Always

the ballbuster, Stephie Girl," he praised, before wandering off to embarrass some other member of the family.

"Thanks," Brody mumbled under his breath, realizing after Pat left that he hadn't had to say a single word.

His sister shrugged. "No one gets to give you a hard time but me." She turned her attention back to the bridal proceedings as Bailey and Anne moved toward the dance floor for their first dance. Then she slanted him a look out of the corner of her eye. "Though *did* she dump your ass?"

"Not that I know of," he answered—and Steph's lips twitched as if he was joking.

She had no way of knowing he hadn't spoken to Valeria since he left Zermatt.

Hiding from his regularly scheduled life.

Their relationship had never been the talk-every-day kind, though. Valeria had her own high-profile career to chase, and sometimes they'd go for days or even weeks just exchanging texts from different time zones. They got along well when they were together, but even after nine months he didn't know how well she actually knew him.

Which was part of why he hadn't known what to say to her since he left. He didn't go to her with problems. Hell, he wasn't used to *having* problems, beyond which wax to use on his skis for race day conditions.

Valeria had her own life when he was competing, but no one liked being ignored, and he wouldn't be able to dodge her forever. It was only a matter of time.

God, he was such a coward. He shouldn't be hoping that his girlfriend of nine months would get fed up and break up with him via text so he wouldn't have to talk to her about his messed-up feelings, but this week nothing had felt like it should.

Except seeing Kendall.

That had been different. He'd felt...*grounded*. Like himself for the first time since Zermatt.

They hadn't really kept in touch the last few years. He'd been so caught up in being the best that even her brother, Kevin, his best friend, only managed to get him on the phone once a month. He and Kev would talk about racing, about Kevin's finance job, about who he'd run into at an après-ski party or who Kevin had met at a posh fundraiser—and somehow Kendall never came up.

Brody's gaze returned to the service door she'd taken him through. She still wasn't back.

The brides opened the dancing, and Brody watched with half of his attention, preoccupied by waiting for Kendall's return. Her family had owned this resort for generations. He'd known he might see her here, but he hadn't expected her to be working the event. The idea of Kendall Walsh sitting behind a desk in an office somewhere felt like an insult to the natural order of the universe.

She'd always been the human embodiment of "Faster, Higher, Stronger." Always pushing. Always moving.

They'd met racing on the mountain when she was seven and he was eight. She'd beaten him down a run and crowed her victory. Then beaten him again. And again.

He'd never met anyone more daring than he was on skis, until Kendall. No one who wanted to win more than he did. She'd been faster than him. Faster than everyone.

But that was before her accident.

Over the last six years since that day in the hospital, he'd probably only seen her a handful of times—he was almost never back in Vermont. He'd texted her a few times after the accident, but when she didn't respond, he'd thought she would reach out when she was ready. Kev had probably told him that Kendall had moved back home. Brody just hadn't realized she was still here. In his head, she'd still been Kendall Walsh, Speed Demon.

Things always changed back home while he was off chasing gold. *People* changed, going on with their lives, settling down when he wasn't looking, but it was still jarring. Especially this time.

His best friend was a partner now at a fancy financial firm, his sister was engaged—and Kendall Walsh worked in an office.

He didn't really know her anymore. He hadn't known her in a long time.

But he still felt, strangely, like she was the only one who would understand if he told her the real reason he'd left Zermatt.

"Taking notes for your wedding?" one of his aunts asked from across the table.

Brody opened his mouth to instinctively protest that he and Valeria weren't even talking about the distant future possibility of getting married—but Steph spoke before he could.

"Absolutely," she said brightly. "Though pretty much everything is already locked in with less than two months to go."

Brody snapped his mouth shut, his cheeks warming as Steph snuck him a glance out of the corner of her eye. The little smirk playing around her mouth let him know that she had absolutely caught his almost denial.

It wasn't that he always thought every question was directed at him—it was just so easy to get into that mindset when he was at things like this and it felt like he was sitting in a spotlight. Steph might tease him for his arrogance, but that attitude was almost a defensive reflex, honed by years of experience.

"It's mostly logistics now," Steph went on. "Figuring out who to ask to drive to Burlington to pick up the centerpieces, since we're getting married up here and Frank and I are both based in Pittsburgh."

"I can pick them up," Brody offered.

Steph almost laughed. "Mom's getting them. It was just an example. Don't worry. We know better than to ask you to do anything that doesn't involve skiing. I'm just glad the World Cup decided to have a competition in Lake Placid that week, so I can have a reasonable chance of my brother showing up."

She was smiling as she spoke, but the words still made him bristle. Yes, he was rarely home. He'd prioritized training and competing—and when he wasn't training and competing, his PR team had encouraged him to do interviews and commercials, even a stint on *Dancing with the Stars* a few years back. Building his brand, attracting sponsors. Becoming the face of US men's downhill skiing.

But the idea that his family *knew better than to ask him for anything* and thought there was only a *reasonable chance* he was going to make it to his only sister's wedding...that grated. Even if it might be a little true.

Everyone thought his life was perfect. All supermodels and fast skiing. Which it was. That was how he'd built it. But he didn't like the idea that he'd trained his loved ones back home not to rely on him. To expect him to never be around, even for the important things. Had he been so focused on gold he'd forgotten to have a life?

"When's your next race?" his aunt asked, pulling him back to the conversation and repeating the question everyone had been asking since he arrived.

"I'm not sure. I might stick around for a while." When

Steph shot him a surprised frown, he added the lie: "I'm rehabbing my knee."

His aunt made a sympathetic face—and across the room Brody caught sight of platinum blond hair in a tight twist. *Kendall.*

"Excuse me for a sec." He was on his feet before he realized the impulse, moving toward her.

As he wove through the crowd, Kendall shifted in and out of his line of sight.

When he reached the place he'd spotted her, she wasn't there, but he caught a glimpse of her across the ballroom again. The side of her face. The sculpted muscle of her arms visible in her sleeveless black outfit. He followed again, smiling as he avoided getting sucked into conversations with friends and family, but he couldn't seem to catch up with her.

Story of his life. He'd never been able to catch Kendall Walsh.

He lost sight of her and found himself on the edge of the dance floor, turning in a slow circle as he scanned the room.

When he completed his circle, his sister was standing waiting for him to finish, arms folded, eyes narrowed. "Okay, what's going on with you?" she demanded.

"I thought I saw someone."

"Not that. You're acting weird."

"Because I volunteered to pick up centerpieces?"

"Because you wanted to come to this wedding. Because you aren't spending every second of every day either working out, skiing, or talking about working out or skiing." Her worried face looked a lot like a glare, but he knew Steph, so he didn't take it personally when she glowered at him. "Exactly how bad is the knee?"

Brody hadn't realized how badly he wanted her to see through his bullshit until she asked that question and something inside him deflated.

"It's fine," he insisted—which was the truth. There was nothing wrong with it. Or at least nothing more wrong than had been since his last surgery. But he didn't know how to talk about what was really wrong.

When you were the guy who had always known exactly what you wanted and been willing to do whatever it took to be the best, how did you tell people you were suddenly having a freaking existential crisis and weren't even sure you knew who you were anymore? That your life suddenly felt empty and *wrong*? How could he explain that in a way that made sense?

He'd fled from the life he'd always wanted, and he didn't know when he was going back. *If* he was going back. He was freaking lost.

But he said what he always said. "I'm fine."

And because he was *the* Brody James and his life was perfect, everyone believed him.

Chapter Three

That night, Kendall walked into her place to find a gaping hole in the carpet beside her couch, with Banner sleeping angelically next to it, and couldn't even find the energy to be upset.

With the day she'd had, coming home to find Banner had dug a hole through the ratty shag carpet and all the way through the carpet pad to the subfloor below just felt like a natural conclusion.

After the near-disaster with the cake, Kendall had decided on impulse not to put Banner in her office—it was too small, and he'd probably destroy it in under thirty minutes—so instead she'd taken him back to the ramshackle old ski lodge that she'd converted into her personal retreat.

The old lodge had been built by her however-many-greats-grandfather when the Pine Hollow Mountain Resort first opened back in the 1920s, but it had been closed to the public for more than half her life. Until she'd moved in, it had mostly been used for storage and teenage parties—like the ones once thrown by her brother when they were in high school.

The rustic A-frame building was mostly one large room in the front, facing the massive windows, with a loft above and offices and storage rooms in the back. It had been renovated and repurposed a few times as the resort expanded, most recently in the early seventies—as evidenced by the dingy orange shag carpet.

The resort now centered around the main lodge with its luxury hotel rooms, giant ballroom, and ski-out access to the new lifts that spanned the sunnier side of the mountain—and the old lodge had been left to fall into neglect.

It was a huge, drafty space for one person. The pipes had a tendency to freeze, it was furnished entirely by mismatched pieces she'd scavenged from the main lodge over the years, and the furnace made an ungodly clanging noise when it came on, but it was her sanctuary. The one place in the resort where she didn't have to worry about anything being perfect.

And the one place where she'd been sure Banner couldn't do any damage.

More the fool her.

Kendall sank down onto the shabby couch she'd appropriated from the lobby when they'd updated the furniture there. She'd always hated that carpet. Having an excuse to replace it wasn't so horrible. Though the last thing she needed right now was one more thing on her to-do list.

God, she was tired.

"Cheer up committee, incoming!"

Kendall looked up from the black hole in her carpet as her two best friends entered, knocking as they were already walking through the door. Charlotte and Magda had known her since kindergarten. She should have known they would realize she was stewing.

"We come bearing champagne and leftover cake," Magda said, holding up their spoils.

The rest of the wedding had gone off—mostly—without a hitch. Her staff had managed to scramble and avert a dessert fork shortage when it was time to cut the cake. No more canine wedding crashers had appeared, and the happy couple had made their getaway with smiles on their faces. But Kendall still felt like she'd barely survived.

She wasn't so sure she was cut out for this wedding planning business, but she didn't see another option. *Something* had to get the resort out of debt. She was so tired of wondering if each season was going to be the one when they finally went under. One bad snow year might be all it took.

Charlotte made herself at home, moving to the old built-in bar and opening the champagne, but as she delivered a flute to Kendall, she froze, staring at the floor. "What happened here?"

"Banner happened."

"*Oh.*" Charlotte sank down beside Kendall on the couch, both of them staring at the hole, as Magda portioned out leftover wedding cake. "Do you hate me?"

That brought Kendall's gaze off the hole and onto Charlotte. "Why would I hate you? You didn't sneak in here and scratch a hole in my floor, did you?"

"I made you foster Banner."

Kendall snorted, accepting cake from Magda, who sat down on her other side. "You can't make me do anything. I wanted to foster him. And I'm not even upset about the floor. Maybe I will be later, when it hits me—but right now, it just feels sort of fitting. The cherry on top of this disaster of a day."

"Anne and Bailey couldn't have cared less about Banner's little sprint across the dance floor," Charlotte assured her.

"And Bailey's parents? The ones footing the bill for this two-hundred-seventy-five-guest black-tie extravaganza that was supposed to be our calling card? We needed good referrals from this."

"And you'll get them. Everyone was happy," Charlotte insisted. "The resort looks like it's doing great."

"Yeah, well, looks can be deceiving. We're hanging on by the skin of our teeth." She took a long drink of champagne, feeling the bubbles all the way down. "I thought weddings would be a way to get us comfortable—but to do them on the scale I want we'd need a dedicated events person, which I thought I could do, but I've just had to fire that idiot Phil when it took me *forever* to convince my dad to hire someone to take over staff management—"

"Wait, you fired Phil?"

Kendall grimaced, reminded of the *other* disaster that had hit today. She'd been on her way back to the ballroom after stashing Banner when she'd run into the ski instructor who was supposed to be watching him.

Ashley had been all apologies—but then she'd admitted that the reason she'd been distracted and lost Banner in the first place had been because she'd been comforting one of the concierges, who was apparently being harassed by the new manager. None of the staff had wanted to bother Kendall with their problems with Phil, but as soon as Ashley started talking, everything had come out.

"He tried to get one of our concierges to sleep with him for better shifts."

"Wow. Asshole." Charlotte reached for the bottle to refill her glass.

"Thank you." Kendall accepted the drink, taking a welcome sip.

Kendall hadn't had time to deal with him until the reception no longer needed her attention, but as soon as she could get away, she'd done some digging and then called Phil to confront him.

Phil had insisted that the concierge had misunderstood him, but he'd openly admitted to giving more shifts to the male ski instructors, because they could "handle it," and leaving some of their best female instructors without enough hours to get benefits. And he'd actually bragged that he would be saving the resort money by cutting the hours of a pregnant maid in an attempt to force her to quit so they wouldn't have to pay maternity leave.

Kendall had never liked the guy—her dad had overruled her when they were hiring him—but now she couldn't help wondering if she'd missed the warning signs that he was even worse than she thought because she hadn't wanted to see them. Because if she saw them, then she had to fire Phil, and she *really* hadn't wanted to fire Phil. Because as soon as she did, all of his duties landed right back on her. She'd *needed* him to be good at his job. She'd been so overwhelmed.

"He was supposed to be the solution." And now she felt like she'd let all of her people down. All the ones who had trusted her to look after them. "He was supposed to make it so I finally had a chance to breathe, and he didn't even make it six weeks." She took a bite of the wedding cake and closed her eyes on a groan. "Oh, Mags, this is amazing. What did you put in here?"

"About twenty-seven pounds of butter and sugar," Magda answered absently, still focused on Kendall's problem. "I feel like we should watch Hallmark movies. There's always a plucky heroine trying to save the family business. We'll get ideas."

"And if there's a big-city developer swooping in to steal your family legacy, you should absolutely jump on him and teach him the meaning of Christmas," Charlotte added, taking her own bite of cake and pausing to groan appreciatively.

"It's January," Kendall reminded them.

Charlotte shrugged. "It's always Christmas in Hallmark-ville."

"If a big-city developer tried to swoop in and buy us out, at this point I might just let him."

Magda looked at her in surprise. "Really?"

It did sound tempting. Freeing. The idea that she wouldn't have to keep running on the treadmill of her family business and could figure out what she *wanted* to do instead. But just walking away from the resort…letting it leave the family, when she was the reason it was even in trouble in the first place…

"No. I don't mean it. I'm just tired," she admitted. "We keep coming up with ways to survive through one more season—and then our solutions only seem to make things worse. Like the conferences. They got us through the summer, but we lost ten percent of our year-round service staff after Bagel Gate because we somehow managed to only book conferences that treated our people like crap. And now this stuff with Phil…I just feel like I'm letting everyone down."

She'd never wanted to do this in the first place. Running the resort had never been her dream. But then her dream had ended, much faster than she was ready for, and the resort had been there. A safe place to fall. And she'd owed her dad so much—both emotionally and financially after he'd drained money from the resort to pay for her treatment. She still owed him.

"Your family relies on you too much," Magda said gently.

Kendall snorted. "Says the pot to the kettle."

"You need to get your groove back," Charlotte proclaimed.

Which sounded great in theory. It was just the reality part that was tricky. "Stella went on a Caribbean vacation to get hers back. How am I supposed to swing that when I can't even get two days off in a row?"

"Okay, not a vacation. Maybe just forget about the big-city developer and jump Brody instead. Did you find out how long he's staying this time?"

"No, because I was too busy being a total jerk to him."

"What?" Charlotte frowned. "Why? You've been obsessed with Brody James since grade school."

"I'm not obsessed."

"Wait, Brody puppy guy from the wedding was *your* Brody?" Magda asked. Mags hadn't been at the wedding. She'd just dropped off the cake, so she hadn't seen the ski god in the flesh. She'd only heard about Puppy Gate after the fact on their group text.

"He isn't *my* Brody," Kendall corrected Magda. "If he's anyone's Brody, he's Kev's. But yes, Brody James is apparently Bailey's cousin—which you could have warned me about." That last part was directed at Charlotte, who held up her hands innocently.

"I didn't know. I got the scoop after you saw him at the reception. Apparently, Brody's aunt married Bailey's dad five years ago and her parents invited *everyone* to the wedding because they were sort of competing with one another to see who could shower her with the most attention. No one really expected Brody to show, because he's always off skiing in Zurich or whatever, but then, like three days before the wedding, he flies back from Europe and decides to come. Everyone was really shocked he was back. And you still have to explain why you were mean to him."

"Because...I don't know," Kendall stalled—though she did know.

She'd hated him seeing what her life was like now. Because then she had to see it.

She'd been so good at just putting one foot in front of the other for the last several years. There were always a million things to do at the resort—and yes, she was frustrated by feeling responsible for everything while also being continually overruled by her dad when it came to making decisions. But she'd kept busy and gotten very good at ignoring the deeper problem.

Her powers of denial were *strong*. Second only to her stubbornness.

The first step might be admitting you had a problem, but Kendall had never been good at that step.

Though she had to admit she wasn't happy. Even if the only people she was willing to admit that to were her two best friends.

"I didn't want him to see me like this," she confessed. "He hasn't really seen me since the accident. It's like he's the only person left in the world who remembers me as I was, and I didn't want him to figure out who I am now."

Her best friends closed their arms around her. "Who you are is *awesome*," Charlotte insisted, and Magda hummed her agreement.

Banner chose that moment to wake up and wriggle up close, his sweet soft head resting on her lap. Just when he seemed like he might be more trouble than he was worth, he looked at her with those big sweet eyes, and she just melted.

"You proud of yourself?" she asked the puppy, who continued to gaze at her lovingly. "You're lucky this place needs a remodel, bub."

Magda bent down, peering more closely at the wood that had been exposed by Banner's attempt to dig to China. "It's actually kind of nice. The hardwood. Is that original?"

"Yeah. This place was something, back in the day. You should see the pictures." She tipped her head back, taking in the exposed rafters and massive windows looking up toward a defunct ski lift from the fifties. "I've wanted to fix it up for a while. Turn it into a secondary event space. For smaller parties that don't need the ballroom but don't want to risk the weather being poor if they book the rooftop space."

"Ooh, that would be amazing," Charlotte enthused. "It'd be a good wedding venue too. Rustic is very in. I'd have gotten married here myself if George didn't have twenty-seven million sisters and we needed the space of the ballroom."

"And if it were actually renovated," Kendall reminded her. "Which requires money. Money my father is never going to invest. He still thinks we shouldn't be trying to attract weddings."

Charlotte and her sister were the only brides Kendall had managed to book. Charlotte had actually come up with the plan to use the two weddings as samples on the resort's website—Anne's in the winter and Charlotte's in the summer, showing off the resort in both seasons. But then one of George's sisters had announced she was pregnant and wouldn't be able to fly for a summer wedding and everything had changed.

Faced with the choice between moving the wedding up or pushing it back until she and baby were able to travel, Charlotte and George had rescheduled for February, leaving them only a few weeks to get everything ready.

"What if you only used money you brought in from the weddings?" Magda suggested. "It wouldn't take much."

"Banner's already started demoing the carpet for you," Charlotte added.

Kendall snorted. "Somehow I don't think my dad is going to see it that way. You know how he is."

Charlotte sighed, her enthusiasm deflating. "It was such a good plan."

"Thank you for your attempt to help me save the family farm," Kendall said, bumping her shoulder against each of her friends in turn. They really were the best. She didn't know what she would have done without them for the last few years.

"We'll think of something," Magda insisted.

"Maybe your dad will go for it," Charlotte said, always the optimist.

"Maybe." But they all knew the truth.

It would take an act of God.

Chapter Four

"The chalet burned down!"

Brody froze with a bite of waffle halfway to his mouth as his sister burst into the kitchen in her pajamas, her eyes wild. "The chalet?" he echoed, wondering if he was supposed to know what that meant.

Brody hadn't kept a place in Vermont in nearly a decade, and his sister was only in town for Bailey's wedding, so they were both staying at their parents' place in Woodland for the weekend. Their mother was over the moon to have them all back under the same roof again—as evidenced by the breakfast spread Brody came downstairs to on Sunday morning.

Waffles, eggs, ham, and fresh fruit covered the kitchen table. It was little much for just the four of them, especially since his dad almost never ate breakfast. When he'd protested, his mother had insisted that she knew how much fuel he needed when he was training...and he hadn't had the heart to tell her he wasn't sure when he was going back to the tour.

"The reception venue?" his mother asked, frowning at the dramatic arrival of her typically undramatic firstborn.

"It's gone," Steph declared, waving her phone. "Burned to the ground."

A dribble of syrup slid down Brody's fork and landed on his hand, reminding him he was eating. He quickly took a bite. "Was anyone hurt?" he asked around a mouthful of waffle.

"How can you eat?" Steph shouted, and his survival instincts made him freeze in place again. "My wedding is in eight weeks!"

"We'll find you another venue," his mother said calmly, drawing Steph's death glare away from Brody.

"Another venue. Like it's that easy. Like we didn't pick this one and schedule it eighteen months in advance. I have been planning this wedding for *two years*." Steph sank down, staring blindly at the overabundance of food on the table. "Oh God, the invitations have already gone out. We have to contact everyone. And figure out where we can host eighty people on eight weeks' notice when every decent wedding venue in the state books at least a year in advance. I have to tell Frankie…"

"Maybe there's a cancellation somewhere," his mother added hopefully. "Somewhere even better."

"Yeah, people call off weddings all the time," Brody said.

"Don't say that!" Steph screeched. "Don't put negative wedding energy out there!"

Brody opened his mouth, at a loss. Steph had never been an "energy" kind of person, but apparently wedding stress had changed her.

She looked at her watch and groaned. "I'm supposed to be on a plane back to Pittsburgh this afternoon. I don't have time to call every venue in the state."

"What about the Pine Hollow Mountain Resort?" Brody suggested. "It was nice for Bailey's thing, and I bet Kev can get us a deal."

Steph moaned. "Our theme was rustic winter wonderland. The chalet was intimate. It was historic. It had *atmosphere*—and yes, Bailey's thing was awesome for her, but Frankie and I never wanted a showplace. We wanted *cozy*."

"Beggars can't be choosers," their mother said gently. "Maybe we ask the Walshes if we can reserve the resort as a backup while we keep looking for something that suits you a little better."

"Right now, I'll take anything," Steph said, defeat in every line of her body.

"I'll call around," their mother assured her. "We'll find something."

"I'll go to Pine Hollow," Brody volunteered. "Talk to Kendall."

His mother and sister both stared at him.

"What?" he asked, checking his face for stray syrup.

"Don't you have to go back to Austria or something?"

His hackles rose again. Okay, he didn't usually help out with troubleshooting family stuff, but that didn't mean he couldn't. He didn't want to be the guy that no one expected to be there for them. "Not right away."

"How bad is your knee?" Steph demanded.

"When do you talk to your physical therapist?" his mother asked. "Lou Johansson wanted me to tell you that you're welcome to use his gym anytime you want—even if they aren't open. He'll have a key made for you if you'd rather work out when there aren't people sneaking photos of you."

"Mom, I'm not that famous," he said. "Except for a few months around the Olympics every four years, hardly anyone recognizes me."

"They'll recognize you here," his mother insisted. "And I thought you might want to train at certain times of day, get yourself on the right time zone so it's less of a shock to your body when you go back. Of course, you probably won't know what time zone to be on until you know when you're rejoining the tour. Is it Lake Louise after Switzerland? Did the doctors give you any sense of how long you need to go easy on your knee?"

Brody sidestepped the issue of his knee by refocusing on Steph. "What matters is I can go to Pine Hollow today."

"I'm not asking—" Steph started, and he interrupted.

"I want to. I want to help."

And if he was around his mom too much, she was definitely going to figure out his knee wasn't nearly as bad as he was feigning.

Not to mention that going back to Pine Hollow gave him an excuse to see Kendall again.

Last night after the happy couple made their getaway, he'd lingered and mingled, wanting to talk to her one more time, even though he wasn't sure what he would have said. Kendall had never reappeared, but if he was asking about a venue for Steph's wedding, who better to speak to than the wedding coordinator?

"Just leave the ballroom up to me."

"No. No more weddings. Let's stick to what we know."

Kendall gritted her teeth and tried to remember what patience felt like. It was Sunday morning, and she'd ambushed her dad in the family suite before he could begin the morning rounds. He'd always liked being the weekend manager, overseeing things and handling any little hiccups, while the weekday manager—which had been Kendall until recently and probably would be again until she could replace Phil—handled all the scheduling and payroll paperwork.

Kendall was technically off today. She could have taken her

time, scheduled a dinner with her dad and stepmom, laid out her strategy over appetizers, but she hadn't wanted to wait to talk to him about her ideas for expanding the wedding business.

Though maybe she should have. She hadn't even mentioned the idea of refurbishing the old lodge yet, and already he was shooting down everything she said.

"*Why?*" Kendall demanded. "The wedding last night was a huge success."

Her father didn't even look up from the tablet where he was scanning the morning reports.

"Kurt," her stepmother interjected softly, prompting him to look up. Laurie always did everything softly. Kendall would have loved to think Laurie was going to intercede on her behalf when she met her husband's eyes and tilted her head slightly toward Kendall, but her stepmother had never once disagreed with Kurt Walsh. His sweetly smiling yes-man.

"We have this gigantic ballroom with gorgeous views, and we need to be using it for more than Christmas parties and the New Year's Eve bash." Kendall pushed when her father frowned and glanced at his watch.

"The conferences love the ballroom," he pointed out, starting for the door to begin his morning ritual of walking the resort, ensuring everything was running smoothly, that everyone was where they were supposed to be, doing what they were supposed to be doing.

"The conferences like the size of the ballroom," Kendall acknowledged, following him out of the family suite to continue making her point, leaving Laurie behind. "But they all complain that we don't have enough smaller rooms for breakout sessions, and the conferences and seminars are constantly negotiating our prices down so they can hold on to as much of the profits for themselves as possible—whereas with high-end weddings Mommy and Daddy love saying 'money is no object.' Especially when they're trying to show off for their friends. We pulled in nearly as much last night as we did for a three-day conference last summer."

"But the conferences sell out the room blocks." He exited the staff hallway, moving toward the Day Lodge, and Kendall hurried to keep up.

"At lowered conference rates. The wedding parties might not stay as many nights, but they pay full freight. And if we make ourselves attractive to the multiday event weddings, with golf packages and heli-ski packages and a chapel on site—"

"Now you want to build a chapel?" he asked incredulously, eyeing the ticket sales lines to make sure enough windows were open and the waits weren't too long. "Pine Hollow already has wedding sites. The Inn at Pine Hollow—"

"Is booked two years out. Weddings are big business, and there are a *lot* of people who want to get married in Vermont. Especially if we can offer them something that the inn can't. Like adventure packages and wine tastings for the wedding party. We could *customize* for the bride and groom."

He still didn't glance in her direction, checking to make sure the equipment rental customers all looked happy as he moved past. "Don't you already do that?"

"Yes, but we aren't *advertising* it. We aren't trying to attract brides and wedding planners. When you google us and weddings, *nothing* comes up." On her tablet, she pulled up the webpage mock-up she'd made after Charlotte and Magda left last night. She caught up to him at the hotel registration desk, where he'd set his own tablet down, and she quickly swapped it for hers. "Look. I took a few shots of the ballroom yesterday before the event and whipped up a little page for the website—just to show you what it could be."

Her father frowned at the screen, but he was swiping. He was *looking*. "This looks expensive."

"It's all stuff we're already doing! And we can charge a premium for it—"

Her father frowned at one of the photos. "What is this? *Get married in rustic splendor?*" he read—and she realized he'd found the photo she'd impulsively added of the exterior of the lodge.

When she'd had a moment of foolish optimism that he would go for the idea of renovating it.

She couldn't stop thinking about it. Last night, she hadn't been able to sleep, her mind spinning with ideas, but now her throat tightened.

He was going to shoot her down. She could feel it. "I just thought if we fixed up the old lodge, we could use it as an alternate wedding venue. For smaller weddings looking for something more intimate than the ballroom—"

Her father glowered, shoving the tablet back at her before picking up his own and starting across the lobby, shutting down as she'd known he would. "Is that why you wanted to meet? So you could ask for money to throw after this ridiculousness?"

"Why is it ridiculous?" she demanded. "Weddings make money. We need money."

Her father shook his head, his mind already made up—like it had been before she said a word. "That isn't what the resort is."

Kendall followed him out the side doors and onto the veranda with a view of the ski lifts. He eyed the lines, checking to make sure everything was running smoothly—though he was carrying a walkie, and if anything had gone down, he would have heard about it over the radio.

"I'm not saying we stop being a ski resort," she argued. "Skiers get married too. Maybe we could even offer a wedding on the slopes. Throw the bouquet at the top of a black diamond. People want different. They want to be able to put something no one else has done before on Instagram."

"Instagram," he scoffed. "I realize you're trying to think outside the box, but we're managing. You don't have to do this."

Kendall wondered at what point it was appropriate to scream at your boss-slash-father that he was a moron. Probably never, but it sounded oh so tempting.

She took a breath, regrouping to start again. "Dad. Things are different than when you took over from Grandpa. And definitely different from when he took over from his dad. We can't keep doing things the same way we did before World War II."

It was the wrong approach. She saw that the second he puffed up. "I'm fully aware of that," he said as he stalked back inside, and she followed him toward the restaurant. "Don't forget who built that ballroom you're so fond of."

"Then let me use it! At least let me try! What does it hurt to put a page on our website advertising us as a wedding venue? Run a few Facebook ads with shots of the ballroom decked out for a reception—you saw how much our lift ticket numbers boosted when you let me start a social media campaign."

He waved a hand at her tablet. "You're advertising what we don't have. What if someone wants the lodge?"

"This was just a mock-up. We don't have to include the lodge on the website." She shouldn't push…she knew she shouldn't push. But she couldn't help it. The words started tumbling out in a rush. "But I ran some numbers last night, and it wouldn't take much to turn it into a venue. There's hardwood under the carpet." Which she now knew, thanks to Banner's investigative digging. "And yes, it's scratched up from skis and poles, but I think people would love the original character. It would really just be about clearing out the seventies crap and reworking a couple of the back rooms so the catering staff could operate there. I would only use the income we brought in from other weddings so it wouldn't affect the resort finances—"

"Where would you live?" he asked, as if throwing down the ultimate trump card. As if Kendall would never have considered that she couldn't crash in the loft anymore if they were using it for weddings.

"Somewhere else," she snapped, at the limit of her patience. "There are one hundred eighty-two rooms at the main lodge, and if we can't spare any of those, there are condos just down the road that are constantly on Vrbo."

"Don't you have enough on your plate since Phil left?"

Her irritation flared, but she forced her voice to remain calm. "He didn't leave. I fired him. Because he was trying to get hand jobs for shift changes. And I will hire someone else as soon as I have a chance. We could promote Michelle tomorrow. I told you I thought she would be a better choice—"

"She's twenty-four."

"So? I wasn't much older when I started managing this place."

"That's different. You're a Walsh. It's your legacy. We should never have hired Phil."

"Dad, I need to be able to focus on events. We have to capitalize on the momentum from the Jenner-Rodriguez wedding."

"I'll think about it."

Kendall barely stopped herself from screaming. She knew that *I'll think about it*. Her father rarely said no outright. He would just argue her into the ground with all the reasons he wouldn't listen to her and then leave her with an *I'll think about it*.

But Kendall had gotten her stubbornness from him. "I'm not going to give up on this. I know I'm right. And I am sick of conferences who try to stiff us on half our bill because they underordered cheese Danish."

"We don't even have conferences in the winter. Enjoy the ski season. We'll talk about the weddings in the spring."

"These events are planned months in advance! The big ones will already have their venues for the spring! And they'll think anyplace that's available last minute isn't worth having."

"I'll think about it."

"Dad!"

"Kendall. I said I would think about it."

She rocked back on her heels, wondering again if screaming might help. Her dad had never been good at dealing with tantrums. Or children in general. He'd always treated them like they were tiny training partners.

He'd loved teaching her and her brother to ski—as a former Olympian himself, he'd always wanted one of them to continue the family skiing dynasty. She knew he loved her, but for most of her life he'd been her coach more than her dad. The taskmaster. Always so certain he was right. That his way was the only way.

Some things never changed.

But some things did—like the fact that she'd gone from being the golden child he butted heads with to the disappointment he never seemed to be able to look directly at.

"Dad—"

"Uh, Kendall?" A tentative voice spoke beside her, and Kendall had the delightful experience of wondering if her *entire* staff had just witnessed her being put in her place by her father as she chased him around the resort, or only seventy percent of it. She winced as she looked to the concierge who had spoken.

"Hey, Nina. What do you need?"

"Brody James is asking to see you? He's in the lobby."

Her father instantly perked up, turning to face Nina. "Brody's here?"

"He was at the wedding last night," Kendall explained. "He probably forgot something."

She turned toward the lobby, and her father fell into step beside her—right when she would just as soon he walk away.

"Why didn't you mention you'd seen him?" he asked.

"It didn't come up." Though maybe if she'd mentioned that weddings could bring Brody James back to the resort, her father would have actually considered them.

As soon as they stepped into the main lodge's cavernous lobby, her dad stepped in front of her to greet the great Brody James, beaming at him like he was the prodigal son, and not just the prodigal son's best friend.

Brody stood in front of the hot cocoa fountain, his winter coat draped over one arm, and looking like a Patagonia ad. Hell, he'd probably been in one. Or several.

"Brody, my boy!" Kurt Walsh exclaimed, throwing his arms open wide—

Right as a golden destruction magnet bolted into the lobby, leash trailing, ears flapping, and tongue lolling joyfully from the side of his mouth as he ran straight for Brody.

"Banner, no!"

Chapter Five

This time Brody didn't see the dog coming.

Kendall's shout was the only warning he had before the golden retriever flung himself at Brody's chest with all the subtlety of a monster truck.

Brody had been half-turned toward the cocoa fountain display and didn't have time to brace himself before impact. He stumbled back a step when the dog landed in his arms, and bumped the edge of the table. The hot cocoa fountain rocked but miraculously stayed upright. Banner twisted in his grip, trying to lick his face and flopping like a fish out of water, and Brody stepped on something he only figured out was a dangling leash after it was tangled around his ankle.

Kendall reached them then and grabbed the dog's harness—but only managed to get twisted up with them as Brody staggered backward into the table, taking Kendall and Banner with him. The leash pulled tight around his ankle—

And he knew he was going down.

Brody had skied long enough that he knew when he was

about to bite it, and the only thing left to do was try to mini-mize the damage—so he turned his back to the chocolate foun-tain, taking the full blast of it as the entire thing tipped over and a chocolate tidal wave broke over his back.

The dog did another contortion, managing to leap from Brody's arms—but the leash was still tangled around his ankle and Kendall's arm—and they all crashed to the floor in a slip-pery, cocoa-covered mass.

Kendall looked over at him and groaned—thankfully sounding more annoyed than pained—and Brody met her eyes from a distance of inches.

"We really have to stop meeting like this."

"Ha," she said grumpily, unimpressed by his attempt at humor. "You okay?" The dog continued flopping like a fish since his leash was too tangled to allow him to get free.

Brody sat up, everything he was wearing drenched in thick, rich cocoa—which thankfully wasn't hot enough to scald his skin.

Kendall's father rushed to help him up. "Brody! Are you all right?"

"I'm good." He looked to Kendall. "You good?"

She grunted as she sat up as well. "No worse than I ever am." The dog eagerly licked her chin, and she shoved him gently away. "Don't lick that, Banner. Chocolate is bad for you."

"His name's Banner?"

"Satan was already taken," she said dryly. "But Banner seems to fit. What with the whole Hulk thing."

"I thought that dog was supposed to be contained," Mr. Walsh said as Kendall and Brody untangled themselves from the leash.

"He was supposed to be on a walk with Marco. Looks like

he got away." Then she eyed Brody and groaned. "I should just start paying for all your dry-cleaning bills."

Brody looked down at himself. The chocolate bath had not been kind to his pale blue Henley. Kendall's clothes had a few splotches as well—but more from where she'd landed in the chocolate puddle than from the fountain going over. He'd definitely taken the brunt of that. "It's just a shirt," he assured her.

She unwound the leash from his ankle, eyeing his leg. "Is that the knee?"

"I'm fine," he insisted, coming to his feet and offering a hand to help Kendall to hers—which she ignored, keeping both hands on Banner's harness so he couldn't wreak any more havoc.

"I assure you this isn't how we usually greet guests," Mr. Walsh said. "Look at you. You're soaked."

"I'm good. It's fine," Brody repeated. "Sorry about the cocoa thingy."

The hotel staff were already cordoning off the area and a mop had appeared, seemingly out of thin air. They all looked to Kendall for direction as they quickly set about cleaning up the mess.

"You're about Kevin's size," Mr. Walsh continued, still focused on Brody. "I bet Kendall can find you some of his things while we have all this laundered. You have to stay for lunch, of course. Gotta catch up with all the World Cup news. Haven't seen you in so long."

"I'd like that," Brody agreed, since driving back to Woodland dripping in chocolate didn't sound ideal. "But I'm actually here to talk about a wedding."

"Are you getting married?" Mr. Walsh bellowed, delighted.

"Steph. My sister," he clarified quickly. "Her reception venue just burned down, and I was hoping the ballroom was available."

"Of course! When's the wedding?" Mr. Walsh asked.

"March second."

Mr. Walsh glanced at Kendall.

"It's not booked," she confirmed—and Brody somehow wasn't surprised she had the resort's entire event schedule stored in her brain.

"It's only eighty people—and we might not even need it," Brody quickly clarified. "Steph really wanted cozy and rustic, so she's gonna keep calling around for cancellations, but if we have the ballroom as a backup—and of course I'll pay whatever deposit you normally ask for—"

"Nonsense! You're family. We're happy to help," Mr. Walsh insisted. "The ballroom is yours. But you know what? We might have something even better. Kendall and I were just talking about our plan to renovate the old lodge—turn it into a smaller event space."

"The old lodge?" Brody repeated, excitement spiking at the idea that he might have actually saved Steph's dream wedding. "Steph would love that. It'd be perfect." They'd had parties there in high school—he didn't remember much about the interior, but he was pretty sure it had been all vaulted hardwood ceilings and giant windows. And it was historic. Exactly what Steph had wanted.

The grouchy line between Kendall's eyebrows deepened as she stared at her father. "You just said you didn't want—"

Mr. Walsh spoke over her. "We can have it done by March, don't you think? You said there wasn't much to do. Clean out the junk, polish it up."

"We still have to get contractors. We don't have any quotes." Kendall adjusted her grip on Banner's leash when he tried to make a break toward a little kid at the other side of the lobby who was fascinated by the chocolate disaster.

"I could help," Brody offered, in the vein of his new I'm-someone-people-can-rely-on kick. "And don't worry about the money. I want to do this for Steph."

"Nonsense. Kendall's got a whole budget worked out."

Kendall frowned. "A budget that planned on doing things over time and doing as much of it as possible myself."

"I'm sure we can make it work," Mr. Walsh insisted. "You tell Steph the old lodge is hers."

"*Dad.*"

"You'll get him all set up on the details, won't you, Kendall?" He beamed, clapping Brody on the shoulder. "I'll go let Laurie know you're here for lunch."

Mr. Walsh gave him one last pat on the shoulder, beaming as he headed toward the original section of the main lodge where he and Kendall's stepmom had their private suite.

Brody looked toward Kendall, expecting to see steam pouring out of her ears, but she just looked resigned. Annoyed. But resigned.

"Off to kill the fatted calf," Kendall drawled when her father was out of earshot. She slanted a look at his cocoa-covered self and sighed. "Come on. Kev left a bunch of his stuff at my place so he doesn't have to pack much when he comes up to ski. I'm sure there's something that'll fit you."

Brody expected her to lead him in the same direction her father had gone, but instead of toward the family suite, she headed out the front doors. He shivered as the cold air hit his cocoa-soaked back, but decided against putting his coat on and getting it cocoa-fied. He'd dropped it when Banner hit him, and the chocolate eruption had missed it.

Without giving him a second look, Kendall crunched across the hardpack at the base of the mountain, heading away from the ski lifts and in the same direction as the old lodge. Brody fell into step beside Kendall and the dog—who seemed to have more of a kamikaze zigzag pattern than a shortest-distance-between-two-points approach to walking.

She seemed irritated—but since Kendall pretty much always seemed low-level aggravated, he couldn't tell if it was about the wedding.

"Your dad kind of volunteered you. Is having Steph's reception at the lodge a problem?"

"We'll make it work," Kendall promised—but she still seemed low-level pissed off.

"You sure?"

Kendall sighed, glancing over at him—her frown deepening when she noticed he was carrying his coat. She wasn't wearing one either, but her thick cable-knit sweater was a lot warmer than his soaked Henley. "By itself it's not a problem," she said. "If my only job was fixing up the lodge and I could find the labor to do it, sure, I'd love to host Steph's reception there. It's just the timing feels impossible, and if this blows up in my face, it's gonna be my fault because I was the one who wanted to make it into a venue—but I wanted to take six months to do it, not two, and we haven't even *started*. And somehow I'm supposed to wave my magic wand and make the old lodge perfect, while also coordinating my friend Charlotte's wedding and planning her bachelorette party—all of which was *supposed* to happen in June, but, as of a week ago, is suddenly happening in February. But no pressure."

"For what it's worth, I don't think Steph needs perfect. She'll just be grateful to have someplace."

"Every bride deserves perfect." She veered suddenly off the paved path, taking the snowy track through the woods toward the old lodge, and Brody scrambled to follow.

"My mom's calling other venues. She might be able to find something else. I don't want to make your life harder—"

"That's just it. I *want* to renovate the lodge. I've wanted to for years, and this is probably the only way I'm gonna get my dad on board to do it. But five minutes before you showed up he was telling me no more weddings, no renovation. Then you walk in and he can't say yes fast enough."

"Oh." He'd definitely had that happen before. People tended to want to do things for celebrities—even minor ones like him.

"It's the same shit he pulls with Kevin," she grumbled, stomping up the path. "He wouldn't even *consider* hiring someone to manage the staff so I could plan events—and then Kev comes home for one weekend and over dinner says, 'Why don't you hire a new manager so Kendall can focus on events?' and suddenly it's 'What a great idea, Kev!'"

"I'm sure he didn't mean—"

"Don't," she snapped. "You don't know. Kevin was the one who told them they should try to attract conferences—which I *hate* running. And now that I had to fire the douchebag we hired to take over staff management so I can freaking *breathe*, I'm back at square one—managing the staff and planning weddings and running a renovation—because God knows I needed one more thing. And I'll probably have to get Kevin to ask my dad to hire a replacement manager before he'll listen. Unless you want to drop it into conversation over lunch today, since God knows he'd listen to *you*."

The old lodge appeared in the clearing ahead of them, with its incredible views of the mountain's first ski trails and a long-since retired chairlift. Just as picturesque as he remembered. Kendall stomped up onto the porch, bending to clip the dog to a line there.

"Or I could do it," he offered.

"That's what I just said," Kendall snapped, stalking to the door of the old lodge and quickly unlocking it.

"No, I mean the job," Brody clarified. "I could do the job. Until you can find someone."

Kendall snorted, looking at him over her shoulder as she entered the lodge. "Right. Because rock-star athletes can't wait to moonlight as mid-level managers."

"Most Olympians have day jobs. You know that," he said as he followed her inside.

Kendall's eyes narrowed. "Most Olympians with multiple medals, movie-star looks, endorsement deals, and sponsors? I know you're doing well, Brody. You don't have to pretend you aren't."

She made a beeline toward a pile of boxes—and he took a moment to consider the old lodge and the project he'd inadvertently signed her up for.

The place had seen better days. There was a hole roughly a foot across where the ugliest carpet on the face of the planet had been ripped up, and the furnishings were all a mishmash of battered hand-me-downs. Like a particularly depressing thrift store. Or the Ghost of Ski Resorts Past.

But under the piles of junk and seventies décor, the bones of the place were still solid. The exposed rafters. The rustic log banisters leading up to the loft area above. Though it did look a little small.

"Can you really fit eighty people in here?"

"It's bigger than it looks."

He glanced toward the pile of bent ski poles. "Hard to get a sense with all the junk."

Kendall met his eyes. "Uh-huh." She shoved a box at him. "That's some of Kev's stuff."

It wasn't until he accepted the box of clothes that Brody remembered what she'd said. About Kev storing some of his stuff *at her place*.

This was her place. She actually lived here. In this ski shop thrift store.

"Do you…?"

Now that he was looking, he could see the signs that it wasn't just a catch-all storage shed. The laptop balancing on one arm of an old leather couch. The dishes in the sink.

"Don't," Kendall snapped.

"Don't what?" he asked, grabbing the first shirt out of the box and straightening.

"Don't get that poor-Kendall-her-life-is-so-pathetic look on your face. I chose this."

"I just didn't realize we were talking about kicking you out of your home."

"We aren't."

"But you—"

The frown line between her eyebrows deepened. "I'll figure it out, okay, Brody? It isn't your problem."

But he wanted it to be. He wanted to help.

She jerked her chin past him. "Bathroom's through there. Second door on the left."

He didn't move. "I was serious," he called as she climbed up into the loft. "About working here for a while. I could help you fix this place up quickly. Turn it into Steph's dream venue."

He didn't know why he suddenly liked the idea so much. Maybe because he wanted to be the hero. Or, more accurately, he didn't want to have to face his own life or his own thoughts just yet. A distraction sounded amazing. A pause button on dealing with his own shit.

"Not your problem," she reminded him. "But you can tell your sister we'll hold the ballroom for her, and I'll see what I can do here. Have her call me or email me about décor and seating and all that. I'm sure she already had a plan with the other venue. We'll try to match that as much as we can."

"I still can't get over you as a wedding planner."

"It defies belief," Kendall said dryly.

Wild child Kendall as a buttoned-up wedding planner. He couldn't wrap his head around it. "Didn't you get married on a dare?"

"Nobody's perfect."

She was up in the loft now, out of sight, and he was standing there, clammy with cold cocoa, but he wasn't ready to give up.

"I'm serious," he called up the stairs. "You should take the offer."

He didn't expect gushy gratitude—this was Kendall. She looked over the railing down at him, her perma-frown deepening. "Aren't you competing this year?"

"I…" He hesitated. "I don't know." It was the simple truth. Right now, he wasn't sure of anything.

He hadn't thought ahead when he packed up and left Zermatt. He hadn't thought at all. He'd just known he couldn't compete, that he needed to get away from his chaotic thoughts after hearing the truth about Oskar. The knee had been a convenient excuse. But then he'd gotten home and people kept asking him when he was going back, and he'd pretended he had an answer, pretended he had it all figured out, because Brody always had a plan. A clear goal so singular it was an obsession. All-or-nothing Brody James.

Except now. He was operating on instinct—which had

tended to work well for him in the past. And his instincts were telling him to stay here.

Kendall's expression turned sympathetic as her gaze went to his knee. "It's that bad?"

It felt deeply shitty, lying to Kendall, whose entire life had been upended by an injury. He didn't want to let her believe the same thing was happening to him, but he didn't have another answer that made sense. Not if he didn't want to tell her about Oskar. "I just need some time. To strengthen it."

"Won't you want to focus on that? You're hardly going to have time to create schedules, do payroll, and rip out the occasional ugly shag carpet if you're trying to get back in shape."

"I can multitask," he said. "There's more to life than skiing, right?"

Her eyebrows flew up. "More to your life?"

"I want to do this," he insisted, a little more sharply than he intended, because he was tired of everyone implying all he was good for was skiing. Tired of it being true. "Show Steph she can count on me. Help you out. And yeah, I'll rehab at the same time. It'll be good. Ripping out carpet will be like cross-training."

"Uh-huh," Kendall said skeptically.

"I know the resort," he reminded her. "You aren't going to find someone else on short notice who knows it like I do."

"Skiing the resort isn't the same as running it. When have you ever managed anything? You think it's so easy?"

"I'm a fast learner. And I can start tomorrow. No one else can say that."

"Unless I promote from within. Which was what I wanted to do in the first place before my dad insisted we hire Phil. The head of our ski school would be perfect."

"So you work on convincing your dad to promote your choice and I fill in the gaps until then," he said, making it all up as he went along, but it sounded good as he said it. It felt right. He *wanted* this, more than he probably should.

"My dad would probably love that," she grumbled. "He won't even care that you don't know what you're doing. And at least I know you won't proposition our ski instructors." At his blank look, she explained. "That's why I had to fire the last guy."

"No propositioning the instructors. Got it."

She cracked a smile at his deadpan delivery—and he grinned at the victory. It had always been a challenge to make Kendall smile.

She disappeared from the visible section of the loft, reappearing on the steps a moment later in a clean sweater and fresh jeans.

"You're serious about this?" she asked, her eyes hard.

He had the sudden feeling that people had let Kendall down. And he very badly wanted to be someone who didn't.

He'd need to call his training team. And Valeria. Let them all know he was taking a break for a little while. He could fob them off with the knee excuse for a few weeks. Until he figured his shit out. And in the meantime, he could be the hero for Steph and Kendall and show them that he wasn't only good for skiing.

He could be useful here. And it would be good to have something other than racing to think about. Something other than Oskar and that gaping hole of panic lurking in the back of his thoughts...

"I need to do something," he said, camouflaging the real reason. "If I don't keep busy, I go crazy. You'd be doing me a favor."

Kendall frowned, studying him—and probably seeing far more than he wanted her to. "I'll talk to my dad. See what he thinks." Brody started to smile, and she held up a finger. "If we do this—and I'm not saying we will, but if we do—give me as much notice as you can when you're gonna leave, okay? Just don't vanish on me. That's all I ask."

"You can count on me," he said, defensive.

"Brody. You're a skier. You'll need to get back to racing. I get it. Just give me as much warning as you can."

"Okay," he promised. Right now, the idea of going back made his brain shy away—but he knew she was right. At some point, he'd need to figure out where he was going next, even if it wasn't back to the tour, and he needed to give her as much warning as possible when he did. "I won't leave you in the lurch. So we're doing this?"

"I'll talk to my dad," she said. "No guarantees."

Chapter Six

Her father was in love with the idea. Because of course he was.

It was like he'd finally gotten his wish and been able to pass the ski resort to his firstborn son, only that son was also an Olympian just like he'd been. Someone who'd never let him down or driven the resort into debt with medical bills. That whole not-actually-biologically-related thing didn't seem to matter nearly as much as the fact that Saint Brody was going to grace them with his presence.

Brody had even somehow convinced her father to increase the budget.

She hadn't seen it—Kendall had worked through lunch, making lists of all the things she would need to accomplish if she was going to turn the lodge into a wedding venue in less than two months—but Brody and her dad had walked out of the restaurant beaming and clapping one another on the back. And she'd walked away with a new personnel manager and a renovation budget triple what she'd thought she'd be able to talk her father into. Her dad even wanted to train Brody personally, so she wouldn't have to make time in her schedule to do it.

She knew she should be grateful—and she was. She finally had a chance to try out one of her plans for the resort. But she had mixed feelings about the entire scenario—and how it had magically set itself up the second Brody decided he wanted to play ski resort manager for a few weeks.

In the middle of the competition season.

When he should have been focused on his recovery.

Something was seriously wrong there.

She had to be ready for him to return to the tour at any time. And on top of that, the man had literally no experience managing people.

Though he was smart. And he had worked in and around ski resorts his entire life. He knew the layout of their resort inside and out from playing with her and Kevin as kids. And the staff would listen to him—if only because most of them would revere him like a god.

He was probably going to be a natural at running the resort.

Which was deeply annoying.

Even though obviously she *wanted* him to be good at it because it would mean she wouldn't have to babysit him and could actually focus on the renovation. But did he have to be so freaking *perfect*?

She was barely able to contain her irritation as she recounted the entire story to Magda and Charlotte later that night.

Charlotte just stared at her, then held up a finger.

"Wait, so Mr. Might Have Been, the sexy ski god you've been secretly comparing all other men to for the last decade, is staying in Vermont and working for you? And might be doing so shirtless because you're going to be renovating your place and turning it into a wedding venue—all of which your father has miraculously agreed to pay for—and you're pissed about this?"

At Charlotte's assessment of the situation, Kendall pulled a face. "I'm not pissed. I'm…fine, yes, I'm pissed. It was just so easy for him! And not just talking my dad into it. I said something about not being sure how much work would need to go into stripping the carpet and refinishing the floors, and he just made a call. Half an hour later, the premier floor guy in the state is looking at the flooring and handing us a bid—with a discount because *the* Brody James was there smiling at him."

"Are you worried that he'll take over?" Magda asked. "That he'll get all the credit?"

"Oh, I'm sure he'll get all the credit," Kendall grumped. "And I'm sure he'll be a great manager and the renovation will be faster and cheaper with him here—which I'm grateful for. It's just the principle of the thing. It *shouldn't* be easier for him. How is that fair?"

The three of them were in Charlotte's condo, surrounded by approximately two hundred tiny bottles of bubbles—since Charlotte and George had decided to forgo rice or confetti. Charlotte had planned to cut costs by making her own wedding favors, but now had substantially less time to make them, so Kendall and Magda, as co–maids of honor, had been drafted to tie tiny little ribbons on tiny little bubble bottles.

When she and George had gotten engaged in September, Charlotte had warned them that she would probably go "full bridezilla," but so far she'd been remarkably calm as they adapted to the sudden change of plans. Either that or she was hiding her stress a lot better than she usually did.

"Did you find out why he's staying?" Charlotte asked now, securing a tiny teal ribbon. Her wedding was going to be an explosion of vivid color—in part because that was who she was and also in an attempt to differentiate it from the muted pastels of Anne's reception in the same venue just one month earlier.

"He says he's rehabbing his knee, but he doesn't seem to be favoring it. Banner keeps ramming into him, and I haven't even seen him wince." Banner and Bingley were fast asleep, after playing themselves out with Magda's pit bull, Cupcake, and George's dog, Duke.

"He should come by the sports med clinic," Charlotte said, referring to the clinic where she and her fiancé both worked part-time, Charlotte as an orthopedist and George in physical therapy. "Though I'm sure he has his own team of doctors."

"That's the thing. He doesn't seem to be worried about physical therapy or doctor's appointments. I'd think he wasn't injured at all, but why would he lie about that?"

"To save face?" Magda suggested.

"Yeah, but about what?" Kendall asked. "I googled him after he left. The knee is the public story, and it does explain why his times so far this season have been off, but it feels like I'm missing something. Why else would he just up and leave the racing circuit when he finally has a shot at winning it all?"

"Didn't he always have a shot?" Charlotte asked.

"Technically, yeah, but no one could ever catch Oskar Isaakson."

Charlotte frowned. "I feel like I've heard that name—"

"He's been gold to Brody's silver for the last decade, but he died last year."

"Oh God, what happened?"

"Some accident when he was home for a break. It didn't even make headlines in the US."

"Poor Brody," Magda said, her empathy on max.

"I don't think they were close," Kendall said. "I wondered if that might be it, why he was taking a break, but he doesn't seem grief-stricken. I'm pretty sure they didn't even like each other. It's just weird that he's not pushing harder, now that he's the heir presumptive to be world number one."

"A mystery." Charlotte widened her eyes dramatically as she reached for another bottle. "I love a mystery. Do you think he's back to profess his undying love to you?"

Kendall snorted. "Brody James has never seen me as anything other than a racer."

Charlotte handed her another bottle to decorate. "Even if he hasn't been secretly pining for you, I still think you should jump on him while he's here. Because you have certainly been secretly pining for him."

"I don't pine," Kendall protested, offended. "I am a pine-free zone. And aren't you the one who insisted we all swear off men?"

Charlotte waved away her argument. "I was drunk. And *you* told me I didn't need to swear off men, just assholes. So now I'm telling you that you don't need to swear off men—just this serial dating where you find and fixate on all the red flags in three dates or less. Love is a function of time—you need to give it a chance to grow."

"I just happen to be very good at reading people, and I don't see the point in wasting my time on relationships that aren't going anywhere," Kendall argued. "I don't need to be with someone just so I'm not alone."

"What you need is someone who makes you forget the logical," Magda said.

"Exactly," Charlotte agreed. "And Mr. Might Have Been is perfect for that."

Kendall frowned repressively. "I'm not going to sexually harass my new employee."

"I'm not telling you to harass him." Charlotte waved a bubble bottle. "I'm just saying don't let a good chance pass you by. This is the perfect time to get all those unrequited feelings out of your system so you're open to the possibility of blissful happiness." She frowned at the ribbon in her hand. "You guys would tell me if the colors were garish rather than cheerful, wouldn't you? You wouldn't let me get married inside a circus tent?"

"The colors are great," Kendall assured her. "It's gonna look fantastic. I promise."

"I wanted it to be different from Anne's, but I don't want to make people's eyes bleed."

"No bleeding retinas," Kendall promised. "You're good."

"Is that why you didn't go with a Jane Austen theme?" Magda asked. "Because Anne had all the Austen quotes on those little cards on the tables at their rehearsal dinner?" Charlotte's entire family was notoriously Austen obsessed.

"That, and I didn't want George to think I'm trying to act out some Austen fantasy. It can't be all about me. It has to feel like *us*."

"What does he think of the colors?" Kendall asked.

"He says he loves them, that it's going to be fun—but it's George. He's going to say he loves whatever I like."

"He might actually love what you like," Kendall reminded her.

"I know." Charlotte sighed and stared at all the colored ribbons around them. "He keeps saying he just wants to marry me. That he doesn't care about the when or the where or the how, as long as his family is there and it's 'fun.' Maybe it's good that we had to move everything up. Four fewer months for me to question every decision and agonize over every little detail. It's just so much pressure! How do people do this?"

"The reception is just a party, and you love parties. It's gonna be great," Magda soothed.

"And even if it's a total disaster, it doesn't matter," Kendall reminded her. "The wedding is just a day. The marriage is the thing. And you and George…you're gonna be fine."

"I know," Charlotte agreed. "I just want it to be special."

"Honey. You're getting married. It's gonna be special."

Charlotte slanted a glance at her. "Was it for you?"

Kendall blinked, startled by the sudden detour into a past they all generally ignored. "My wedding was a fiasco because I was twenty-three and marrying someone I barely knew to prove a point. Don't worry. Yours will be nothing like mine." She quickly changed the subject. "And the colors are going to be perfect."

"Is that why you won't give anyone a chance?" Charlotte pressed, refusing to be distracted. "Because of your ex? I know he cheated and it was all public and awful—"

"It wasn't like that," Kendall argued. She didn't even blame Carter anymore. "We were both young and stupid."

Magda and Charlotte hadn't been at her wedding. Not even her family had been there. It had been the rashest of rash decisions, back when she was a different person who thought the riskier something was, the more fun it had to be. Skydiving. Free-climbing. Marrying near-strangers.

And yes, her divorce had been a fiasco, and it had made the worst year of her life even harder, but she'd also learned a lot from the experience, even if she hadn't recognized it at the time.

She knew what she wanted now. And what she wasn't willing to settle for. She knew that she would rather be alone than with the wrong person. She wanted someone who made her *more*. Someone she couldn't live without. Because otherwise what was the point? Why bother?

"I just want you to be open to the possibility of falling madly in love," Charlotte said. "To put yourself out there."

"I'm very open," Kendall promised—though she wasn't entirely sure she was telling the truth. "But I don't have time right now to put myself anywhere. I already need more hours in the day."

And the absolute last thing she needed was to be distracted by Brody James.

Chapter Seven

I'm sorry. Explain to me again how you went there looking for a wedding venue and came home with a job?"

Brody was unfazed by his sister's sarcasm. Of everyone he'd told about his sudden change of plans, so far she'd actually been the least shocked.

"I also got you the wedding venue," he reminded Steph, speaking into his rental's Bluetooth as he drove through the winding mountain passes between Woodland and Pine Hollow. He was on his way to his first day of work, and he was surprised how *excited* he was. "A rustic lodge just like you wanted. It was already being refurbished," he said, bending the truth slightly. "But since I'll be working there, I can help out and make sure the venue is ready before your big day."

"You didn't have to put yourself into indentured service to get me a venue, you know. We would have found something else."

"I know," Brody assured her. "I wanted to do this."

"Why?" Steph asked. "Seriously, Brody, what's going on? You usually can't wait to get back to racing."

Why?

It was the same question everyone had been asking when he said he was going to work at the Pine Hollow resort for a while. His coach had sounded gruffly suspicious—like Brody was trying to conceal a serious injury. His mother had been overtly worried—scanning him as if she could psychically detect some invisible illness. And Valeria had been mildly horrified—she could understand taking a break from skiing, but *choosing* to work as a ski resort manager in the middle of nowhere when he could be doing literally anything else defied belief.

He was fully aware that what he was doing didn't make any sense from the outside. People didn't walk away from successful athletic careers to go be low-level managers at country ski resorts. And it was especially out of character for Brody, who had always put racing first. And second. And sometimes third.

But when he thought about going back to Switzerland, about stepping back into that bubble where all that mattered was his times, his chest would get tight and he wouldn't be able to get a full breath. He'd see Oskar in his mind's eye, checking his gear as he got ready for a run—and something inside him would jerk back, away from the image.

But when he thought about working at the resort—being of use, helping Kendall and seeing her every day—it just felt right. Like he was exactly where he was supposed to be.

So that was what he was going to do.

"Nothing's going on. This is just something I need to do right now," he said to Steph, by way of explanation, as he pulled into the staff parking lot tucked away behind the main lodge. "I've gotta go. Don't want to be late for my first day of work."

Steph snorted. "You're the novelty manager they hired so

they could put your picture on the wall and attract more customers. They aren't going to care if you're late."

"I care." He knew no one really took this foray into employment seriously, but he wanted to do it right. "I'll send pictures of the lodge later. Bye, Steph."

He climbed out of the car, smoothing the shirt he had spent way too long picking out. He'd never tried to look managerial before. But it was a ski resort, and he was pretty sure he'd never seen Mr. Walsh in any clothing that wasn't made by North Face, so he'd gone for the kind of outfit he would have worn for an interview after a race. Winter semi-casual.

He started toward the staff entrance—and as soon as he stepped through the doors, he realized that news of his arrival must have already been spreading through the staff.

Ski instructors and hotel staff seemed to have clustered in common areas, lingering and watching him. Most smiled or waved. "Sup, Rocket!" one guy with the same ski-bum haircut he'd had all through his teens called out as he walked past.

Brody was used to the reactions. Like he'd told his mom, he wasn't famous. Except for a few months around the Olympics every four years, he could go to the grocery store and no one would give him a second glance. But put him at a ski resort and all bets were off. He was the Rocket here.

"Brody, my boy!"

Kendall and Kev's father strode toward him, beaming.

"How are you, Mr. Walsh?" he asked, shaking the extended hand.

"Kurt, please."

"Of course. Sorry, sir." At his look, Brody amended, "Kurt."

"There you go. And I'm great. Just great." Mr. Walsh clapped him on the shoulder. "Come on. Let me show you the ropes."

* * *

The job wasn't hard.

It was mostly people, and Brody had always been good with people. All he really needed to do was oversee everything that happened on the mountain, keep up with paperwork, and make sure the ski report went out on time.

He knew his way around the resort already—thanks to years skiing here and running through the back corridors with Kendall and Kev. Most of the staff had changed since then, but he recognized a few faces as Mr. Walsh introduced him around.

He spent the rest of the morning learning the systems Kendall had put into place. Her father kept saying "we" created these databases, but he could see Kendall's fingerprints on every organizational chart. When she did something, she *did* it.

She'd come up with spreadsheets for tracking her racing times and logging her workouts to maximize results when she was twelve. And now she'd developed systems to minimize staffing issues. She'd done her best to make them idiot-proof. And Brody badly wanted to prove to her that he wasn't an idiot.

After lunch, a supply order needed Kendall's signature, so he leapt at the flimsy excuse to head out to the old lodge—since he'd promised Steph he'd check in on things at her venue. And yes, because he hadn't seen Kendall all day.

He crunched up the snowy path to the old lodge and was still several feet away from the clearing when he heard Banner barking. Brody emerged from the woods to find Kendall struggling to heft the corner section of her ratty old couch into the back of her Jeep, while the dog bounced at her side.

"Whoa, whoa, whoa!" Brody called out as he jogged up to grab the other side of the sectional. "Where's your spotter?"

Kendall had always been one of the strongest people he

knew. Her arms were shaped by muscle—but he'd heard Kev say her back still gave her trouble.

"I've got it," Kendall insisted, grunting as she shoved her side and managed to wedge the sectional piece into the back of her Jeep. Whether the tailgate would close remained to be seen. "Chill, Trouble," she said to the dog, who stopped barking but kept wiggling in between them, trying to be in the middle of everything.

"I thought your dad wanted to hire someone to clear out the junk."

"He does, but if he had his way, he'd throw it all in a dumpster." She reached down, ruffling the ears of the dog she professed to barely tolerate. "I arranged for a storage unit this morning—for the stuff that might come in handy when we're ready to set up the space."

"You think someone's going to want a beat-up sectional at their reception?"

"I think if we're using the lodge for weddings, as well as receptions, then we'll need dedicated back rooms for both sides of the wedding party where they can get ready—and a perfectly comfortable sectional that only needs a new slipcover might save us some money furnishing them. Also, I might want it myself, once I get settled."

"I assumed you'd be moving into the main lodge." When they were kids, Brody had thought it was so magical when he came to play with Kendall and Kev that they lived in a special suite in the hotel.

"Yeah, I'm not moving back into the family suite," Kendall said firmly. "I figure we do the loft last. I'll stay there as long as construction will allow."

"I didn't expect you to move back in with your parents. I

thought one of the other hotel rooms—your dad offered me one so I don't have to commute back and forth to Woodland. Is that not normal for the manager?"

Kendall snorted. "He just wants the great Brody James under his roof. You should take it, though. We're almost never booked solid. I figured I'd borrow one of the empty rooms as a last resort if I can't find a place when I need to be out of here."

Brody trailed her back into the lodge, where the piles of used items from the resort still cluttered the space. "I think you might need a U-Haul. And a team of movers."

"The more I can do myself, the more of the budget I save for the things I can't." She pointed upward. "I'm worried we might have to redo the wiring, which is going to kill my chandelier budget unless I can economize elsewhere."

She had it all figured out. "How long have you been planning this?"

"Since Saturday."

"And you already know your chandelier budget?"

"I wouldn't have gone to my father with this without a plan," she explained, picking up what looked like an old ski binding and tossing it onto a pile—which sent Banner leaping onto the pile after it. "The logistics make it real."

Brody smiled at the familiarity. "You always were the girl with the plans."

"Yeah, right up until they blow up in my face."

Brody hesitated. He never knew quite what to say when they drifted too close to the topic of her accident. Did she want him to ask about it? Would she shut down if he did? Or maybe she wasn't even thinking about that day. Maybe he was the one who couldn't forget the sight of her in that hospital bed.

"Leave that, Banner. *Banner*," Kendall repeated, dragging

the dog away from the binding pile, which was now scattered across the floor. "He's been getting into everything today."

"Do you have a crate for him? Somewhere he can be safely out of the way when there's construction?"

"He's not staying," Kendall reminded him. "I'm just fostering him until he's adopted again."

She'd said that, but he hadn't thought she really meant it. "Even if he's not permanent, he can't run wild during construction. We could put the crate in my room when it's not safe for him to be here."

Her perma-frown line deepened. "I can't ask you to do that."

"No one wants to ask me for anything, but I'm standing here offering. Didn't I promise to help? To be your minion on this project?"

"I don't think that includes dog sitting," she said. "You're already helping by taking care of the manager crap so I don't have to. Just keep my dad happy—and preferably out of my hair."

She shoved at a box, grunting, and he quickly moved to help. "You shouldn't do the heavy lifting on your own. At least let me be the muscle. I can borrow my dad's old truck. He never uses it, and it'll fit a lot more than your Jeep." Kendall had never liked to be helped, but he knew how to appeal to her—with logic.

She eyed him, and he could see the moment she relented before she spoke. "Give me a day to figure out what I'm keeping, and then yes," she said, reluctance in every word. "Thank you. I'll take you up on your offer."

Brody beamed. He'd just committed himself to who knew how many hours of manual labor clearing this place out—so he didn't know why he felt like he'd just won the lottery.

"It's a date," he said—and Kendall shot him a strange look.

"Yeah. Okay. Now get back to work before my dad accuses me of distracting you."

"You got it, boss."

She shook her head, but that little smile was tugging at her lips when he left, so Brody felt like he'd won the lottery all over again.

Chapter Eight

Kendall groaned in relief as she sank into the resort's twelve-person outdoor hot tub, breathing in the steam rising off the surface. Her back was killing her. She'd definitely pushed too hard these last couple of days, but she'd had a mission, and when she had a mission, she had a tendency to forget that her body couldn't always keep up with her mind anymore.

She'd moved all her brother's boxes to the storage unit, along with the locked trunk containing all her skiing memorabilia. The bar area had been cleared out—along with the coffeepot and microwave that were her version of a kitchenette.

Contractors had been coming by all week, lured out by Brody's fame, to give them estimates and squeeze them into their busy schedules. So far, it was looking like they might finish early and under budget.

This whole thing might actually work.

She'd arranged with Brody to come by with his dad's truck tomorrow to help her clear out the things she hadn't been able to manage on her own, but other than those things, the first floor of the lodge was nearly empty—and ready to have the carpet ripped out.

Provided she could still lift her arms tomorrow.

The warm water sank into her muscles, and she closed her eyes, letting her head fall back to rest against the lip of the hot tub. It was a gorgeous clear night, bracingly cold, but that only made the heat of the hot tub that much more welcome.

There were two other outdoor hot tubs on the other side of the main building, just outside the indoor pool area and the saunas, with views of the lights from the ski lifts. Most of the tourists went there, leaving this one empty more often than not. Even at ten thirty on a perfect night.

The other two were enclosed by pergolas and bedecked with twinkle lights, giving them a festive atmosphere, but this one, which was a short walk up a gravel path to a clearing in the woods, had been Kendall's favorite ever since they put it in—with its peaceful quiet and uninterrupted view of the stars.

"Mind if I join you?"

Kendall opened her eyes and could just make out Brody in the golden light of the brazier that warmed the hot tub pad. He was wearing a Pine Hollow Mountain Resort monogrammed bathrobe and a cautious expression.

"I think there's room," Kendall said lightly, nodding toward the rest of the oversized hot tub.

Brody smiled and shrugged off the robe, revealing a pair of dark board shorts—and the body of an Olympian.

Which was only logical, since he *was* one.

There was an Olympic rings tattoo to one side of his washboard abs, and a couple other tats on his upper arms. Kendall averted her gaze to avoid the blatant objectification of her new employee—but her unruly eyes kept sneaking glances at him from beneath her eyelashes. So she focused on his feet. Those weren't sexual. She could stare at feet.

But then those feet stepped into the water, the rest of his body following, and Kendall made herself look away again—but not before she saw the line of scars along the side of his knee. And his wince. Reminding her that his body was battered by the sport they both loved. Not like hers was, but he'd taken some hits.

"Knee acting up?"

"Not too bad."

He was fully immersed now, so Kendall let herself look back at him—which was a mistake. He'd stretched out his arms to either side. Curves of muscle bunched from his shoulders and along his arms, outlined in the dim golden light of the brazier.

Kendall distracted herself by focusing on the thin white scar on one shoulder. "Looks like you had a good surgeon. You can barely see that one."

Brody snorted. "My agent requested a plastic surgeon do the stitches. He was trying to get me some beachwear ad campaign and didn't want to damage the goods."

And the goods were very good indeed.

Kendall cleared her throat, looking pointedly into the woods. "How are you liking being one of the working stiffs? Settling in okay?" It had been four days now. He'd moved his stuff into one of the rooms at the main lodge, but the staff were still in awe of him. So much so that they still came to Kendall when they had problems—but at least he'd taken over some of the paperwork nonsense that sucked up her time.

"Is it weird that I love it?" Brody asked.

"Yes," Kendall said without hesitation. "Though I suppose it's different when you can go back to being a ski god as soon as the novelty wears off."

"I don't know. It's kind of fun," he said.

"Better you than me."

"You don't *really* hate it," Brody argued.

"Oh, I do. I never wanted to be a manager. You know me. I'm the opposite of a people person."

"Says the woman who wants to run weddings?" Humor was thick in his voice.

"That's different."

"How exactly?"

"It just is." She glared at him, and he grinned.

"I still can't get over you as a wedding planner. You don't even like weddings."

"I don't dislike them." At his look, she admitted, "Okay, fine, yes, I kind of hate them. I'm the anti-romantic. But I'm good at planning. At coordinating things and keeping them organized."

"Yeah, but why weddings?"

"Because anything is better than the conferences," she said with feeling. At his blank look, she asked, "Have you heard about Bagel Gate yet?"

"Bagel Gate?" he echoed, his lips twitching.

"You laugh, but it was very serious business at one of the motivational corporate conference thingies we hosted last summer."

"Well, now I have to know."

"It was stupid," she insisted. "The conference had advertised they would provide breakfast both days, but they were trying to cut costs, so they didn't want to order enough bagels for every attendee—assuming some people would go for eggs or yogurt or muffins instead. Shouldn't be a problem, right? But the first day of the conference, they ran out of bagels, and there were complaints."

"That's it?"

"Oh no," Kendall assured him. "See, lots of attendees had

only eaten half of their bagel, leaving the rest, so we offered to cut the bagels in half for the second day. People who still wanted a full bagel could just take two halves, but we'd have enough for everyone to have some."

"Okay…"

"You would think we were chopping kittens in half based on the reactions. One of the conference attendees actually started screaming at my staff. About *bagels*."

"Wait, so how did you chop them? Like to make a bagel sandwich or to make little Cs?"

"Does it matter?"

"I'm just saying there's a natural way to cut a bagel—"

"Don't defend the Bagel Gaters. Four of my best servers quit that day."

"Because of bagels?"

"Because they were sick of being yelled at for things that weren't their fault—like the chicken being cold because some seminar ran an hour later than the conference organizers had planned and they failed to tell us that they would need to push back lunch." Kendall's back twinged—and she forced herself to relax the tension in her shoulders that always tightened up when she talked about last summer. "We never should have been trying to attract conferences to begin with."

"Then why were you?"

"Because *Kevin* wanted to. His company sent him to some corporate retreat in Vail and he thought, 'This will save the resort!' and my father is convinced that everything Kevin says is genius because he's a fancy business guy now—even though he's never worked at the resort a day in his life—unlike those of us who are trapped here. Who spend our entire freaking lives on this mountain and yet are systematically ignored when we point out that we want to be a destination for *adventurers*. We want people to come here to *celebrate*, because yes, those people might be demanding, but they're also *happy* and they're going to talk about what a great time they had and want to come back, for anniversaries and vacations. We need to capitalize on what we have." She shoved a finger toward the mountain. "We're secluded! We're over an hour from the nearest airport! And my dad is out there offering free shuttles to and from Burlington to lure in people who don't even *ski*."

She didn't blame her brother—Kevin had left Pine Hollow at eighteen and never looked back. It wasn't his fault he'd become the rising star at his financial firm at the exact same time Kendall's star had been falling. And it certainly wasn't his fault their father had suddenly started listening to him at the same time he'd started blocking Kendall out. Success was their father's love language.

"Your dad's listening now," Brody pointed out. "You're fixing up the lodge…"

"Because Saint Brody asked him to." An Olympian. A champion. How could he resist?

"I'm sure he listens to you—"

"Don't," she snapped, irritation spiking. "Our relationship is…complicated." It always had been.

Her father had never been an overtly affectionate man. Always the taskmaster, always pushing a little harder, but since she'd stopped skiing, it was like he'd stopped being able to look at her. The failure. And she'd been trying desperately to make it up to him.

Brody didn't know what it was like. He didn't understand the pressure to carry on the family name, that elusive feeling of chasing her father's pride, *knowing* that she had disappointed him on the largest scale possible—not just because he'd nearly bankrupted them for her medical bills, but because she'd had the audacity to walk away.

Her dad thought she'd given up. And maybe part of her did too. Maybe that was why it was so hard to see his disappointment—because it reflected hers. Because deep down she wondered if she should have kept trying, no matter how many times she told herself that she'd tried as long as she could, as hard as she could without permanently reinjuring herself.

Maybe he only would have been happy if she had.

"He loves you like crazy."

"I know." She did know. Her dad wasn't into hugs or talking about feelings, but he really did love her. Even if he'd never been big on showing it. But sometimes that didn't help.

Brody shifted, dropping his arms into the water and sinking up to his chin. "Do you really feel trapped here? I thought you loved the resort."

"I do," she said. "I just never thought this would be my life. I never wanted to work here."

Brody frowned, confused. "I remember you always working around the resort. Even when we were teenagers. Teaching ski school. Running the lifts. You've done this almost as long as I've known you."

"But it wasn't who I was. It wasn't *all* I was. I was training. I was racing. The resort was what I did on the side, but I was going to the Olympics. That was *me*." She shrugged. "And then it wasn't. And I needed to do something so I would stop thinking about everything I couldn't do anymore, and I owed my dad, all those medical bills—so I did this. I came home and I did what was safe. I moved into the old lodge. I worked at the resort. And I stopped looking forward."

Brody was watching her now. She didn't know why it was

so easy to tell him secrets she hadn't even admitted to Charlotte and Magda. Maybe it was the quiet of the night or the hot water. Maybe it was just Brody.

But she kept going. "I used to be in such a hurry, and now I'm not going anywhere. Sometimes when I meet someone new, it feels like they can't see me—like there's this giant piece of me that they don't know. Because that isn't me anymore. I don't know when I stopped being me."

"You're always you."

"No. I changed. And I don't know who I am now. My dad was a skier. My grandfather was a skier. Kevin was supposed to be, but he was never great. *I* was great. I was the best. It was all I wanted. And now it's like I don't know how to want things anymore. Like I forgot how to take risks. So I just stay. I play it safe. I work at this job, where my dad is my boss and doesn't listen to me. Where we're always one bad season away from having to sell. And I constantly feel like I'm letting everyone down."

"For the record, the staff all love you. They know you're the one who really runs this place, and they've all told me how great you are."

She shook her head, even though the words were good to hear.

"I'm sorry to be driving you out of the old lodge," he said after a moment of only the night birds talking.

"You aren't driving me anywhere. You just gave me the opportunity to change things. Well. You and Banner." She glanced toward the trees in the direction of the old lodge, where she'd left the troublemaker sleeping. "I never planned to live there so long. I just sort of...got stuck. And I always thought that carpet was hideous. I knew the lodge could be incredible if I fixed it up, but something always stopped me. Like if I renovated it to live in, it would be admitting I was really staying. Even though obviously I'm not going anywhere."

"You could."

She met his eyes across the span of the hot tub and didn't answer. She'd never told anyone half the things she'd just told him. She hadn't even let herself think them. But somehow she didn't regret a word of it.

"Truth or dare?"

Kendall looked at him sharply at the light question.

They'd played that game a thousand times when they were little. It had always been about one-upping each other. The bigger dare. A challenge to see who would yield first. Or which one of them would need to be rushed to urgent care for stitches.

Once he'd hit high school, they hadn't played as often. He'd figured out that the pretty, giggly girls liked him and stopped being her best friend and became Kevin's. He'd still played truth or dare—but then it was in the hot tub with Kevin and those girls in bikinis with the sweet, high-pitched voices. Kendall had only played with him a few times—and only once without Kevin around.

Only once when it was just the two of them, and she'd wanted so badly to dare him to kiss her…but she hadn't had the nerve.

She'd had such a crush on him…and then he'd gone off to join the World Cup tour and the giggly girls had become pouty-lipped models, and they'd stopped playing altogether. Even after she'd joined the tour herself.

"Haven't you had enough truth for one night?" she asked.

"Truth or dare?" he repeated.

She shook her head. "I'm not going first."

"There's nothing wrong with my knee."

Kendall blinked. "What?"

Chapter Nine

Brody hadn't meant to blurt that out, but something unknotted in his chest as soon as he did, and he heard himself explaining. "I'm not hurt. At least not any more than I've ever been."

Kendall stared at him, wide-eyed. "That isn't how the game works. You're supposed to pick truth or dare."

"I know." But the truth had just come out and now that he'd said it, he felt inexplicably relieved. Like a weight had been lifted just saying it out loud.

"What are you doing here if you're not injured?"

"Hiding from my life," he admitted. "I felt off all season. I haven't been racing the way I normally do, and then in Switzerland, I just skied out. I was on a training run, and I missed a gate. And then, I left."

"You just left?" she asked incredulously.

"I packed my things, bought a ticket on my way to the airport. It wasn't a plan. It had nothing to do with Bailey's wedding. Or Steph's. I just suddenly couldn't be there."

"Why?"

"I didn't want it anymore. Not like I used to. I'd been pushing so hard for so long. I was standing there in my hotel room, looking at the life I'd built, and suddenly it all felt so empty. So pointless. And I had to go. I wasn't thinking. Only reacting."

She watched him, her eyes dark. "Is this about Oskar?"

"No," he said too quickly, hoping she didn't hear the lie. He didn't want it to be about Oskar. He didn't want to think about that. "I mean, it was tragic, but..." He shook away the thought. "It was me. I just needed to get away. All I did was ski. My whole life was about trying to be the best—and I couldn't even figure out why I was doing it anymore. I needed to be something else for a while. So I came here. And then I saw you. And I thought...I thought if I stayed here, I could figure it out. I know it doesn't make any sense."

Kendall watched him, something inscrutable in her eyes. "It kind of sounds like burnout."

"I guess. Maybe. I—" Brody broke off and started again. "You know how you, um, you said you were always in a hurry when you were chasing gold?"

"Yeah. It's all that matters."

"Exactly." He'd known she would get it. Because Kendall had always been *him*. The daredevil. The fastest on the mountain. And the one who wanted Olympic gold more than anything in the world. The only person who worked harder than him in training. Except Oskar. "You don't let yourself think about anything else. And then you look up and it's ten years later and you're still fighting, still reaching, but everybody else has changed. Steph's getting married. Kev is some hotshot financial analyst in New York. You're—"

"Right where I always was?"

"A wedding planner. The glue that holds this whole place together. And I'm the guy people know better than to ask for things. I'm the one they know won't be there. Because that's all I am. The racer."

"But they understand why. We all understand why."

He grimaced. "It's not like I'm curing cancer."

"No. But we still support you. You don't have to feel guilty for prioritizing your dreams."

"I don't. I'm just…"

"Having a midlife crisis?"

He huffed out a soft laugh. "Yeah, maybe." He met her eyes in the darkness.

"Have you talked to anyone?" she asked gently.

"Like a therapist?"

"I had a really good sports psychologist after my accident. They could help."

"Yeah. But then I'd have to tell someone that the problem isn't my knee. It's my head."

"That's okay," she insisted, her voice surprisingly soft. "You're human."

He'd thought, when he first saw her at the wedding, that she hadn't changed a bit—and in some ways she hadn't. But there was something different about her. Something that made it hard to look away from the understanding in her eyes.

She knew him. She always had.

"Truth or dare?" he asked.

After a moment, she smiled slightly. "Fine. Truth."

"Really?" She'd *always* said dare.

"I'm too old to go roll in the snow or whatever other dare you've got queued up. I'm mature now."

His lips twitched. "How disappointing."

"You got a truth or what?"

He met her eyes, reading the challenge in them. She was going to judge him by his question. It needed to be something real. But not too real.

"Did you really get married on a dare?"

She groaned, rolling her eyes. "Don't you know this story?"

"I've heard it, but never from you."

She held his gaze for a moment. "Yes, okay? I did."

He arched his eyebrows, waiting, and Kendall groaned, half-laughing—which was exactly what he'd hoped for.

"In my defense, I was twenty-three."

He made a gimme gesture with one hand. "Story."

"Fine!" She sighed. "I had been dating Carter for about three weeks—"

Brody groaned.

"I know! Shut up," Kendall snapped. "Anyway, as I was saying, Carter and I had been dating for a *while*—"

He snorted.

"—and my dad *hated* it. He hated anything that he thought detracted from my focus. It was an Olympic year. But Carter was *fun*. He was a good time. And yes, in retrospect, he was also immature and self-absorbed and more interested in me as 'the best' than in me as a person—but in his defense, so was I. And he was an athlete too, so he got it, you know? I never had to defend my priorities."

"And the dare?"

"It was right after a competition. I won, but I was so pissed at my dad—I don't even remember about what. He was my coach and my manager, and it felt like he tried to control my entire life. So I snuck out. Carter and I were out drinking with some friends, doing stupid shit, challenging one another, and then—I don't know who said it, one of Carter's friends, I think—but someone said something about how I wouldn't *really* defy my father. Like, I'll complain about him, but then I'll always do what he wants me to."

"Uh-oh."

"Yeah. I saw red. And I said, 'Name it.'"

"'Name it'?"

"Yeah, I told them to name it and I'll do it. Whatever you think I won't do, because it would piss my dad off, watch me do it. And they said marry Carter. So I did. That night. Probably wouldn't have happened if we'd been competing anywhere other than Tahoe—but Nevada was right there. And that was it."

He smiled. Not even a little surprised by the course of the story. "They didn't know you at all. The only thing you like better than a dare is pissing your dad off."

Kendall sobered. "Yeah, back then. 'Course it didn't really work out all that well for me. Crashed a month later. Carter stuck it out seven whole weeks before he cheated on me while I was rehabbing. Though in his defense, I'm pretty sure he married the girl he cheated on me with, so maybe they really loved each other. He's got a YouTube channel now."

"Your ex was a dumbass."

Brody had only met Carter a handful of times—one of them being when he'd gone to see Kendall in the hospital after the crash. She'd been disoriented, concussed, and unable to remember the entire day of the accident. Every time she woke up, she would struggle to get out of bed, convinced it was the morning of the Olympic trials and she was going to be late. They'd had to tell her over and over again that her Olympic dreams were over. That she was lucky to be alive. That she would have months of rehab before she'd be able to walk again, let alone ski.

And Carter had been making cracks about "visiting the red room" and what a "total yard sale" Kendall's crash had been.

Every skier knew injuries were possible—hell, they were a way of life when you were rocketing down a mountain at eighty miles per hour and a split second could change everything. They all developed a macabre sense of humor. The "red room" meant the barriers on either side of the course, and every skier knew how much caroming into them hurt. A "yard sale" was when you hit the ground so hard your bindings popped and your skis, poles, hell, even your gloves and goggles, went flying off and scattered, until it looked like you were throwing a yard sale with all your gear.

Brody had heard the terms his entire career—and he'd never wanted to beat someone senseless for using them until that day with Carter cracking jokes over Kendall's hospital bed.

Everything in him had hurt, seeing her there. His invincible friend, the one he'd always been chasing down the mountain, suddenly unable to move.

"We were both young and stupid. Luckily, I'm mature now." Kendall lifted her hand from the water, holding her fingertips up to the light. "And on that note, I should go in. Banner's probably digging another hole in the carpet, and I'm getting all pruney."

Brody rose when she did, shoving down a flash of disappointment. "I'll see you tomorrow? To clear out the lodge?"

"You bet. We've got work to do." Kendall climbed out, shivering in the cold air in her simple black one-piece suit, long legs pale in the moonlight. Brody quickly looked away when he caught himself staring. This was Kendall. Kevin's sister. He didn't ogle her legs.

But he wasn't blind.

"Have a good night, Brody," she said, and he looked back to see she'd wrapped up in a towel. She lifted one hand in a wave, already heading up the path toward the old lodge, her Crocs squelching in the snow.

He watched her walk away, with her words echoing softly in his mind.

More interested in me as "the best" than in me as a person…

He wasn't sure anything had ever so perfectly described his relationship with Valeria. They'd met at a party celebrating his US Championship last year. She was gorgeous. She was charming, so composed and elegant. Everything had been easy and surface level. When her schedule had allowed, she'd come to see him race, which both of their PR teams loved, but they lived their own lives, satisfied with that.

He was an athlete and she was a model, and they were both obsessed with reaching the pinnacle of their chosen careers. Just like Kendall said, he'd never had to explain his priorities, which he'd thought made them perfect for one another, but it had also kept a comfortable distance between them. Even when they were alone together, they were frequently in their own worlds. Both on their phones.

What did they really have in common? What did they really know about one another?

It hadn't even occurred to him to talk to her about what he was going through. About his quest to get a life. About the fact that he wasn't sure he wanted to go back to skiing anytime soon. If at all.

What were they if he wasn't a champion anymore? What if he never got back that competitive edge?

It was five in the morning in Italy, but he suddenly wanted very badly to call her. They hadn't talked or even texted much since he'd told her he was staying in Vermont. Maybe she just didn't understand how serious he was.

Brody let himself into his hotel room—the one he'd moved into this week to avoid having to explain to his parents every morning why he wasn't going back to the tour. He stripped off his swimsuit and took a quick shower, but then couldn't wait anymore. He grabbed his phone and wrote Valeria a text.

We should talk. I'm not sure how long I'll be here.

He considered adding an invitation for her to come to Vermont, but then decided against it.

He hesitated with his thumb over Send. He didn't want to wake her, but she probably had her Do Not Disturb on anyway. And he didn't trust himself to send it if he waited until the morning. It was always easier to be honest at midnight.

A knee injury was quantifiable. Whatever the hell was going on in his head…how could he measure recovery time? What if this was it? What if he never went back?

He tapped Send, expecting no response, but almost immediately three little dots appeared.

Shit.

She must have an early shoot. Or maybe she wasn't in Italy right now. She could be anywhere.

Anxiety had him watching those dots. So he saw the moment the message arrived.

I don't think this is working anymore. I'm sorry.

Brody stared at the words.

Had she just broken up with him via text? She knew he was

awake. She could easily have called him back, but she'd chosen text.

And yes, he'd already bailed on their relationship when he flew back to the States without so much as a word—he was definitely the one who'd lit the match to set their paper-thin relationship on fire—but a little voice whispered at the back of his thoughts, telling him she'd run for the door the second it had become apparent he might not be the great Brody James anymore. That he was worthless without the titles.

His throat tightened.

Who the hell *was* he, if he wasn't an Olympian?

He wasn't good with insecurity. He wasn't used to introspection and questioning himself. He'd always been racing forward so fast and pushing so hard that he never gave the doubts a chance to catch up.

Kendall had joked about a midlife crisis, and she wasn't wrong.

He didn't know what he was doing or where he was going, but he was here now.

And tomorrow he would help Kendall. Until he figured the rest out.

Chapter Ten

"All right. I think we're good. Everything else goes in the dumpster."

Brody dusted off his hands, surveying their work, and Kendall resisted the urge to ogle, as she'd been doing all day. They'd finally finished running things to the storage unit in his dad's old truck.

"Except the poles," she pointed out.

Brody looked at her like she'd lost her mind. "Kendall. No one needs two hundred broken ski poles."

"They aren't for me. There's an artist nearby who works with found materials. I've been saving them for him," she explained. "If you help me load them into my Jeep, I'll take them out there tomorrow."

"An artist." He nodded. "That makes a lot more sense."

She bumped his shoulder with hers. "You thought I was a hoarder, didn't you? My dad certainly does."

"I mean, I wasn't going to say *hoarder*."

She released a short, involuntary laugh at his expression. "I just hate wasting things. People are too quick to throw things away the second they aren't useful."

"I get that." He met her eyes, his smile softening, and she held his gaze a little too long.

Then his stomach growled.

She blushed, taking a step back, when she realized how close they were standing. "We should stop for lunch. You like burritos? There's a truck that sets up near chair five most days. I can run over and grab some. Jamie always gives me extra guac." And leaving Brody here would give her a break from the laughing and ogling. She'd been doing entirely too much of both.

"Who am I to turn down extra guac?" He nodded toward the pile of poles. "I'll get started loading these. We're so close to being done."

"Just with this part," she reminded him. "We still have a long way to go." She started toward the door. "I'll text you a picture of the menu and you can tell me what you want. C'mon, Banner."

"You can leave him here. I'll keep an eye on him," Brody offered when Banner didn't immediately leap to follow. Brody frowned as he watched the dog doing a weird little cha-cha against the wall. "What is he doing?"

"Butt dances. I have a bunch of videos on my phone of him doing that. He loves being scratched just above his tail, and when there's no one around to oblige, he rubs his hind end against the wall trying to scratch it. You sure you want him to stay?"

"Go," Brody insisted. "I've got him."

Brody reached for an armful of poles—and Kendall escaped down the path toward chair five before he could start lifting things, with his muscles being all *muscley*.

Last night in the hot tub had just been two old friends talking. It didn't mean anything, even if he had made her feel all fluttery. He had a girlfriend. And even if he didn't, he would be going back to the World Cup tour as soon as he got past his current burnout.

It made sense now, why he was here. He'd always pushed himself too hard. His coaches used to have to stop him from training too hard because he'd drive himself to the point of collapse. When he was on, he was on, but if he missed one gate, he missed seven. All-or-nothing Brody James.

Last night in the hot tub, he'd talked about skiing being all he was and pushing himself so hard, and it had all clicked into place.

He was burned out now, but it wouldn't be long before he'd bounce back. With a knee, she'd figured he might be here for weeks, maybe even until Steph's wedding, but without a physical obstacle, Brody James wouldn't hang around. That itch would strike again, his on-off switch would flip, and he'd be on a plane within a week or two. When people decided they were done with Pine Hollow, it happened fast. She'd learned that lesson early.

So there was no point in feeling like a starry-eyed teenager over him. He didn't see her that way, he had a girlfriend, and he was leaving. The unavailability trifecta.

It had just been too long since she'd been with anyone else. That was all this was.

Last March, Charlotte had broken up with her awful ex-boyfriend and suggested they all take a man detox. Kendall had protested the lack of booty calls—but since her last no-strings arrangement had moved to Washington, she hadn't exactly had much to give up. And she'd been so busy over the summer with those awful conferences that she hadn't had time to find anyone new.

She periodically tried dating but hadn't made it past the third date in years. Friends with benefits was better—but she had to be so careful about who she hooked up with. No employees of the resort, no matter how much some of the ski instructors flirted with her. No one who might catch feelings or get annoyed that she didn't want to be vulnerable or play the girlfriend. No one who would get too pissy or demanding of her time when she prioritized the resort. She didn't want to navigate manly feels. She just wanted a mutually satisfying arrangement that stayed simple—but no matter how much men might say they wanted that too, they always ended up wanting more.

So it had been months. Getting close to a freaking year. And she had *needs*, damn it.

Which had to be why she kept getting all hot and bothered looking at Brody. Well, that and the fact that he was built like a freaking Greek statue.

What she needed was a date.

She arrived at the burrito truck and took a pic of the menu, texting it to Brody before joining the line. Jamie glanced over the crowd as he handed one customer their food, and he flashed her a big toothy grin when he saw her waiting.

Jamie, who always gave her extra guac. Jamie, who Magda was convinced had the hots for Kendall.

It was hard to take him seriously as a romantic prospect—he was seven years younger than she was and she had distinct memories of teaching him when he was still in ski school—but he was legal. Old enough to drink even. And she wasn't looking for romance.

Maybe Jamie was exactly what she needed.

Brody texted back his order, and Kendall shuffled forward in the line, studying Jamie the entire time. He was sort of goofy.

Always smiling. Always wearing a T-shirt that looked like it was one wash away from falling apart. He'd never paid attention in ski school, and he talked to all of his customers longer than Kendall preferred—she liked efficiency. Keep the line moving. Less chitchat. But the food was good and fairly priced.

No one hated Jamie. That was a nice quality in a hookup.

"Hey, Kendall," Jamie said with a big grin when she got to the front of the line. "I hear you're working on some big project."

"You hear right. The usual for me and a Vermonter."

"Coming right up," Jamie promised, disappearing into the depths of his truck. She swiped her card through the reader, paying while he cooked, and his voice floated out, even though she could no longer see him. "Is it true you hired Brody James? That guy's my idol."

"It's just temporary," Kendall called back.

"Still, it's wild. Puttin' Pine Hollow on the map. I bet people'd come from all over for ski lessons with Brody James."

"He's not teaching. He's just…doing us a favor." And he would be leaving soon.

"Right, 'cuz you, like, know him. That's so wild." Jamie appeared back in the window, grinning, probably getting ready to ask her what Brody was *really* like, but Kendall didn't want to talk about Brody. She didn't want to *think* about Brody.

She needed a distraction.

So she blurted out the first thing that popped into her mind. "Do you want to get a drink tonight?"

Jamie's eyes widened. "Whoa. Yeah. Like a date?"

"Like a date," Kendall confirmed.

"Wild," Jamie said, grinning. "Yeah."

"Tipsy Moose? Eight o'clock?"

"Yeah," Jamie confirmed, handing over the burritos with a wink. "I gave you extra guac."

"Thanks, Jamie. See you tonight."

Kendall started back toward the old lodge, already wondering if she was going to regret asking him out.

She was lost in her thoughts, but must have been glowering, because as soon as Brody saw her tromping up the path, he frowned. "What's wrong?"

Kendall tried to clear her glare. "Nothing."

"Did something happen?"

"No, I just, I have a date, okay?" She hadn't meant that to sound quite so belligerent.

He blinked, visibly startled. "Oh. Like, now?"

"Tonight. It just sort of happened."

"Yeah, dates are tricky like that."

Her lips twitched. "Shut up. You know what I mean."

"Do you want me to watch Banner?"

She shook her head. "I can't ask you to do that."

"People need to start asking me for things. Besides, I'm offering. It's not like I have anything else going on." He patted his back pocket, frowning. "Have you seen my phone?"

Dread slammed into Kendall. "Where's Banner?"

"He was inside—" Brody broke off as Kendall bolted for the door.

"Banner, no!" She caught him with his front paws on a bar stool, stretching to reach the cellphone resting on top of the bar. The dog froze in place—as if by not moving she wouldn't notice he was guilty as hell—and Kendall snatched the cellphone off the bar.

"He eats cellphones," Kendall explained, shoving Brody's top-of-the-line iPhone at him. "I should have warned you. It's why he was returned to the shelter so many times."

"Expensive habit, buddy," Brody said to the dog as the golden slunk down from his perch, trying to look nonchalant and innocent.

"Hopefully one he'll grow out of." She knelt down, cupping Banner's furry face between her hands. "Cellphones are not chew toys, you menace." But he looked at her with those *who me?* big dark eyes and she couldn't be mad. "You're the worst," she grumbled, ruffling his ears.

"That'll teach him."

"Ha." Kendall straightened and shoved a burrito at Brody.

"So what time should I come by to pet sit for your date? He obviously can't be left unsupervised."

She considered arguing, but she didn't trust Banner not to wreak havoc while she was gone, and she still hadn't gotten him a puppy crate—because that would be too much of a sign that she was keeping him. He was temporary.

But he needed a minder.

"Quarter to eight?"

"I'll be here."

Chapter Eleven

Brody may have made a tactical error.

It wasn't Banner. Watching Banner was easy. Before coming over tonight, Brody had swung by Furry Friends in town and picked up a ball-flinger and a Kong. When Kendall had left for her date, he'd introduced Banner to the toys—using the flinger to throw a ball up the hill beside the old lodge until the dog was exhausted from leaping through the snow, and then putting some peanut butter inside the Kong to keep him occupied when they came inside.

The entire lower level had been cleared now—no couch, no television, just the ugliest orange shag carpet in the world, waiting to be ripped up. And Brody alone with his thoughts.

He hadn't expected the idea of Kendall out on a date to bother him. It never had before. But maybe it was something about being here when Kev wasn't. Like he needed to fill the role of big brother and watch over her. Look out for her interests. Not that he'd ever felt particularly big brotherly toward her, but it was the only explanation he had as to why he felt so unsettled knowing she was out with some guy right now.

He'd brought his phone. He tried sitting at the bar and streaming something on it, but he couldn't focus on *Rick and Morty*.

Banner finished his Kong and padded over to sniff at the hole he'd made in the carpet, pawing at it and gripping a single loose carpet fiber with his mouth, yanking until it came up with a jerk. The dog growled, eagerly attacking another thread.

Brody should probably try to get him to stop—allowing him to rip holes in rugs was a terrible precedent to set, but the carpet needed to go anyway, and Brody could understand the restless energy that made the dog want to shred it.

"You know what?" he told the golden, rising from the bar. "That's a great idea."

So while Kendall was off dating that guy, Banner and Brody ripped out the carpet.

He hadn't come here planning to do manual labor tonight, but he needed to do *something*. He knew Kendall was an adult. She was an attractive woman. She'd probably been on hundreds of dates in her life. But it hit differently, knowing she was on one *right now*.

Banner loved the game, growling and pouncing on the remnants as Brody jerked up long swaths of ugly orange shag. The physical exertion felt fantastic, but he hadn't worn the right shirt for yanking up carpet, so he stripped it off and kept going. He propped his phone on the bar, playing his pump-up playlist. He tried to focus on the music and not what Kendall might be doing right now as he fell into the rhythm of yanking up carpet and using a box cutter to slice it into pieces.

This was good. This was purposeful. He wasn't avoiding his mental quicksand—he was *helping*.

"Brody?"

Brody spun to face the door, feeling like he'd been caught in the act of something nefarious as he saw Kendall standing in the doorway. "Hey."

There was a shirtless Olympian in her house.

A *sweaty* shirtless Olympian. It was like something out of a sports drink ad campaign, all muscles and flexing. The man was freaking *glistening*.

And Kendall felt more in a single second of watching him manhandling carpet than she had in her entire date with Jamie. Apparently her plan to avoid having inappropriate feelings for Brody by getting a little stress relief with someone else was fundamentally flawed.

The gods were laughing at her.

"You're back early."

"Am I?" she asked, the words sharper than she'd intended. She was just so annoyed. With herself more than anyone. She didn't *want* to be feeling hot and bothered for Brody Freaking James.

Banner bounced over to greet her, and she gave him a quick cuddle hello before heading toward the stairs to the loft, avoiding carpet remnants scattered over the floor. The dog wove around her legs eagerly. "I thought the contractor agreed to rip out the carpet."

"It's like you said—anything we can do ourselves saves money for other things. And I needed the exercise."

She glanced over at him, reminded by his physique alone how much exercise he normally got. "Why haven't you been skiing? I know you're telling everyone you're here because of your knee, but you could still take a few runs."

"I've been busy. And I haven't been here that long."

She frowned. They both knew how quickly conditioning could slip.

"How was your date?" he asked, in a blatant attempt to change the subject, and she glowered.

"It was fine." She stomped up the stairs, stripping off her coat and scarf.

"Just fine?"

"I screwed up my guac connection," she snapped without looking back.

"That bad?"

"No, it was fine, I just…"

She'd felt guilty. Because she'd been planning on using Jamie. Using him to make herself feel better. To offload some stress. And using him to push away things she didn't want to be feeling for Brody.

It hadn't occurred to her that Jamie might want anything other than a hookup until he'd shown up at the Tipsy Moose—freshly shaven, with his hair slicked back, in a button-down shirt that for once didn't look like it was falling apart at the seams.

But it wasn't even the obvious effort he'd put into his appearance. It was how *nervous* he looked. How excited.

And she'd felt like the worst possible human because to him this was real. And she didn't want real. She didn't have the mental energy for real. And she didn't trust it.

"You just what?" Brody prompted from below.

Kendall looked over the balcony at Brody standing shirtless amid the half-removed carpet. There was something incredibly satisfying about seeing it being ripped out. "You want a hand with that?" she asked instead of answering his question.

He glanced at the wreckage around him. "Sure."

Kendall threw down her bag.

Twenty minutes later, she was sweaty and sticky—and smiling with satisfaction as she planted her hands on her hips and surveyed the carpetless floor. The hardwood underneath the carpet pad wasn't in terrible shape. It would look better after it was refinished next week, but it was already a huge improvement.

The room looked bigger without the carpet—and without all the crap that had been cluttering it up. It was easy to envision it as an event space now. Some new lighting. Fix up the back rooms. Clear out the loft.

"God, that feels good," she said aloud.

"Hell yes, it does," Brody agreed at her side, shirtless and filthy and beaming.

Banner was asleep in the corner on a pile of discarded carpet. He'd loved the carpet ripping at first, leaping on the pieces as they tore them up, but had finally conked out.

"Steph's gonna love it," Brody commented, looking around at the space.

The place still needed a lot of work, but they could see it now. What it was going to be.

"It always bothered me that we let the lodge fall into disrepair," Kendall said. "This whole section of the mountain got bypassed when we put in the new lifts, and it made sense for everything to center around the main lodge, where it's all shiny and new. But this is our history. And it's still perfectly good."

"It's freaking amazing."

Kendall glanced down at herself, then over at Brody, feeling the first twinge in her back from overexertion but not regretting it for a second. "Hot tub?" she asked.

He met her eyes. "Hot tub," he agreed.

* * *

The forest-clearing hot tub was empty again when Kendall sank into it with a satisfied sigh. Brody had run back to the main lodge to get his suit, so she'd made it here first.

She closed her eyes, sinking into the warmth, and trying not to feel guilty about Jamie or the fact that Brody had bought more toys for Banner than she had, or the fact that she was taking advantage of Brody for free labor and ogling him the entire time.

She didn't open her eyes more than a slit when she heard Brody approach, letting him think she couldn't see him as he climbed in opposite her with a relieved groan.

"You gonna tell me about Guac Guy?"

She opened one eye at his question. "You really wanna know?"

"Just if I need to beat him up as your honorary big brother."

Kendall closed her eye again. *Honorary big brother.* That was deflating. "You aren't my brother," she reminded him. "And he was great. It was me."

"I doubt that."

"Charlotte thinks I don't give people a chance." Kendall sighed, opening her eyes. "She's probably not wrong."

They just hadn't clicked. Jamie had missed all of her references. He didn't have any ambition—didn't seem to *want* anything. And he kept calling everything *wild*. It had been tempting to turn it into a drinking game, except that probably would have led to even worse decisions.

And then he kept bringing up Brody with hero worship gleaming in his eyes—which hadn't exactly helped in her plan to forget he existed for one night.

"You went out with him. That's a chance."

"And I spent the entire date cataloguing all the reasons why we would never work. That's my superpower," she said. "I can determine what will go wrong in every potential relationship in three dates or less."

"The commentators did always say you must be psychic."

She smiled slightly. She'd actually forgotten that. The way the skiing commentators had marveled at her instincts on the course. The way she seemed to know what was coming even if she'd never skied a mountain before.

"I'm not sure it's a good thing," she admitted. "It's like this red flag reflex. I can't help it."

"So what were Guac Guy's red flags?"

He wasn't you. She shook her head. "It doesn't matter. I can't go out with him again. I'd be leading him on. He likes me too much."

"And liking you too much is a problem?"

"It is when all I wanted was to use him for sex."

Brody made a choking noise, and suddenly his face was bright red.

"Are you blushing?" she demanded. "The playboy of the World Cup circuit?"

"I was not a playboy. I just…"

"Got around."

If possible, his face got even redder. "Women like me."

"Oh, I remember. Carolina Vasquez…Brittany Luther… was there a cheerleader you didn't date in high school?"

Poor Brody's face was going to combust. "If they asked me out, it would be rude to say no."

"God, the giggling. So. Much. Giggling." She eyed him. "Let me guess, Valeria is a giggler."

"You guess wrong."

"Have you evolved to sexy pouting? That's your type now?"

He grimaced, then took a breath, watching her for a moment before admitting, "We broke up."

"What?"

"Valeria and I. We broke up."

"When? I thought—"

"Last night, actually."

"Oh. Wow." She was officially an asshole. Giving him shit about his taste on the heels of a breakup. "I'm sorry, Brody."

"I'm not." He frowned as he spoke. "I definitely should be, but I'm not. We were just going through the motions of being together. I'm not sure she ever really knew me. And I certainly didn't know her. We were both so busy with our careers—but it turns out at least one of you has to put in some effort if you want a relationship to work."

"Yeah. Probably."

And then a stupid thought popped into her head.

He was single.

He was still leaving, and he just called himself her honorary big brother, but sitting in the hot tub with him suddenly felt different. Kendall shifted, her breath going a little short.

"So—"

He spoke at the same time. "You should give Guac Guy another chance."

"What?"

"You never used to be afraid of taking chances. With your heart or anything else."

She met his eyes, irritable that he thought he still knew her. "Maybe I learned my lesson."

"Maybe you're doing exactly what you hate when other people do."

"Excuse me?"

He shrugged, unbothered by the sharpness in her voice. "The lodge, the dog, the ski poles, all of that junk in the storage unit—you *hate* when people throw things away the second they aren't perfect. Isn't that what you're doing when you won't give people a second chance?"

Her irritation built that much faster because he might have a point. "You don't know me," she snapped. "You haven't known me in years. You're off living your perfect life and now you come back and think you can just sweep in and fix everything, including me, because you're Saint Brody, everyone's hero—"

"I never said—"

"I don't need you to fix me. I didn't ask for your advice."

"Truth or dare?" he demanded.

"What?" she snapped.

"Truth or dare?"

"No." She was so not in the mood to play.

"Are you happy?"

"Are *you*?" she snarled.

"I don't know."

The simple honesty of his statement slammed the brakes on her anger.

He held her gaze as he repeated: "I don't know."

She was surprised he'd said it, even if the game was truth. "Really?"

"I should be," he said. "I'm supposed to be. How many people would trade places with me in a heartbeat?" He met her eyes, and the knowledge that *she* would fill the air between them. "I'm grateful. I got to stand on an Olympic podium, even if they weren't playing my national anthem, and that's supposed to make everything else good, right? I have a great family, who support me. A girlfriend—until last night—who always understood my dedication, my priorities. These are the things that are supposed to make you happy, right? It's like I've been telling myself I am because I could check all the boxes and I didn't realize I wasn't until…" He trailed off, shaking his head. "I don't know. Zermatt."

Her instincts twinged. "Did something happen?"

"Nothing that hadn't already…" He shook his head and met her eyes. "I'm not Saint Brody. And I'm not trying to fix you. I know you aren't the one who needs to be fixed."

Aren't I? He'd asked if she was happy, and the words had felt like an attack.

"I shouldn't have—I'm sorry I yelled at you."

"No, I was being a dick." He held out a hand across the hot water. "Truce?"

She shook it, a little zing trying to travel up her arm. "Truce."

"So what's on tap for tomorrow?" he asked as he resumed his spot with his arms stretched out to either side. "Ripping out the weird half wall in the back office?"

Kendall made a face. "I can't. I have a shower tomorrow."

"I have a bath next week."

She snorted. "A wedding shower. For Charlotte. Magda's in charge of planning it, but I need to help set up. It's a whole thing."

"I thought you were the maid of honor."

"We're sharing the duties. Magda took the shower, and I took the bachelorette party—since Mags wouldn't know how to go wild if she tried."

"And you do?"

Kendall's eyes flared with offense. "Excuse me. I believe you are talking to the woman who once skied Sugarloaf in a swimsuit because *someone* dared me."

"You're the one who said you forgot how to take risks."

"Is that a challenge?"

He smiled. "I wouldn't dare."

"Then I guess you're taking truth."

"Fire away."

The air felt like it was sparking between them, and she couldn't fight the challenging smile on her face. *God,* it was fun. Facing off with him. The up and down of it. Pushing against someone she knew would never let her win. Who would always challenge her to push herself a little further. She'd *missed* him.

"Where did you lose your virginity?" she asked.

"Olympic Village," he said without missing a beat.

An involuntary laugh burst out even as she splashed him with a wave of water. "Liar." He'd been twenty-four at his first Olympics, and Kendall didn't buy for a second that he'd waited that long.

"Okay, that was a lie," Brody admitted. "But it makes a good story, doesn't it? And I didn't get nearly as much action as everyone thought. I was virtuously focused on my training."

"You have to do a dare if you don't answer the question," she reminded him.

He nodded, running his tongue along his teeth.

"Well?" she demanded. "Do I need to think of a dare?"

He sighed, then admitted, "The old lodge."

This time Kendall believed him, and her jaw dropped. *"My* old lodge?"

"Your loft, actually."

"Oh my God."

"We used to have all those parties there, and one night Brittany Luther and I stayed after everyone else left…"

"Brittany Luther. I should have known. She was cute. But God, the *giggles*."

"She was a giggler," Brody acknowledged. "But she rocked my seventeen-year-old world." He looked over at her. "Truth or dare?"

"Truth," she said—because right now, that felt more daring. Being honest with him. Daring him to ask her something that would keep this simmering feeling bubbling beneath the surface.

He smiled, lolling against the edge of the hot tub, and asked, "What's your favorite alcoholic drink?"

Kendall tried not to visibly sag in on herself.

They both knew how this game was played. How he'd played it with those giggling girls in high school. If you liked someone, if you were using the game to flirt with them, you asked them questions about first crushes and first kisses and sexual attraction. If you were trying to let them down easy, you asked literally anything else.

He was letting her down easy.

"I actually really like beer. IPAs. Local microbrews. That kind of stuff," Kendall answered, trying to mask the disappointment she shouldn't be feeling.

Hadn't she been telling herself for days that nothing was ever going to happen with Brody? So why was she even remotely surprised?

He was her brother's best friend. He was leaving. And she had much more important things to worry about. Like her best friend's wedding.

Chapter Twelve

The wedding shower was a couplefest.

Kendall had known it was going to be. George and Charlotte had elected to do a coed wedding shower with all their friends, but Kendall hadn't realized how lovey-dovey all the romantic stuff was going to make everyone.

She probably should have, but she'd been too busy helping Magda and Charlotte's sisters get everything ready for the party to think much about whether she was going to spend the entire afternoon surrounded by cooing lovebirds.

Charlotte's sisters were there, with their spouses, and George's poker buddies with theirs. Charlotte's dad had brought his girlfriend, and George's bandmates had brought theirs. Even most of George's sisters, who had joined via Skype, were cuddled up with their husbands.

It seemed like the only single people at the party were Magda, who was hosting; Mac, who was doing everything he could to needle Magda; and Kendall, who had long thought Mac and Magda should just get a freaking room. Though she'd never dare say that to Magda's face.

The parlor of the Bluebell Inn was overflowing with love—which was pretty perfect for a wedding shower, so Kendall tried to squash her romantic cynicism. Magda stood next to the piano, the dog-eared notebook in which Kendall had helped her plan the party clasped in her hands, as she hosted a quiz to see who knew George and Charlotte best.

"Question five," Magda announced. "Where did Charlotte and George get engaged?"

"Too easy! It was right here in this room!" Mac called out from the back—earning groans from the rest of the shower guests and a death glare from Magda.

"No shouting out answers," Charlotte's brother-in-law, Levi, reminded him.

"It's the wrong answer anyway," Charlotte commented from her position on the love seat with George.

"No hints!" Magda scolded.

Around the room, couples bent over their answer sheets, but Kendall just leaned against a wall and watched. She'd helped Magda come up with the questions, so it wouldn't be fair of her to play, but right now, she was wishing she had something else to do. Some necessary distraction.

To her left, George's friend Ben whispered something to his extremely pregnant wife, which made her blush. Not far from them, Connor and Deenie, another pair of soon-to-be parents, were laughing together over some private joke.

"Question six: Which book did George give Charlotte to tell her he was in love with her?"

Charlotte met George's eyes and smiled as around the room the various competitors whispered their answers to one another.

Kendall had never envied relationships, in and of themselves. She knew that a lot of couples weren't nearly as happy as they wanted everyone to think. She'd seen her parents' shouting matches in private, even when they'd played the perfect family in public. The whole town had been shocked when her mother suddenly left before Kendall's eighth birthday—everyone except Kendall and Kev. They'd felt a lot of things, but surprise had never been one of them. No, Kendall didn't trust the illusion of romance.

But she did envy Charlotte and George. They had something special. Kendall had never wanted to be with someone just to have a relationship. She was a perfectly whole human all on her own. Happier without the drama. But that something special... part of her secretly longed for that. It was the only reason she kept putting herself through the pain-in-the-ass that was dating.

"Question seven: What is George's nickname for Charlotte's dog?"

"Ooh, I know this one," George joked, and Charlotte giggled as if he'd said the funniest thing in the world.

Kendall watched them, her throat going tight again—though this time not from envy.

Charlotte was getting married. It was really happening.

Charlotte and George had been friends for months before they started dating, and anyone with eyes had been able to see they were crazy about one another. Charlotte might have been trying to swear off men, but she'd always been a hopeless romantic and George was perfect for her. Their engagement had surprised exactly no one. Marriage was just the natural next step down the road to their happy life.

So why was it hitting Kendall all of a sudden that this was real?

Charlotte and George already lived together. They'd acted like an old married couple since before they were even officially dating. Nothing was really going to change. So why did this feel momentous?

Her best friend was getting *married*.

The quiz continued, and Kendall squashed down whatever this nonsense she was feeling was.

As soon as Mags started reading the answers, to many cheers and groans—with Magda and Mac bristling at one another the entire time while he argued for half credit—Kendall took the chance to escape to the kitchen of the inn to get the cake Mags had made for the occasion.

It was wonderfully quiet in the kitchen. Kendall unboxed the cake as cautiously as if she was handling priceless china, careful not to bump the flawlessly designed icing.

Magda had outdone herself.

Charlotte hadn't wanted a Jane Austen wedding, but Magda knew how much the author's work meant to Charlotte and the role it had played in her relationship with George, so she'd made an exquisite two-tiered Austen-themed cake for the shower.

The bottom layer was pristine white fondant, accented by inky black script with all of Charlotte's favorite quotes from the books, and the top had been painstakingly designed to look like a stack of books covered in buttercream roses.

Kendall couldn't imagine the hours that had gone into the cake—and she almost hated to see it cut up and eaten, though she knew the flavors inside would be just as impressive. Magda had been in self-imposed training for months now, getting ready to audition for *The Great American Cake-Off*. Kendall knew she had a second interview with the show coming up, but she'd been very hush-hush about when.

With work like this, there was no way she wasn't getting on the show.

Kendall took a moment to take pictures of the cake from every angle, and even a video where she walked all the way around it. She was flipping through her shots to make sure none of them were blurry when Magda walked in.

"Hey. I thought you were getting the cake."

"I was, but got distracted admiring your masterpiece. Mags, this is incredible."

Magda flushed, smiling her sweet shy smile. "I was pretty pleased with how it came out."

"Pretty pleased, she says. As if she's not a freaking genius."

"I just hope Charlotte likes it. And genius or not, the people are hungry. Let's go. Before Mac convinces George to give him any more half points for answers he clearly got wrong."

Kendall's lips twitched, and she trailed Magda back into the den of love.

"You guys are the best friends ever in the history of friends, you know that?"

"It was all Magda," Kendall said as she bent to pick up a stray cocktail napkin that had somehow ended up beneath the piano. The inn had let them use the parlor for next to nothing because Charlotte's sister Anne worked there, on the condition that they leave it exactly as they'd found it.

Magda and Kendall were on cleanup duty, and Charlotte had lingered behind to help, no matter how much Magda kept insisting the bride wasn't supposed to clean up after her own shower. George was on his way back to their condo with his car full of presents—and Charlotte was glowing with happiness and twitterpated love.

"It wasn't a solo effort," Magda protested. "Kendall did a lot, and your sisters helped a ton."

"Well, it was perfect," Charlotte insisted, doing a little twirl in the middle of the room.

"And no random dog to try to eat the cake," Kendall said dryly.

"The *cake*." Charlotte clasped her hands. "It was so gorgeous, Mags. Did we get pictures? I was so caught up in just enjoying everything that I didn't take any—"

"Don't worry," Kendall assured her. "Everyone took pictures. And videos."

Charlotte twirled again. "I think Elinor is regretting her courthouse wedding with no frills. She could have had an Austen cake. A *Magda* Austen cake, which is clearly the best kind."

"I was actually thinking about your dog and the cake the other day," Magda said to Kendall, steering the conversation away from uncomfortable praise.

"He isn't my dog. I'm just fostering."

"Any interested parties?" Charlotte asked.

"Not yet. I think the disclaimer about the cellphone obsession on the Furry Friends website is scaring people off—though I can understand why Ally put it there, since he was returned to the shelter twice for the same offense. He nearly got Brody's phone the other day."

Charlotte's eyes glittered. "And how are things with the great Brody James?"

"Good," Kendall said, trying to keep all traces of weirdness out of her voice. "We ripped out the carpet. You guys should see the lodge. It already looks so much better."

"So you haven't jumped him yet?"

"I have no intention of jumping him," Kendall reminded her. "I never did."

"What I want to know is what's going on with Jamie," Magda said.

"Jamie?" Charlotte echoed, perking up.

Magda grinned as she stacked cake plates. "I heard Kendall and Jamie are dating. It's all over town."

"Seriously?" Kendall groaned. "This town and the rumors. We went out yesterday. *One time.*"

"And will you be going out again?" Charlotte asked.

When Kendall didn't respond, Charlotte and Magda exchanged a look.

"Poor Jamie," Magda mumbled.

"Kendall Walsh, the one-date wonder." Charlotte sighed.

"Why is it poor Jamie? Why can't it just be that we aren't right for each other?"

"I just feel bad for him," Magda said. "He's had a crush on you forever. You probably broke the poor guy's heart."

"I can't control his crushes."

Magda held her gaze until she started to squirm. Mags was the gentlest of them. The kindest. But that didn't mean she let them get away with anything. "We both know how much it sucks to have feelings for someone who doesn't have them back," Magda said softly. "I hope you let him down easy."

"I did," Kendall insisted, but she was no longer feeling quite so confident she hadn't been a little quick to brush Jamie off. She actually felt a little guilty.

"Were you comparing him to Brody?" Charlotte asked.

"This is not about Brody!" Kendall said, a little too loudly. "But if I had been comparing him, it would only be because Jamie wouldn't stop talking about how awesome Brody was."

Charlotte nodded sagely. "Classic mistake. Don't bring up the guy she has shoes for when you're trying to woo."

"I do not have shoes for Brody James!" she insisted, lying her ass off.

Shoes had been their code back in high school. Their way of talking about mushy feelings stuff in public.

"Wasn't Brody the original shoes?" Charlotte asked, with her annoyingly good memory.

"I think he was," Magda confirmed—and Kendall glared at both of them.

Because they were right.

It had all started because of Brody. They'd been at a party at the old lodge—one of the ones her brother threw, which they'd been convinced their dad and Laurie didn't know about.

Kendall had been watching Brody flirt with Brittany Luther. She'd been feeling all sorts of angsty, teenage feels, and she'd told Charlotte and Magda that she had an *issue*—a stupid crush that refused to go away—keeping her voice down because she hadn't wanted Brody or Brittany or, God forbid, *Kev* to overhear. But she'd been so quiet, Magda had misheard her and thought they were talking about shoes.

It had become their code for feelings they didn't know what to do with. Feelings that they knew could never go anywhere but that stubbornly refused to leave.

And she still had freaking massive shoes for Brody James.

No more truth or dare. She'd been entirely too truthful with him in that damn hot tub. And she didn't even want to think about what she might be tempted to dare him to do if they kept playing that ridiculous game.

They weren't teenagers anymore. She had obligations, and so did he. Even if most of his were half a world away and he was doing his best to ignore them. The tour had moved on. They were in Canada now—and yet Brody was still here. Yes, he was burned out, but she expected every day to be the day he announced he was going back. This couldn't last.

"You never said why you were thinking about Banner and the cake," she said to Magda—in a blatant attempt to change the subject.

"You're not going to give us anything about Brody?" Charlotte asked.

"There's nothing to give," Kendall said firmly. She turned to Magda. "So why were you thinking of the Golden Destroyer?"

Magda clearly wanted to say more on the Brody subject, but she sighed. "Pupcakes."

"Pupcakes?"

"Like cupcakes for dogs," Magda explained. "After Anne's wedding, and seeing how Banner kept trying to get at the leftover cake, I started looking into some dog-safe recipes. At first it was just for Cupcake," she said, referring to her own rescue pit bull, "but then I thought, what if I sold them in the shop?"

"Okay, that's brilliant," Charlotte declared.

"Really?" Magda asked, something soft and hopeful on her face. "You like it?"

"It's really smart, Mags," Kendall confirmed. "People in this town are nuts for their dogs. And I love you, so I'm not even going to ask for a cut, even though it was clearly my dog who gave you the idea."

"I thought he wasn't your dog," Charlotte argued. "And by that logic I should get a cut because I told you to foster him."

"But I *agreed* to foster him. And sustained all the duress from his cake adventures."

The conversation devolved from there. It was kind of perfect, being here with her two best friends, being ridiculous and forgetting about the foolish angst she'd felt for Brody in the last few days.

Kendall wasn't romantic. She didn't get distracted by stupid teenage crushes. She was going to make an amazing wedding venue for Steph and a fabulous wedding for Charlotte, and bring the resort back to full profitability. No more dares. No more temptation. Everything else was just noise. And she didn't need it.

Chapter Thirteen

The next two weeks were a blur.

Brody settled into the new job and continued to work on the old lodge in all his spare time, doing his best to keep himself too busy and too tired to think about anything other than putting one foot in front of the other. A plumber came out to work on the pipes and an electrician to look at the wiring. Brody and Kendall ripped out one of the walls in the warren of back rooms to make a bigger prep space for catering, and the floors throughout were set to be refinished next week. Tiles had been ordered for the bathrooms, and they had a guy coming in on Tuesday to service the clanging furnace.

His sister's wedding was still over a month out, but Steph had dropped by to check out the venue on the weekend. Even though it was mostly an empty space at the moment, she'd stood in the middle of the old lodge, looking out over the snowy mountain with the single rusted ski lift chair listing in the view, and clasped her hands together happily. She'd declared it perfect, telling him he'd done well, and Brody had felt like he'd just won a race. Better, actually.

Steph had grilled him about when he was going back to the tour, and he'd played up the knee thing again, feeling bad about lying, but not knowing what else to say. He was missing races. He hadn't even skied since he got here, and he wasn't doing anything close to his normal training regimen.

His training team kept calling him, trying to figure out what the hell was going on, and he kept putting them off. They'd spread the story about rehabbing an injury he'd gotten during training and everyone was buying it, but the people who worked with him, whose jobs revolved around making him great, couldn't figure out why he wasn't seeing specialists and fighting to get back on the mountain. They all worked with other athletes. They didn't depend solely on him. But this was supposed to be his year, and they all knew it.

And he was in Vermont. Playing at being a ski resort manager. Which had gotten out on social media. People had spotted him, and rumors were swirling. Though none of them came close to the truth—that he was hiding from his life. Letting everyone down because he didn't know how to talk about the real reason he was here. About Oskar…and maybe not wanting to be a professional skier anymore.

Some speculated that he was nursing a broken heart, since Valeria had been seen with some guy in Milan. And personally, he liked that story, since it made him seem much more sensitive and romantic than he actually was. He hadn't felt a thing when he'd seen her with another guy. Not at all like he'd felt watching Kendall go on a date. Though that was obviously a protective instinct. She was family.

Which must also be why it ate at him so much to see her turn herself into a hermit.

He hadn't run into her at the hot tub again since their last episode of truth or dare, but they worked side by side most days—and he couldn't stop thinking about her. About how *wrong* it felt that she didn't see herself as adventurous anymore. It bothered him that she felt trapped here. Bothered him that the daredevil part of her, that fierce, wild, free part of her, seemed to have gone into hibernation.

He wanted to wake her up again. Remind her how it felt to leap before you looked.

And one Saturday morning, he finally saw his chance.

He found Kendall sitting on the busted ski lift chair in front of the old lodge, using the ball flinger he'd gotten Banner—though the dog was standing a dozen feet away with the ball at his feet, staring at the sky.

The pup continued to get into trouble whenever he wasn't watched like a hawk, but all of the ski lift operators, instructors, and ski patrol had started taking turns keeping an eye on him. He was quickly becoming the mascot of the mountain. And Brody had noticed that the only time Banner seemed to run away from his minders was when he was trying to find Kendall. The golden's favorite place to be was so close to Kendall that he practically tripped her when she walked—though she'd started taking him to Canine Good Citizen classes at Furry Friends in town so he'd learn to heel.

Kendall insisted the classes were part of being a responsible foster mom—so he'd be ready to be adopted—but Brody could see Banner burrowing his way into her heart. Brody had bought the dog a crate, since he had a feeling he was still going to be there when the construction began in earnest, and when he'd set it up in the loft, he'd seen the little golden hairs all over Kendall's bed, evidence she let the dog sleep up there. And there was a distinctly fond note in her voice every time she called him to her with a whistle and a "Come on, Trouble."

"What's he looking at?" Brody asked as he approached now.

Kendall glanced over at him. "Aliens?" she suggested. "He does this a lot. He's a very strange dog."

He heard the affection in her voice and smiled. "You sure you aren't keeping him?" She'd started keeping treats in her pockets and playing with him when she thought no one was looking.

"Charlotte will tell you I don't let myself get emotionally attached to living creatures," Kendall said glibly. "Though I do feel a little guilty that you've bought more stuff for my foster than I have. He loves the crate, by the way. He associates it with treats. I need to pay you back for it."

"My treat." The dog spun in a circle and barked at the sky. "Have you figured out where you and Banner are going to stay next week to avoid the floor fumes?"

"Probably the main lodge. We aren't fully booked, and it'll be easier to coordinate things for Charlotte's bachelorette if I'm not at some Vrbo across town." She picked up the ball flinger that had been resting beside her to make space for him.

Brody eyed the rickety lift chair she was sitting on. "Is that thing safe for two?"

"Probably not. You wanna risk it?"

"Speaking of risks…" He gingerly settled beside her—and miraculously the rusty chair didn't collapse. "I have a dare for you."

"Are you daring me to take a whole day off and not worry about the resort for twenty-four hours? Because that's what I was daring myself."

"You'll need a bathing suit."

Her blond eyebrows arched up. "Does this dare involve a hot tub?"

"It does not. And that's all the hints you're getting."

She narrowed her eyes—and he kept his expression as harmless as he could, willing her to be tempted.

Finally, she murmured, "Okay, I'm intrigued."

He grinned, and jerked his head toward the old lodge, where she still had her stuff. "Get your suit. I'll get Banner."

"Oh no. Absolutely not."

Brody caught Kendall's arm before she could make a break back toward the parking lot.

A banner reading PINE HOLLOW POLAR PLUNGE had been stretched over a dock at the edge of the lake, and Kendall had taken one look at it and spun back toward the car. Banner romped around their legs, excited by all the activity on the shore of the partially frozen lake.

"Why not?" Brody demanded. "We used to do this stuff all the time when we were kids."

"And we were insane. It's freezing."

"It's for charity," he reminded her.

"I'll make a donation."

"Not the same." He met her eyes. "Come on. I dare you."

She cocked her head, faux haughty. "I am no longer susceptible to dares."

"How disappointing." He reached for the zipper on his jacket. "Either way, I'm doing it. If you're just too chicken…"

"You are not going to goad me into this. I'm not seventeen anymore."

"You have to be seventeen to have fun?"

She pointed at the frosty lake. "This is your definition of fun?"

He flashed her a huge smile. "With you? Hell yes."

Her lips twitched. She looked from his smiling face to the lake and back again. Then she shook her head, a rueful smile spreading across her face. "I'm gonna regret this."

Brody whooped, that won-the-lottery feeling rushing back again as he grabbed her hand and dragged her over to the registration desk. He'd already signed them both up online, so it was a quick process, and before long they were waiting in line for their turn to leap into a frozen lake.

Around them, other members of the community were waiting as well—either to jump into the lake or to cheer on those who did. Banner strained at the end of his leash, trying to get pets from every single person there.

"I can't believe I let you talk me into this," Kendall grumbled, already shivering and they hadn't even jumped in yet. They were both wearing bathing suits beneath the winter coats they would shed at the last minute.

"I can't believe I had to talk you into this. Old Kendall would have been dragging me toward the lake."

"Old Kendall was nuts."

"And fun."

She glanced at him out of the corner of her eye, but whatever rebuttal she might have made was lost as the line shuffled forward—only one more group before it was their turn. They watched as the five teenagers from the local community theater—all wearing Shakespearean costumes for some reason—joined hands and screamed, leaping into the water.

"Oh God," Kendall groaned. "This is such a bad idea."

"Moment of truth," Brody said with a grin.

He stripped off his jacket and boots, handing them along with his cellphone—with the camera app open—to the volunteer at the side of the dock. Kendall handed her coat and boots to the volunteer at the other side, along with Banner's leash. "Thanks," she murmured.

Brody held out his hand to her, palm up. "You ready for this?"

"Not remotely."

His grin grew wider. "You gonna go anyway?"

She grabbed his hand and her grin matched his. "Hell yes."

Her grip tightened, and she jumped.

He was a fraction of a second behind her, off the dock and into the water—always chasing Kendall Walsh.

The frigid water hit like a thousand needles jabbing into his skin at the same time. Closing over his head and making his lungs ache like he'd forgotten how to breathe. *Damn*, it was cold.

And he'd never felt more alive.

Kendall's hand yanked him upward, and they both broke the surface, gasping and swearing. The group at the lake's edge cheered—and Banner leapt into the water, his splash hitting both of them in the face with another blast of icy water before he began paddling happily in circles.

"I hate you," Kendall gasped as they treaded water. "You are evil, and I will never forgive you."

Brody would have laughed if his teeth hadn't been chattering too hard to manage it.

They swam to the edge of the area that had been cordoned off for the plunge, and volunteers helped them out of the water, wrapping them—and Banner—in warm towels. They shoved their feet into their boots and accepted the rest of their belongings from the volunteers before shuffling quickly toward the little hut that had been set up for the plungers to warm up.

The hut was ringing with laughter and loud conversation, as

if the bracing cold of the water had left everyone shouting—but it was blissfully warm. Kendall and Brody huddled close to one of the heaters as she rubbed Banner down, and he pulled up the photo app on his phone.

"Still mad at me?" He turned his phone to face Kendall.

The action shot was fantastic. The volunteer had caught them as they were jumping up—Kendall a little higher than he was, her eyes squeezed closed tight, but her mouth open in the biggest laughing smile he'd ever seen. She looked like joy. Pure joy.

Her reluctant smile twitched as she looked at the photo. "That's a good one."

"I'll send it to you."

She nodded, her mouth twisting to one side as she looked at him. "This might have been fun."

He mock gasped. "Are you admitting I'm a genius? I feel like you're admitting I'm a genius."

"Don't get excited. You occasionally have a decent idea. We're not to genius territory yet."

"Genius," he marveled. "Pure genius."

She snorted, shaking her head. "All right, egomaniac. I'm gonna go get dressed. Can you keep an eye on Banner?"

"I've got him," he promised.

He knew he should get dressed too, but he watched her walk away instead, grinning like a fool.

"Kendall! I didn't know you were doing the plunge!"

Kendall froze at the shout as she exited the changing rooms. She was still buzzy with adrenaline from her leap into the lake, feeling freaking *fantastic*, but some of that giddy so-alive-you-can-barely-stand-it feeling retreated when Jamie called out to her.

"Hey, Jamie," she said, awkwardness trying to climb up the back of her throat.

She'd been avoiding thinking about him. That had been her primary mode for that last two weeks—do what needed to be done and ignore everything else. She hadn't been by Jamie's burrito truck, and she'd been doing her level best to keep her distance from Brody—which hadn't exactly been easy when she was refurbishing the old lodge side by side with him and also overseeing everything he did at the resort to make sure they didn't have another Phil situation. Not that she thought he would hit on the instructors, but she didn't want to let her people down again.

So she'd been supervising him, and working with him, while also avoiding talking to him about anything not work related. And avoiding the hot tub because she couldn't seem to keep her guard up around him there.

Jamie, if she was honest, had barely been on her radar—but now that he was right in front of her, she couldn't help remembering what Magda had said about him having a crush on her. Though the burrito-slinging ski bum didn't look heartbroken as he threw out his arms in greeting.

"How you doing? Haven't seen you for a minute."

"It's been busy," she said, trying to see if he was putting on a good front. "How've you been?"

"So great. Did the plunge. It's wild, amirite?"

"Wild," she confirmed. "Look, Jamie, I, uh, I wanted to apologize if I…" She trailed off, searching for words, and Jamie just watched her like an eager puppy. "I'm sorry I kind of ghosted you after our date. I've been really buried—"

"Oh, no, don't worry about it. I totally get it."

She blinked. "You do?"

"Yeah. I mean, I was psyched that you wanted to get a drink, 'cuz, like, I don't know if you know, but I had like the biggest crush on you when I was thirteen. You were, like, the hottest thing on the planet, and going out with you in real life was *wild*, you know. But, like, Brody James. I get it."

Kendall blinked, not following. "What—Brody?"

"Saw you guys jump in together. And people been, like, talking around the resort—"

"People have been talking?" she asked sharply.

"I mean, like I said, I get it. I'd date Brody James. He's freaking Brody James."

"But we're not—"

"Not dating. Gotcha." Jamie winked a little too emphatically. "But good for you, right? And good for him! He deserves some TLC after that model chick dumped him."

"I don't think that's what—"

"Kendall!"

Kendall jerked, spinning toward the sound of Brody's voice. Thank God he was far enough away he probably hadn't heard what all of the resort apparently thought was happening between them.

"Yo, Brody!" Jamie shouted, raising one arm in bro salute.

"I gotta go," Kendall said, on a mission to keep Jamie from talking to Brody.

"Gotcha." Jamie nodded. "See ya round."

"Yep. Bye, Jamie!" she shouted over her shoulder, already booking it up the shore toward Brody and Banner.

Brody glanced past her, frowning slightly. "That's Jamie? Guac Guy?"

"Yeah, he was doing the plunge too," she said, grabbing Brody's arm and pulling him toward the parking lot. He was fully dressed and had Banner all dried off, no reason for them to hang around long enough for Brody to hear rumors she *really* didn't need him to hear.

Brody slowed, looking over his shoulder. "You aren't going out with him again, are you?"

In another world, she might have thought he sounded jealous. But this was the real world, and she knew he was only pulling that big-brother crap. "Nope. My virtue is safe."

"Not that you can't go out with him," Brody tried to backpedal as they reached the parking lot and climbed into his truck. "You can date whoever you want."

"Thanks for the permission." She loaded Banner into the car, clipping him to his seat belt.

Brody winced. "Okay, that was patronizing, but I only meant—"

"Brody. We're good. Let's just go."

He turned on the truck, glancing over at her as he pulled out of the parking lot. "Did you at least have fun?"

The slight frown she hadn't realized she was nursing instantly vanished. "I did. This was a great idea."

"So I'm not evil?"

"Oh, no, you're still evil," she confirmed instantly, before adding, "But I forgot how much fun it can be to have a devil on my shoulder telling me to do all the things I know I shouldn't."

He chuckled darkly. "Now that you've admitted that, I'm going to have to come up with new ways to tempt you."

Kendall's face heated as she thought of several ways she wouldn't mind being tempted. She looked away from his movie-star profile and out the window at the passing trees as he drove. Trying to think virtuous thoughts.

It didn't take long for them to get back to the resort. The lake wasn't far.

Brody pulled into his usual space in the staff lot and shut off the truck, but Kendall didn't move to get out. She glanced across the cab at him while Banner whined to be released.

She'd been trying to avoid him for weeks, but he'd done this for her, and she suddenly wanted to do something for him.

"Were you still looking for a wedding present for Steph? I need to go pick up a chandelier on Wednesday. For the lodge. From that found materials artist I was telling you about. He has a lot of cool stuff, if you wanna come with me."

"Yeah." Brody's grin was huge. "Yeah, that'd be great."

"If it's okay with you, can we take the truck? I'm not sure the chandelier would fit in the back of my Jeep."

"Using me for my wheels. I see how it is."

Kendall smiled. "You're just so helpful."

He met her eyes, something sincere shifting in them, though his response was light. "I try."

Chapter Fourteen

The Vermont countryside stretched around them in fields of white bisected by scattered country roads. They'd left the mountains behind twenty minutes ago and were now in farm country, passing long swaths of snow-covered fields, occasionally pocketed with barns.

Kendall seemed to know where they were going, which was a good thing, since Brody didn't have a clue where they were and they'd long since lost cell service. The sky was a cloudy gray today, making everything look dingy and moody.

"How did you meet this guy?" Brody asked as they drove farther and farther into the middle of nowhere.

"I ran into him at a farmers market a few years back, selling things out of the back of his truck—he had these chairs made out of old skis, and I fell in love with them. I wanted to buy twenty for the lodge, but my dad didn't think they worked with our aesthetic." She made a face. "Anyway, I got to talking with Alan, and I told him about all the busted gear people leave behind at the resort, and he asked if I could save some of it for him. The stuff he makes," she marveled. "The way he sees the world…there's so much potential in it, you know?"

She directed him through a turn down another narrow lane. "He doesn't come to the farmers markets anymore. He's kind of a hermit. Says he doesn't like people—which works, 'cuz I don't much like people either."

"Liar," Brody accused softly.

"Excuse me?"

"You love people. You're just picky. You love your staff. Your friends. Family. You'd do anything for them. You just don't like dealing with strangers. Which does make you a strange fit for customer service."

Kendall snorted. "Okay, fine. I like some people. Jury's still out on you."

"You know you love me," he gloated.

"Sure thing, egomaniac." She pointed through the windshield. "That's it there. The big barn."

Brody slowed the truck as they approached, taking in the scene.

The barn was huge, plenty of workspace and storage for an artist—or a hoarder. The house beside it was much more modest. A little bungalow with an empty front porch. Beside the barn was a frozen-over pond, the ice crisp and white. And beside the pond, a single Adirondack chair sat facing the water. There wasn't another property as far as the eye could see. Just farmland and countryside. And that empty chair.

Brody pulled into the gravel driveway, and Kendall leapt out, shouting a greeting as she tromped toward the barn, where a man with a scraggly white beard appeared in the doorway. Brody hung back, moving more slowly, his gaze going again and again to that solitary Adirondack chair. Off all by itself in this lonely little pocket of the world.

"Brody? You coming?"

"Yeah." He shook himself, hurrying to catch up. "I'm right behind you."

Alan was a genius.

He was also snarky and irritable and reluctant to part with any of his work.

Brody could see why Kendall loved him.

The chandelier he'd fashioned for Kendall was magnificent—constructed entirely of old fireplace pokers, but still elegant and seeming to flow, while perfectly matching the rustic aesthetic of the old lodge. He'd also set aside a small sculpture of a skier in a racing tuck, molded out of an old bent ski pole—which he insisted Kendall take as "payment" for all the supplies she brought him.

Brody could have spent hours poking through all his work, but Kendall pointed him toward an end table made from recycled maple syrup kegs, into which Alan had branded the state seal of Vermont—and he knew nothing would remind Steph of home so perfectly.

They headed back out to the truck to load up their purchases, and while Kendall lingered to chat with Alan about other décor ideas for the lodge, Brody found himself once again staring at that single chair, facing the edge of the pond.

Something about it bothered him. It kept niggling at him as they finished loading and said their goodbyes to Alan, and even afterward, when they were on the road headed home, the miles disappearing beneath the tires. He couldn't let the sight of it go.

It was just so *lonely*, that chair.

Alan probably liked it that way, the peace, the solitude, but it ate at Brody. The idea of a man sitting alone. So alone that there wasn't even a chair for other people when they came to visit. Because no one would ever visit.

Had Oskar had a chair like that?

Oskar. Sitting alone at the edge of the training runs. Focused. Isolated.

He'd had a reputation for being aloof. And emotionless. Commentators talked about him like he was a robot. The Norwegian Machine.

But something about the description bothered Brody. Everything was bothering him today.

"Brody?" Kendall asked, and something in her tone made him think she'd tried to get his attention already. "You okay?"

"Everyone keeps asking what I'm doing here," he blurted out suddenly, not even sure what he was going to say until he was saying it. "You were the only one who asked me if it was about Oskar."

"And you said it wasn't."

"I lied."

When Kendall sucked in a breath softly, he flexed his hands on the wheel, barely seeing the road in front of him, his thoughts a continent away. "He died months ago, and it was a tragedy. He was such a great skier. But it didn't really touch me. Except it opened a door, you know. I'd spent my entire career chasing him."

"It's okay if you felt like it was an opportunity—"

"It wasn't an accident," he blurted out the words he hadn't told anyone, feeling a sudden, sharp relief as soon as Kendall knew. "They said it was an accident. Most people don't know, but it was suicide. He died by suicide."

"Oh my God, Brody—"

"I found out at Christmas. I was talking to one of his old coaches, trying to get training tips," he said with a tinge of bitterness. "And he let it slip. It had already happened. Months earlier. It's not like anything changed because I suddenly knew. But it didn't make any sense. He was the best in the world. Seven gold medals at the Olympics. Impossible to beat. I wanted to *be* him. He was my beacon. But he was miserable. And no one knew."

Brody had wanted to be the best more than anything in the world—he'd told himself he *had* to want it with single-minded focus or he would never get it—but what had he thought would happen when he got it? Would he even have been happy? Fulfilled? Oskar hadn't been.

"Maybe it was the pressure to keep being the best. To represent his country. To bring home gold because it was expected of him. I don't know. I didn't talk to him. No one talked to him. He was so alone."

His voice broke on the words and Kendall leaned over, putting a hand on his arm. "Pull over."

Since he hadn't even been aware he was still driving, that was probably a good idea. There was no shoulder here and no cars for miles, so Brody just stopped in the road, putting on his flashers.

"It wasn't your fault," Kendall murmured, her hand still on his bicep. The weight of it a connection, a comfort.

He looked over, meeting her eyes. "I thought he was an asshole. What if he was just lonely? They called him the machine. The robot. Everyone said no one as good as he was could possibly be human—but he was. He was just a man. He was always training, and I used to think he was like us—that he didn't know when to stop pushing—but what if he just didn't know who he was if he stopped? What if he didn't think he *could* stop?"

"Is that why you stopped?" she asked softly. "To prove you could?"

"No, I…Maybe…" He shook his head, trying to find the words to explain. The words that had been evading him ever since he left Zermatt. "Skiing wasn't just what I did. It was who I was—*all* I was. Effort. Struggle. Fighting for gold. But all of a sudden I couldn't figure out *why*. Why any of it mattered. Why I even wanted it. I didn't know who I was without skiing—and it scared me shitless. I spent my entire career trying to be him—and he just…" Brody shook his head.

"You couldn't have known."

"Because I never talked to him. Too busy assuming he had it all. *Envying* him. And no one knows. His family didn't want people to know, so I can't even talk about it. But who would I have even told? I had my team around me, Valeria, but none of them really knew me. I hadn't let them. I'd made my entire life, all of my relationships, about winning. And suddenly the idea of it just felt…empty. What was it all for? Did it even mean anything?"

That day in training in Zermatt came back to him. The moment he'd missed that gate…

"I hadn't been sharp since he died, and then to find out how it happened…" He shook his head. "I skied off the course, packed my things, didn't say anything to anyone. Came home trying to find…I don't know, purpose? *Meaning?* At Bailey's wedding, Steph kept talking about how they know better than to ask me for things, and I hated that. I wanted to…matter."

"You do. God, Brody. You are so loved."

"I know. But I've spent my entire adult life teaching the people who love me that I'm never around. That they can't rely on me. That they don't matter to me as much as a freaking medal." He met her eyes. "I didn't want it to be about him, but it is. That's why I'm here. Why I want to fix up the venue and help at the resort. Why I don't want to go back. Maybe not ever."

She went still as he said those words. "You don't mean that."

"No? When I skied out in Zermatt, I wasn't thinking I needed a break. I was thinking I was done. For good."

"There might be a middle ground, all-or-nothing Brody James," Kendall said gently, her eyes soft with understanding. "Have you thought any more about talking to someone?"

"I've been trying not to think about anything." He'd been entirely focused on their projects for the last three weeks. It had been easy to ignore his real life. To put off facing the future.

"As an expert on avoiding your problems, I can tell you they don't get better if you pretend they aren't there. Just sayin'."

"You gonna take the plunge with me? Talk to someone?"

She moved her hand from his arm, glancing out the windshield. "I'm good. We should probably get back before they send out a search party."

He didn't push her. Kendall would let down her walls when she was ready and not a second before.

He turned off the flashers and put the truck into gear, still unsettled, but also feeling a whisper of relief. He wasn't sure he could have said any of that to anyone but Kendall. He'd just known—he'd always known—that Kendall would understand. That she wouldn't judge.

Maybe he should talk things out more often. Find some quiet in his mind.

He wasn't sure he deserved peace. He wasn't sure he would

ever stop wondering if he could have done something. If he could have changed things for Oskar if he hadn't listened to all the hype about how superhuman he was. If he'd only done more to be his friend.

He'd never thought anything would matter more than gold, but that did.

He was still scared to think about what came next. If he did really retire…

He worried that his only value was as a skier. That he didn't know who he was without it. He'd have to think about that at some point. But for the moment, he would just put one foot in front of the other and try to keep doing his best. Whatever that was these days.

Chapter Fifteen

They drove back to the resort in silence, both lost in their thoughts. At one point, Brody turned on the radio, and they listened to a Simon and Garfunkel marathon as they wended through the Vermont countryside.

When they pulled into the resort parking lot, Kendall's phone buzzed. She ignored it as they climbed out, both of them focused on silently unloading the truck. Only after they'd stashed the chandelier, the sculpture, and the end table in Brody's hotel room for safekeeping did Kendall remember her phone and fish it out of her pocket.

Brody was still quiet, preoccupied, as she brought up her notifications.

As soon as she saw the flurry of texts, she realized something must have happened while she was out of range.

"Do you want to get dinner?" Brody asked.

Kendall didn't look up from her phone, rapidly scanning the texts. "I'm sorry." She glanced up, shaking her head. "I have to go. It's Magda."

Worry instantly pinched his face. "Is she okay?"

"Yeah. I just...I need to be there." Kendall moved toward

the door—feeling weirdly like she ought to hug him, even though they'd never said hello or goodbye with hugs before. "I'll see you later?"

"You'll probably find me at the hot tub."

"I'll look for you there," she promised.

Kendall stepped out of his hotel room, and as soon as the door closed behind her, she broke into a jog. She sent a text as she rode the elevator down, letting Charlotte and Magda know she was on her way.

Charlotte had texted that they were at Magda's, so Kendall headed for the parking lot and raced her Jeep along the curvy road that connected the ski resort to the center of Pine Hollow. Her thoughts were still spinning from everything that Brody had told her, but she didn't have time to think about any of that right now.

Magda's Bakery was dark when Kendall reached the town square—but it was well after normal business hours, so there was nothing strange about that. Kendall parked in the alley behind the shop and used her spare key to open the back door, climbing the stairs to the little apartment above. It was tiny, and the hot water heater had a tendency to go on the fritz, but Magda loved it. She'd always dreamed of living in a cozy little apartment above her bakery.

Kendall knocked at the apartment door at the top of the stairs, and Charlotte opened it instantly, proving they'd heard her on the stairs. "How is she?" she asked, looking past Charlotte into the apartment.

Magda sat on the floor beside her couch, cuddling her big sweetie of a pit bull, Cupcake. Her face was dry—no tear streaks in sight, and her expression was resigned.

"I'm fine," she insisted. "I feel silly. I shouldn't have said anything."

"Of course you should have said something!" Charlotte insisted, returning to the couch and sinking down next to where Magda leaned against it. "You are completely entitled to be heartbroken. If it was me, I'd be bawling. There would be *extremely* dramatic tears. And probably a bonfire."

Magda huffed out a soft, wry breath as Kendall joined them, sitting down on the floor in front of Mags.

"So it was a no?" she asked gently.

Magda made a face, scrunching up her nose. "It's official. The *Cake-Off* doesn't want me."

"*This* time," Charlotte insisted. "They don't want you for *this* season."

"Did they say why?" Kendall asked.

Magda shook her head.

Last year, when they'd all made their drunken and ridiculous pact to swear off men, Magda had decided she wanted to focus her energy on something else instead. She'd confessed to them that she had always dreamed of going on the baking reality show *The Great American Cake-Off*, and that she was going to actively work toward getting on.

She'd been training all year, trying out new recipes, learning new techniques. She'd *worked* for this. Planned for it. Everything had been building toward this audition.

"They just said, thank you, try again next time—"

"So you try again next time!" Kendall insisted, echoing Charlotte.

"I don't think it was my food," Magda said quietly, her hands constantly stroking Cupcake's smooth head—and reminding Kendall that Banner hadn't been out in far too long and she needed to ask Brody to go by to check on him when she had a moment. "I think it was me."

"What do you mean it was you?"

"The interview. I think I was too boring. I just…I didn't know what to say, and I could tell they wanted me to, I don't know, be dramatic—but it's like you said. I don't know how to be anything other than pleasant. All the time."

"I'm sure I didn't say that," Kendall argued—though she wasn't entirely sure. Magda *was* pleasant. And Kendall had never been good at hiding her opinion that Mags needed to cut loose once in a while.

"They would have cast you," Magda said, looking at both of them. "You would have said something snarky and clever and they would have loved your bite," she said to Kendall. "And you would have been dramatic and flamboyant and fun and they would have loved your energy," she added to Charlotte. "I was just too…me."

"*You* are perfect," Charlotte insisted.

"Not for *Cake-Off*."

"Then they're idiots," Kendall said staunchly. "You're amazing."

"I just thought this was going to be my thing," Magda said softly.

"It can still be your thing," Kendall insisted. "And if it's not, who cares? You don't need them to be awesome."

"But that's the point. I'm not awesome."

Kendall and Charlotte both loudly protested that ridiculousness, but Magda talked over them.

"You don't understand. You guys always had these huge dreams. For as long as I've known you. You were so impressive. So driven. You were always going to be an Olympian, and Charlotte was skipping grades and going to med school, and I was just regular old Magda."

"You are *not* regular," Charlotte said, visibly offended.

"Or old," Kendall added. "And I haven't been an Olympic hopeful for years. Dreams change."

"I know," Magda said. "I didn't mean...It's just...I love you guys, but I've never been impressive like you."

"I'm sorry," Charlotte interrupted. "Who went to freaking *France* to learn pastry stuff when she was eighteen, even though she didn't speak a word of French and had never left Vermont before?"

"And who started her own business when she was only twenty-three and made it *the* premium bakery of Pine Hollow?" Kendall added. "You just need to see yourself the way we see you. You're a total badass, Mags."

"I just really wanted this," Magda admitted. "And then I blew it by being bland."

"So you try again," Kendall reminded her. "You should have Mac audition with you. You're never bland or pleasant around him."

Magda made a face. "His breads are better than mine. With my luck, they'd take him and not me."

"Oh please. He's a hobby baker compared to you," Kendall insisted loyally. The diner owner was more chef than baker anyway. Though his dessert specials were legendary.

"What you need is a platform," Charlotte said, grabbing her phone. "Everyone is into food porn these days. I can spend hours watching people make delicious things on Instagram. If you had a rabid social media following, they would never turn you down."

"The bakery is on social media," Magda reminded her.

"Yeah, but it's mostly pictures of your regular items and notices about sales and specials. You need to suck people in with the oh-holy-shit-how-did-she-make-that stuff. Like the Austen cake from my shower! That thing was insane. Here, give me your phone."

Magda had to get up to go get it, since she rarely kept it on her. "I don't want to be obsessing over whether people have liked my latest post. That sounds like torture."

"So you let me run it for you for a few weeks," Charlotte offered. "It'll be fun."

"Are you forgetting that you're getting married this weekend?"

"I'll multitask," Charlotte said. "I want to do this for you. I bet we can get Ally on board too—you could pay her in Pupcakes to take professional quality photos for you. Or maybe even do a joint campaign with the animal shelter! People love dog pics almost as much as food porn."

"This sounds like a lot of work."

"Trust me," Charlotte insisted. "We'll have you going viral in no time."

"Maybe we should hold off until you and George get back from your honeymoon."

Charlotte snorted. "Our honeymoon is two days in Quebec—at least until this summer when we can take the trip to England that we originally planned. But sure. If you wanna wait a week or two, we can wait a week or two. But I'm serious. This could be a game changer."

"I'm just worried that no big social media following is going to change *me*, and they'll still say no."

"You don't need to change," Kendall insisted. "You're perfect."

"You're biased."

"Well, *yeah*. What are friends for?"

Magda finally cracked a smile at that. "Okay. We'll try the social media thing—*after* Charlotte's wedding. And if that doesn't work, I'll just find a new dream."

* * *

Find a new dream.

The words chased Kendall back to the resort that night, after she left Magda and Charlotte binge-watching old seasons of *Cake-Off* and analyzing why each of the various contestants had been selected.

She was in a strange mood, her thoughts swirling like she was right on the edge of some epiphany that hadn't hit yet.

Banner's crate was empty—they hadn't taken him with them to Alan's, since Chaos Banner didn't need to be anywhere near welding torches, and Brody had texted her earlier that he was stealing her dog when she'd asked him to look in on the pup. She should go by his hotel room and get Banner, but instead she found herself sitting on the broken-down lift chair in front of the old lodge, staring up at the mountain.

She texted Brody that she was back and asked when she should swing by to get Banner, and then set her phone on the seat beside her and just stared up at the oldest run on the mountain. The resort had started here. All that history. The Walsh legacy stretching back a hundred years. No pressure. Just a freaking dynasty.

"Hey."

She didn't know how long she'd been sitting there, but she somehow wasn't the least surprised to see Banner romping toward her through the snow, half-dragging Brody with him.

"How's Magda?" Brody asked as they grew closer.

"She's good," Kendall assured him, bending to greet Banner, who nearly toppled the chair in his eagerness to cuddle before flinging himself onto his back on the snow. "Thanks for looking after Banner."

"It was fun," Brody said as Banner began thrashing on his back and growling at an imaginary enemy. "I was actually thinking I might get a dog."

"This one's available," Kendall reminded him as Banner began to shove himself across the snow on his side. Her lips twitched at his antics. He took such joy in everything. The goofball. "He doesn't get many points for grace, but he grows on you."

"You sure you're not keeping him for yourself?"

"I'm not sure of anything tonight," Kendall admitted.

His boots crunched closer and she picked up her phone to make space for him beside her.

Brody took the silent invitation, the chair groaning slightly beneath the added weight. He offered her one of the beers he'd brought. A local microbrew. She accepted it with a little smile.

"Did something happen?" he asked as he handed over the bottle opener on his keychain.

Kendall popped the top before handing it back. "Magda's been trying to get on this reality baking show, *The Great American Cake-Off*. She's been super focused about it, and she found out today that they aren't going to cast her in the next season."

"That sucks," he said softly. "I'm sorry."

"Charlotte and I rallied around her because we know how much this meant to her, but she was incredible. I mean— disappointed, obviously. But she wasn't dwelling on it, you know? Not a lot anyway. Not as much I would have."

"You don't strike me as a dweller," Brody commented, taking a swig of beer.

"But I am," Kendall said, picking at the label on her bottle. "I have wallowed in the dream I lost for the last six years. Magda found out she might not get her dream six hours ago, and she's already thinking, 'Okay, might need to find a new dream.'" Kendall looked up at the mountain. "She's not giving up, and she's, you know, upset, but she's ready to pivot if she needs to."

She shook her head, trying to find the words. "Whereas I am letting this one broken dream define my entire life."

"You're wedding planning," Brody reminded her. "That's a pivot."

"But it wasn't a dream. It was a reaction. An attempt to solve a problem. I didn't *want* this. I mean, I did, but only because it was what I thought was best for the resort, and I *owe* them. I owe them so much."

"I'm sure your family doesn't think—"

Kendall shook her head. "You don't get it. I know you said you don't have this perfect life, but…"

"It's the life you wanted," he said, understanding perfectly.

"Yeah." The Olympics had been her dream. Racing for a living. Courting the sponsors and smiling in the Nordica ads. She wasn't bitter, most days. But she did get a nasty case of the could-have-beens from time to time. Especially when she looked at Brody. "It all changed so fast, and I don't even remember it. That whole day is just gone. I don't even know what I did wrong."

"It wasn't anything you did."

"You don't know that. No one does. All we can do is watch the tape. Was I too fast? Too reckless? Did I lose my focus?" She shook her head. "I still dream about it sometimes. Not the accident. I dream about waking up on the morning of the trials, knowing I'm going to win. I'm so excited, but it's like even in the dream there's this thing hanging over me. Like my subconscious knows what's coming."

"Do you still ski?" he asked softly.

She shook her head, looking up at the mountain and its familiar runs. "No. Not anymore."

Chapter Sixteen

Brody's chest ached at the unfairness of it as he watched Kendall gaze up at the mountain.

She'd been the fastest thing he'd ever seen. No one could touch her instinct for finding the tightest line down a course or her ability to stay just on the right side of control when going faster than anyone else dared to go.

"I wanted to win for you," he confessed. "I promised I would, do you remember? When I visited you in the hospital?"

"Yeah. I watched you take silver," she said. "And I was *so* jealous."

"I wasn't sure you'd seen it." He couldn't seem to stop looking at her profile. "I don't think I would have been able to watch, if I'd been in your shoes."

"It motivated me," Kendall said. "There was this one skier that year—he didn't medal, he didn't even come close—but the commentators were obsessed with him. They kept talking about how inspirational he was. *How can you not be inspired by the courage of this young man, pushing through the pain...*" She dropped the cheesy announcer voice. "We've heard those stories all our lives. How they glorify the comeback, the ones who ski hurt. The commentators worship them for fighting through the pain, for risking reinjury. And that was going to be me. They were going to show the footage of my accident, only to show how far I'd come. What a miracle it was." Bitterness was thick in her voice before she looked down with a twist of a smile. "Laurie begged me not to go back. Even Kevin told me not to," she said, her voice low. "They were all so scared."

"You didn't wake up for almost two days," he reminded her gently.

"I know. Seventeen broken bones. Cracked skull. I've seen what my helmet looked like. I know it was terrifying for them."

"It was terrifying for all of us," Brody said softly.

He hadn't seen the crash live.

The downhill half of the women's alpine combined had been the first race of the day, and Brody had slept in, focusing entirely on maximizing his own physical and mental conditioning. It was the freaking Olympic trials. He'd been laser focused. Good night's sleep. Good breakfast. No cellphone. No distractions. The alpine combined wasn't the event Kendall was most heavily favored in anyway—he'd planned to watch her dominate her primary event after his first ski.

The sound of the helicopter they'd used to medevac her to the hospital had woken him up, but he'd thought it must be some bigwig sponsor flexing as they arrived to watch the trials.

The news of a bad crash had rippled across the mountain, but he'd superstitiously avoided hearing the details of it as he went about his prep, as if that would keep it from happening to him. Trying to keep his head clear and his concentration sharp.

Until he found out it was her.

Kendall Walsh. The little speed demon. The blond braid he'd been chasing down the mountain since he was eight years old.

It had never occurred to him that it might be her. She was so invincible. The one the commentators called psychic because she seemed to know about every bump and icy patch in advance. He'd been sure there was some mistake.

He'd watched the video that was going viral on Twitter then—and thrown up his good breakfast.

The commentators' silence said it all as they struggled to find something reassuring to say to the home audience. *Yes, her max speed had been clocked at eighty-six miles per hour, but they were pretty sure she'd only been doing seventy-four or seventy-five when she went flying into the barrier at the finish line. Yes, she was unconscious and unresponsive, but it might just be a concussion—and surely her helmet had protected her from the worst of it.*

The entire trials had ground to a halt for half an hour while they medevac'd her.

"Laurie couldn't understand why I would risk it, why I would ever want to go back, but my dad was right there with me. All the best doctors. The best physical therapists. Spare no expense. Pour money from the resort into my recovery—money we couldn't spare—it would all be worth it when I made my comeback. Two years of that." She shook her head. "The way my spine was fused, the damage to my hips—I'd lost some feeling, some reaction time, and I couldn't hold a tight tuck. I kept asking my physical therapist, 'When am I going to get it back? I have to get it back.' I was supposed to be a comeback story. But I wasn't."

His chest ached as she went on.

"I wasn't fast. I was never going to be fast again. I just…

my body wouldn't do it. So I stopped skiing." She held up a hand when he opened his mouth. "And I know what you're going to say. That maybe I just needed longer to heal. Maybe I didn't try long enough or hard enough, but I spent years trying. Even after I told my dad we were done, I still trained in secret sometimes. Hoping something would change. No one wanted it more than me."

"I know," he said.

"I was so close."

"I know," he repeated.

She'd been less than a hundred yards from the finish line. Almost two seconds ahead of her closest competitor. An insurmountable lead. An unheard-of lead. No one else had even come close. And then it had all been over.

"It took me a long time to accept that I was never going to get back—and the hospital bills were insane. I owed my dad so much. The resort was barely hanging on because he took every penny he could from it to help me. And he kept saying it would be worth it when I was the best again. But then I couldn't compete—I let him down."

"I'm sure he doesn't think—"

"Don't be sure, Brody," she interrupted, the words resigned. "I had this therapist. Sports psychologist my dad hired to help with my comeback. He fired her after she told me that sometimes the bravest thing to do was walk away."

The words snagged at his brain. Sometimes it *was* brave to walk away—so why did it feel like his own retreat from the sport was cowardice? Why was he so scared to tell anyone he was done?

She shook her head. "We couldn't afford her anyway. But that was when I started to see the toxicity, you know? We all love the person who overcomes the odds, but is it healthy to praise those who fight through pain for glory and give themselves arthritis by the time they're thirty?"

"Or worse," he said softly, thinking not only of her injury, but of Oskar.

Kendall sobered. "Exactly. And yet I would have given anything to be one of those people fighting through the pain. God, I wanted it. You tell me, Brody, is it worth it?"

"I don't know." He met her eyes in the darkness. "Sometimes?"

After a moment, she mumbled, "I didn't mean to talk about any of this."

"Do you talk to anyone about it?" She shook her head, and he grimaced. "Yeah. Me neither."

"I've just been putting one foot in front of the other, doing whatever needed to be done for the resort, and I never stopped to think about what I wanted to be doing."

"Sometimes you have to slow down to see what you really want," Brody murmured.

Kendall met his eyes, something shifting in her gaze.

"And what is it that you want, Brody?" she asked, her voice low.

There seemed to be a weight behind the words. A tension. Her blue eyes held his steadily, a sort of challenge in the look, and Brody suddenly found that he wasn't feeling the cold anymore. There was a sort of warm, heavy feeling in his blood—one that he would almost think was attraction, but this was *Kendall*. He shouldn't be feeling this for her...

He opened his mouth, not even sure what he was going to say—but before he could respond, Banner landed suddenly in his lap.

Brody caught the golden retriever instinctively with the hand that wasn't holding his beer—but the chair rattled, the rusty bar beneath the cushion groaning in warning. Kendall had time to yelp Banner's name in alarm, which made the dog attempt to flip onto her lap—and the entire chair collapsed beneath them.

Brody tried to reach for Kendall, but his arms were full of dog and beer. She shrieked as they all went tumbling backward into the snow in a pile of warped metal, the filaments of rust that had been holding everything together seeming to evaporate as the chair fell to pieces around them.

Brody groaned as Banner wiggled around frantically, delighted that they were all on the ground. "Are you all right?"

"Just wet," Kendall said, holding up her now-empty beer bottle. "And bruised. You?"

"Same." He gently shoved Banner off and turned his head to look over at her. "Sorry about your chair."

"It had a good run," she said as Banner romped off to leap into the snow and then romped back. "This might be the universe telling me that there's a limit to how much I can cling to old things and nurse them along."

"I'm not sure the universe speaks in rusty old ski lift chairs."

"Probably not," she agreed.

His jeans were soaked with beer, and there was something metal poking into his side, but Brody made no move to get up. The backrest cushion had somehow landed beneath her head, and her blond hair was spread out around it. His chest tightened strangely.

"Hot tub?" he asked.

Kendall eyed him, considering the offer for far longer than he expected before she finally murmured, "Yeah. Hot tub."

* * *

She was too honest in the hot tub. Stupid things always happened there. But Kendall kind of wanted stupid tonight. She was feeling reckless, after everything that had happened today.

Brody had brought his swim trunks with him, and they had miraculously escaped the beer shower, so he changed into them in the downstairs bathroom while Kendall went up to the loft to put Banner in his crate and put on her own bathing suit.

On impulse, she reached past her usual one piece and grabbed the black string bikini Charlotte had convinced her to buy when they were talking about taking a girls trip to Cabo that they'd never taken.

She unbraided her hair—then realized if she left it down it would get all wet in the water and quickly put it up in a sloppy knot on top of her head. The Instagram elite could make that look effortless and elegant, but Kendall's hair was so fine the knot was weirdly small and tilted to one side.

Whatever. It was fine. It wasn't like he didn't know what she looked like.

She shook the treat bag to lure Banner into his crate, the dog practically tripping himself in his eagerness to get inside the box and get the liver snack. She rubbed his ears and told him he was a good baby—even if he was a little chaos monster who had destroyed her favorite chair and completely ruined a moment—before shutting the crate.

One last glance in the mirror confirmed that, scar tissue and all, she looked pretty damn hot.

"Make good choices," she told her reflection, and headed down from the loft, grabbing the fuzzy towel the size of a small European country that she always wrapped up in when she went to the hot tub.

She slung it around her shoulders, somewhat ruining the effect of the skimpy bikini, and shoved her feet into her battered old green Crocs as Brody emerged from the bathroom.

"Hey," she said, in a fit of linguistic brilliance.

"Hey." His gaze flicked down to the gap in the towel, where her bare stomach was visible, but he looked away without comment. She almost wished he would have teased her, tried to play big brother again, and given her an excuse to remind him that they weren't related.

Neither of them spoke as they headed outside and walked down the path toward the hot tub. The forest clearing was closer to the main lodge than to the old part of the mountain, but Brody didn't seem to be in a hurry and neither was she. It had warmed up a bit. The temperature was hovering right around freezing, but after the extreme cold of the last few days, it almost felt warm.

Or maybe that was just her. Kendall had to resist the urge to fan herself as they crunched through the snow.

They were still a dozen yards away from the clearing when she started to hear voices. It took her a moment to realize that their hot tub oasis had been invaded tonight. Kendall almost hesitated, she almost turned back, but she didn't want Brody to think the only reason she'd wanted to go to the hot tub with him was so they could be alone and she could dare herself to do something reckless.

Even if that was exactly why she'd wanted to go.

They emerged into the clearing to find half a dozen people already in the hot tub—an older couple who called out greetings and introduced themselves, and four others who Kendall discovered were their three adult children and one son-in-law.

The mood was festive. One of the sons instantly recognized

Brody, though he tried to play it cool and waited until Kendall and Brody had slipped into the hot tub before asking, "I'm sorry, you aren't Brody James, are you?"

"I am," Brody confirmed, taking a place beside Kendall rather than across from her as usual. "You follow skiing?"

"Only every four years. We're big Olympics fans," the mother replied. "We heard a rumor you'd been spotted around the resort."

Brody chatted easily with the family, and occasionally his arm would brush hers, but the mood from the lift chair was gone, leaving uneasiness in its wake.

Why had she told him all that, about her accident? And then put on a skimpy little bikini and come out here with him to a freaking *public* hot tub—what had she thought would happen?

It was bad enough she'd apparently felt the need to unload all of her accident baggage onto him, but then she'd what? Decided to flirt with him? Brody who could not have been any clearer about the fact that she wasn't his type?

What had she been *thinking*?

Thank God the hot tub had been crowded. Nothing had actually happened. She hadn't actually done anything. She'd just cracked her chest open and spilled all her feelings.

And the longer she sat here thinking about it, the worse she felt.

She needed to get out of here. Before the family decided to go back to the lodge and they lost their buffer.

Kendall stood. "I think I've about hit my limit."

The mother's face creased with worry. "We aren't running you off with all our Olympics talk, are we?"

"Oh no," Kendall assured her. "I just, uh, have a busy day tomorrow. Need to get going."

Brody shifted, starting to get up as well. "I should probably—"

"I'll see you tomorrow," she interrupted before he could get any ideas about following her.

He hesitated. "Right. See you tomorrow."

Kendall quickly wrapped up in her towel and shoved her feet into her Crocs, forcing what she hoped was a cheerful smile and a wave for the paying customers.

She'd been spending too much time with him, sharing too much with him. She'd just gotten confused. Her old stupid crush all mixed up with the fact that he was always there, looking strong and capable and willing to help her with whatever she needed. But he was leaving. He was Kevin's best friend. And he had never seen her the way she saw him.

She'd just gotten confused. That look in his eyes…that was her imagination running away with her. And she knew better than to let it run too far.

Chapter Seventeen

Something was beeping.

Kendall groaned. Her head felt thick. Foggy and wrong. She couldn't afford to have a cold. The trials were today. She needed to be sharp. She'd pound as much cold medicine as her system could handle without triggering a drug test, but she was not missing her shot. This was her year. Everyone said so.

The beeping grew louder. She tried to reach for it, but nothing happened. Her body wouldn't respond. She felt heavy. Smothered. She tried to lift her arm again—and panic hit.

It's an anxiety dream, she tried to tell herself. She had them sometimes on the night before a big race. That was why she couldn't move. She just needed to wake up.

The beeping was faster now.

"Kendall? Are you awake?"

No. I'm having a nightmare.

She couldn't move. Nothing would move.

"Kendall." A hand closed over hers—she could feel that. Her hand tightened spasmodically around it—and she opened her eyes.

The room was too bright. White everywhere. And Brody James was holding her hand.

"I'm so sorry."

She looked down at herself—at the casts and tubes, the hospital bed—

Kendall jerked upright in her bed in the old lodge. *"Fuck!"* She shoved her hair back from her face. Sweat made her sleep shirt cling moistly to her skin.

Banner was suddenly there, whining softly and licking her face, and Kendall petted him, soothing the dog she'd disturbed with her nightmare. "It's okay," she assured him. "I'm okay."

Her breathing was still coming too fast, and she tried repeatedly to get a single full breath, but her chest still felt tight.

She hadn't dreamed of the hospital in a while. Much more often she'd dream she was late for the trials, being physically restrained from getting there, but this had practically been a memory.

Brody really had visited her in the hospital. She didn't think he'd ever held her hand like that or told her he was sorry, but it could have happened. Her memories of that time were all jumbled.

That was what happened with major head trauma, apparently.

She finally managed to get a deep breath and lie back down, Banner wriggling close to her side.

Talking to Brody about the accident last night must have stirred everything up. Why had she done that? She never talked about it. But after everything with Magda and what he'd shared about Oskar and then Brody being right there...she'd just spilled everything.

It had been the alpine combined. She'd never been as good

at the slalom portion, so she'd known she needed a huge lead in the downhill to guarantee her spot. She'd been *flying*. And then she'd really been flying—tumbling through the air. Kendall had watched the video a thousand times, but she couldn't seem to remember it. It felt like it was happening to someone else. But it was her career that had ended. Her body that had never fully recovered.

Four years prior, she'd barely missed making the Olympic team because of a poorly timed ACL sprain, but that year...

She'd been the presumptive gold medalist, expected not just to make the Olympic team but to win it all. She'd been *the* story. And then her dream had ended and Brody had become a household name. Just like that.

Kendall grabbed the pillow beside her and smashed it down on her face, groaning into it.

God, why had she brought that up? She didn't talk about her accident with *anyone*. Not for years. She'd mentally put it in a box and put that box on a shelf and built a new wall in front of that shelf.

She was pretty sure her old therapist wouldn't have approved of the bury-it-deep-and-pretend-it-doesn't-exist approach, but Kendall hadn't been able to find a local therapist who took her insurance, and dealing with her issues had become a luxury she couldn't afford these last few years. So she'd avoided her drama. Made it a problem to be unpacked another day.

And then Brody had blown into her life, and all her freaking baggage had come rocketing out of her hidden places like he was some kind of magnet for her issues.

Just how every woman wanted to behave in front of the man she'd had a crush on since she discovered what crushes were.

Banner whined, trying to wriggle his nose underneath the

pillow she was pressing to her face, and Kendall sighed, lifting the pillow so the dog could nose her face good morning.

"You're right," she told the dog. "No sense wallowing here. Work to be done."

Today was floor day, and tonight was Charlotte's bachelorette party. There was much too much to do to bother with feelings.

George's family was flying in today, and Kendall needed to be fully focused on the lodge and her maid-of-honor duties. So back in the box, on the shelf, behind that new wall went all the things she didn't want to think about right now. Including Brody.

It was a big resort. There was no reason she should run into him.

So of course she saw him the second she arrived at the main lodge's staff entrance with Banner and all her stuff to move into the room she was using while the floors were being refinished.

"Hey!" Brody jogged out to take Banner's empty crate—and thankfully the dog didn't run circles around him in greeting, because Kendall didn't have a free hand to manage him.

Pushing one roller bag and with a massive camping backpack on her back and the garment bag with her bridesmaid dress hooked to it so it didn't drag on the ground, she was a delicately balanced ecosystem of stuff.

"You should have called me," Brody admonished. "I would have helped you schlep all this."

"You were working. And I didn't need help." The bag of silly bachelorette party favors for tonight chose that moment to slip off the pile of things on top of her roller bag, undermining her insistence that she had it handled.

Brody picked up the bag and held the employee door open

for her, and she avoided looking directly at him as she maneu-vered herself inside. At least he hadn't brought up last night.

"I'm glad I ran into you. I wanted to talk about last night—"

Kendall wished for a volcano to open up beneath her in that moment and swallow her before Brody could finish his sentence—and then something just as seismic occurred.

A shiny black BMW convertible coupe screeched into the parking lot, fishtailing slightly on an icy patch before correcting and zipping into a parking space amid all the four-wheel-drive vehicles with ski racks.

Brody broke off as both of them recognized the car—and the man who leapt out of the driver's seat, throwing his arms wide and bellowing when he saw Brody still holding the staff door.

"Broseph!"

"Kev!" Brody called back, his smile huge as he set down Banner's crate.

The prodigal son had returned.

Brody and Kevin thumped one another on the back, bro-hugging and laughing—and Kendall was reminded of exactly how she'd felt when she was eleven and her annoying thirteen-year-old brother had stolen her best friend. Yes, she'd wanted to be saved from talking to Brody about the awkward feelings crap, but Kevin brought his own whole solar system of feelings she was trying to avoid.

Then her brother turned to her, bellowing, "Kenny!" and slung his arm around her shoulder above the camping pack, giv-ing her a shake in a jostling side hug.

"Hey, Kev."

"All my favorite people! Come on. I've got news."

* * *

"Dude, *what* are you doing here?"

Brody had heard the same question a hundred times over the last few weeks—usually from skiers who recognized him around the resort and couldn't believe their favorite Olympian was actually breathing the same air they were. It hit a little differently when it was Kev. But the truth still stuck in his throat.

They stood beside one of the fire pits in front of the lodge, a bucket of beer resting on the stone ledge and one in each of their hands, since Kevin had insisted his news was going to call for a toast. Kendall had gone to drop Banner and her things in her room with the help of one of the housekeepers, promising she would find her dad and Laurie and bring them out to the fire pits while Kev and Brody caught up.

Brody had thought he might be getting a sneak preview of the news, whatever it was, but Kev was taking the chance to interrogate him instead.

"I'm just taking a little time off," he said. He needed to stop lying, but he couldn't seem to make himself talk about the truth with anyone but Kendall.

"Your agent called me," Kev said. "He said your knee was messed up, but you wouldn't even talk to your team. That you just bailed."

"I just need some time," he repeated. "Steph's getting married in a few weeks, and I realized, you know, I was missing it. All the family stuff. Having a life outside skiing." That was close to the truth.

"Okay, but why are you playing manager at my dad's resort? You could be doing anything."

"Steph needed a wedding venue, and this was a way for me to help out. Kendall had just fired that guy—"

"So she would've hired someone new. And Steph would have booked the venue. You didn't have to work here."

"No, I know. I just, I wanted to."

Kev looked at him as if he'd lost his mind. "There has gotta be more to it than that. Is it a woman? Oh God, this isn't about Kendall, is it? 'Cuz you gotta be careful there, man. She had the hugest crush on you in high school. You're like my brother, but she *is* my sister, and I can't let you break my little sister's heart."

"No. It's not like that," Brody protested. "We're just—I don't think she ever—we don't—"

"Good," Kev saved him, by cutting him off. "Good."

A shout from the resort entrance distracted them then. Kurt and Laurie Walsh had exited the building, and Kevin turned toward his dad and stepmom, throwing out his arms as they hurried toward him. Kendall trailed more slowly in their wake.

Kurt was bursting with pride, while Laurie fussed over Kevin, asking if he was getting enough sleep. Brody watched the family reunion with a slight smile, then his gaze landed on Kendall and awkwardness rose up.

He hadn't felt awkward with her once in the last few weeks—everything was always easy with Kendall, even when she was arguing with him and had that frown line grooved between her eyes. But he'd never suspected she'd had a crush on him. Was that just Kev being full of shit? Or had she really liked him, once upon a time?

She couldn't *still* like him. Not like that. She was practically family. They'd known one another forever. And yeah, he'd felt weird when she'd gone out with that other guy, and when he'd seen her talking to him at the polar plunge, but that was just because he was protective. Because he wanted the best for her, and not because *he* wanted her. She was *Kendall*. She hardly ever smiled at him. Not exactly the behavior of a woman who was interested in him, at least in his experience. Those women were all smiles.

But then last night something had shifted. There'd been that electric current, that intensity simmering beneath everything before they'd been interrupted by Banner. He'd told himself it was nothing, but now he couldn't stop replaying it...and every other moment in the last few weeks.

"All right, now that we're all here, let's do this!" Kev bellowed, yanking Brody's attention off Kendall.

Kev had never been a subtle human. He grabbed the bucket of beers, handing them out to his parents and Kendall. Once everyone had one, he stepped back and grinned hugely, throwing out his arms. "I'm doing it! I'm getting married!"

"Whoa," Brody said inadvertently. He'd expected Kev to say he'd gotten promoted again, or bought some penthouse in a high-rise. Marriage wouldn't even have been in his top twenty guesses.

He hadn't even known Kev was seriously dating anyone. He wasn't sure Kev had *ever* dated anyone seriously. And from the other exclamations of surprise, Brody wasn't the only one who was caught off guard by Kevin's declaration.

"Honey! Wow. Congratulations! Who is she?" Laurie asked, confirming they were all equally in the dark.

"Her name's Alba. She wanted to come up here with me to meet you all, but she couldn't get out of work, and I couldn't wait to tell you. You're gonna love her. She keeps me on my toes. Knows exactly what she wants. And we're not wasting time. We're thinking April for the wedding. In New York."

"*This* April?" Laurie yelped. "When did you meet?"

"New York?" her husband said at the same time. "Don't

you want to get married here? Kendall's doing a whole wedding thing now."

Kendall shot her father a look.

"Our lives are in the city, you know?" Kev explained. "I love Pine Hollow, but New York is home now. And Alba's never been here. I want her to have her dream. There was a cancellation at this place she loves, and we didn't want to wait. So we just grabbed it."

"How long have you guys been seeing each other?" Kendall asked.

"Couple months. When you know, you know."

"You haven't even mentioned her," Laurie said, equal parts worried and quietly hurt.

"Kev…" Kendall's eyes were wide with alarm.

"April is so soon," Laurie murmured.

Kevin held up his hands, laughing and utterly unconcerned by their worry. "I get it. It's fast. And I'm not Mr. Marriage. But if she was here, you guys would be asking why I'm waiting so long to lock it down. Trust me."

He turned to Brody and clapped him on the shoulder. "I know you're probably going back to the tour soon, so I asked Alba's brother to be my best man—but you've gotta be at the wedding. It's after the season's over, so you have no excuse."

"Of course," Brody agreed, trying not to bristle at Kev's assumption that he might not make it to the wedding. "I wouldn't miss it."

Kev beamed, bellowing, "I'm getting married!"

Brody toasted him with everyone else, all of their faces more worried than joyful—especially Kendall's.

* * *

"Okay, what's the hurry? Why April?" Brody asked as soon as he had Kevin alone. Kendall had left to go get ready for Charlotte's bachelorette party, and Kurt and Laurie had given them a moment alone at the bar after shooting Brody very meaningful looks, as if it was his job to talk some sense into his friend.

"Why are you here?" Kevin countered. "Why does anyone do anything?"

"I didn't think you even believed in marriage. And certainly not hasty ones. You overthink everything."

"I know. It's why my dad thought I was a shitty skier. No instincts. All thinking, no doing. You'd think he'd be proud of me for doing something." Kevin shrugged, taking a drink of his beer. "He will be. In the long run." He tapped his bottle. "I figured at least Kendall would understand."

Brody gave Kev an incredulous look. "Really? You can't think of any reason why spontaneously marrying someone you barely know might concern her? No reason at all?"

"I'm not twenty-three. And yes, Kendall jumped in too fast with her idiot ex, and my parents barely knew each other when they got married and it completely blew up in their faces, but I'm not them. I know Alba. She had us do this whole questionnaire thing, like I was interviewing to be allowed to date her. And we're gonna have a prenup, if that's what you guys are worried about. She's a lawyer. She insisted."

"She's a lawyer?"

"For a nonprofit. Lots of pro bono stuff. Making the world a better place. We met at a fundraiser, and I'm just…well, shit, man, I'm just hoping she never wakes up and realizes she's way too good for me. I really love her."

Brody studied Kevin's face, the naked sincerity in his eyes, and something shifted in his chest—something that felt a lot more like envy than worry. Kevin was in love. He was being rash and quite possibly rushing too fast, but Brody kind of respected that he was taking that leap.

"You're going to have to talk to Kendall," Brody reminded him.

"I will," Kev assured him.

Brody shook his head, starting to smile. "Shit. Congratulations."

"Thanks." Kevin grinned. "Just so you know, I'm expecting you to be at my bachelor party."

"I'm not going anywhere," he promised.

Kev snorted. "Sure you aren't."

He couldn't really blame Kev for his doubt. He'd conditioned his friends and family not to trust him to be around—and these last few weeks, he hadn't exactly been easy to reach. He'd been hiding from anyone he was afraid would ask why he was here. Which hadn't helped him build the connections he'd supposedly come here for.

The only person he'd gotten really close to was Kendall.

Kendall…

He couldn't seem to stop thinking about that moment on the chairlift last night ever since Kev had mentioned she used to have a crush on him. He didn't know if she still had those feelings…but he was starting to wonder if he might. Was that what that spark had been? The excitement to see her every day? The reason he couldn't wait to wake up every morning?

Obviously, she was attractive. He'd certainly noticed, every time they went to the hot tub. And when she smiled at him, or frowned at him, something inside him went sharp and alert and leaned in, urging him to brush against her when he didn't technically need to…

Unless was he just latching onto her because it was easier than facing his own baggage.

He needed to see her again to find out.

And to see if that thing that had almost happened on the lift chair was going to happen again.

Then maybe he'd know what he wanted. The answers always seemed to be with Kendall.

Chapter Eighteen

"Oh no," Kendall declared, plucking the cellphone from Charlotte's hand. "Definitely not. Texting the fiancé is a clear violation of the bachelorette party rules of engagement."

"Do you see this sash?" Charlotte demanded, pointing to her chest. "It says 'bride,' and that means for the next seventy-two hours, I am queen of everything, and if I ask Magda to record my rendition of 'Marry You' so I can text it to my sweetie, you are honor bound as maid of honor to let me." She made a grab for the phone, snatching it back.

Kendall sighed. "I never should have given you a sash."

"Nonsense," Charlotte insisted. "I love my sash, and I love you. This has been the perfect night."

Kendall smiled—Charlotte had downed multiple glasses of champagne, but she wasn't yet to the *I-love-you-guys* stage of drunkenness, so her appreciation was genuine.

The bachelorette party was currently in stage two of Kendall's three-stage plan. The private tasting and dinner at a local winery had been a hit, and the entire group had then loaded onto the party bus for their second stop—karaoke.

Charlotte was a more-the-merrier kind of person, so Kendall had invited all of George's sisters, Charlotte's sisters, and several of Charlotte's friends from town—including a couple of seniors from the retirement community where she worked.

Kendall had expected that at least a couple attend-ees would tap out after the first stop—particularly the septuagenarians—but Vivian Weisman was currently standing on the karaoke stage belting out "The Greatest Love of All" with remarkable enthusiasm, if not terribly accurate pitch. Everyone in the group adored Charlotte and George, and that had been all it took for them to gel. Though it probably also helped that the champagne was flowing freely.

Charlotte was definitely milking the whole bride thing for all it was worth, but she was so clearly *happy* that it was impossi-ble to be annoyed by her playacting the diva bride.

"I'm glad you like it," Kendall said. "We have about a half hour before we need to move on to our next stop."

"Then *you* have a half hour to have fun," Charlotte insisted, shoving a full champagne glass toward Kendall. As the orga-nizer, she hadn't had more than a couple sips of champagne, busy trying to make sure everything ran smoothly and Char-lotte had the best possible time.

"I am having fun." Kendall slid the glass back toward Charlotte.

"You're being the wedding planner," Charlotte complained. "I want you to be Fun Kendall."

"I am Fun Kendall," she said, feeling a little defensive and remembering Brody's incredulity about her knowing how to go wild.

"I don't care if everything is perfect. As the bride, I forbid you from lifting a finger for my wedding if it means you aren't going to enjoy yourself."

Kendall arched her eyebrows skeptically. "You don't care if everything is perfect?"

Charlotte rolled her eyes. "Okay, that was a massive lie. Obviously I want to have the best wedding in the history of weddings—but I feel like I finally get what George was saying about wanting it to be fun. It doesn't mean anything if the people I love aren't going to be able to have a good time because they're so worried about making it perfect for me."

"I *want* to make it perfect for you."

"And I want you to sing."

Kendall blinked. "What?"

Charlotte thrust a finger toward the stage. "Karaoke. I want ridiculous and over the top. *Enjoy* yourself."

"I know how to have fun," Kendall insisted.

"Oh?" Charlotte batted her eyes with mock innocence. "You remember back that far?"

There was clear challenge in her eyes—and Kendall had never been able to resist a challenge. She stood, making her way to the karaoke jockey's desk. A few quick words and a generous tip added her to the queue, and a few minutes later, the opening bars of "Dancing Queen" sounded to a chorus of cheers as Kendall stepped onstage.

Kendall looked out over the crowd—about a third of which was their rowdy group—and locked eyes with Charlotte, who was probably the only person in the room not beaming. Instead, she looked like she might cry from happiness. All wobbly and touched.

Kendall sang the familiar opening, never taking her eyes off the bride. She didn't need to read the lyrics. This had been their song, in high school. Or one of them. She could remember summer nights when they were sixteen, standing on the same dock where they'd had the polar plunge, playing "Dancing Queen" on repeat and making up an entire dance routine with Charlotte and Mags.

Charlotte had graduated early and was about to go off to college. Kendall was finally old enough to compete in the Junior World Championships. It had felt like their entire lives were in front of them and anything was possible. And they'd danced on that dock until they'd nearly fallen off laughing.

When the chorus hit, the entire bar began singing along with her and Kendall grinned, but she didn't take her eyes off Charlotte, pointing straight to the bride as she sketched her way through the dance steps they'd made up all those years ago.

No matter what happened, Charlotte and Mags would always have her back. And she would have theirs. She directed the second verse at Magda, who had been sitting with George's sisters but was now standing up and doing the same ridiculous dance moves as Kendall.

Charlotte was on her feet as well—and when the rest of the bachelorette party realized it was a dance routine, they practically carried Charlotte and Magda to the stage. Kendall grabbed their hands, tugging them up with her, and the three of them finished the song, dancing, grinning hugely, and bellowing the lyrics into a single microphone.

They took their bows, laughing and leaning on one another, to roars of applause. Kendall handed off the microphone and stumbled off stage with Magda and Charlotte hanging off her arms.

"I love you so much," Charlotte gushed.

"I love you too, loser," Kendall said.

"Was that so painful?" Charlotte asked. "Having a little fun?"

"I have fun," Kendall insisted as the three of them returned to Charlotte's table and one of George's sisters launched into "Your Song." She appealed to Magda for reinforcements, but Mags winced like she did when she was about to disagree with someone.

"I haven't seen you laugh in forever," she said.

"I laugh!" Kendall insisted. But they were right. It had been a while. She'd just been so *busy*.

"You've been getting more and more tense these last few years. And less likely to try things," Charlotte said. "You don't let anyone get close to you, and sometimes it feels like you even keep us at a distance."

"It's like you've been slowly closing yourself off more and more," Magda agreed.

Neither Magda nor Charlotte was drunk, per se, but they'd had enough vino to access the veritas. They were both a little looser with their words. A little more honest.

Kendall looked at her friends, her throat tight. "I never meant to push you two away," she said softly. "And I know I've been stressed about the resort, but I'm fine—"

"Kendall."

"Okay, yes, maybe I could be more open to things." She'd always made snap judgments—it was what had made her a great skier. She didn't question her decisions. She committed. Fast. All in, all on instinct. But lately those snap judgments had shifted. They'd become about avoiding risk. About not getting hurt again.

Not physically. She wasn't scared of another injury. She was scared of letting herself hope. Letting herself want things. And being disappointed again.

She hadn't just stopped believing in her dreams. She'd stopped believing in anything that exposed her to disappointment. Love. Adventure. All of it. She'd loved throwing herself into the teeth of fear before—reckless and wild and fun. But then she'd changed.

"I'm sorry I'm not fun anymore," she said to her friends.

"Hey," Charlotte interrupted. "That is not what we said. I don't need you to *be* fun. I need you to *have* fun. To be happy. And these last couple years, it's like you've become so worried about not taking any chances that you don't let yourself just say screw it, this might blow up in my face, but okay, let's freaking do this. You're playing it safe, but avoiding risk isn't keeping you from being unhappy."

"I'm not unhappy," she protested.

But she also wasn't *happy*. She was…safe.

And Kendall didn't actually like safe. These last few weeks with Brody she'd had flashes when she felt like herself—and they weren't the safe moments. They were when he threw down a challenge and she felt that fire in her gut, that click of oh-we-are-*doing*-this.

They were the moments when she dared.

"I just…" She trailed off, searching for the words. "I feel like something changed in my brain. Not necessarily with the accident, but when I realized I wasn't going to be a racer anymore. I couldn't be who I always thought I was, so I put everything that made me that person in a box, and I think it might have taken me a while to realize I'm not the person I've been trying to make myself be for the last few years. But I'm not the racer anymore either. I'm something else, and I'm just starting to figure out who that is." She made a face. "Kevin showed up this afternoon and told us he's marrying some girl he just met—and I had no idea how I felt about that. I've always trusted my instincts with people, and it turns out *I'm* the one I can't figure out."

Charlotte squeezed her hand. "Join the club. We're all messes here."

"And we love all the versions of you," Magda assured her, linking their arms on the table.

Kendall groaned. "Oh my God, the sappy feelings stuff. *Stop.*"

"You know you love it," Charlotte taunted. And Kendall smiled, because yeah, they might be cheesy and ridiculous, but they were *hers*, and she'd always known that.

When Kevin had swept in and stolen Brody's friendship during their teen years, Magda and Charlotte had been there. They'd *always* been there for her. Even when Charlotte was in med school and Magda was at some fancy pastry academy in France.

"Whatever," Kendall griped, because she had a reputation as the unemotional one to maintain. "I'm going to start gathering people up. We have a drag show to get to."

Chapter Nineteen

The drag show was freaking amazing. The queens brought Charlotte up onstage and made a ridiculous fuss over her—which she could not have loved more.

Things had been relatively restrained at the wine tasting and dinner. They'd gotten fun—but not *too* rowdy—at karaoke. But after the drag show, all bets were off. All the "To the bride!" shots had finally hit Charlotte, and she was *hammered*. They'd had to get her down off the bar to pour her back into the party bus, where the septuagenarians had surprised them all by leading a chorus of "Single Ladies" on the drive home.

As bachelorette parties went, it was very Charlotte.

But now Kendall found herself with one *extremely* drunk bride and the job of getting her from the resort parking lot back to her condo. The condo was less than a mile away, so normally it wouldn't be a problem, but maneuvering Charlotte at the moment was a little like trying to convince a particularly unhelpful blanket to walk. She'd draped herself over Kendall's shoulders and showed no signs of moving.

"Are you sure you're good?" George's sister Beks asked, swaying on her feet.

The party bus had stopped at the Summerland Estates Retirement Community, and then downtown Pine Hollow to drop off the locals, but George's sisters and their families were all staying at the resort for the wedding. The others had already headed inside, but Beks hung back, looking exhausted, but still offering to help.

"I've got her," Kendall assured her. "Get some sleep. And hydrate!"

Beks waved one hand, starting toward the doors, and Kendall steered a very unhelpful Charlotte toward the staff lot—driving her half a mile seemed like a much better idea than trying to get Drunko McDrunkerton to walk along icy paths.

At least it seemed like a better idea until she finally had Charlotte buckled into the passenger seat and the Jeep refused to start. It had been giving her fits on particularly cold mornings, but she hadn't had the time—or the money—to take it in to get looked at.

"Shit," Kendall muttered—as Charlotte released a soft snore from the passenger seat. "I guess we're walking."

Her phone buzzed at that moment, and Kendall fished it out—just in case a miracle had occurred and her guardian angel wanted to sweep in and carry Charlotte back to the NetZero Village for her.

But the text was from Brody.

> Not checking up on you. It was Banner. He was worried and wanted to make sure you'd made it home okay.

Attached was a picture of Banner, fast asleep on Brody's stomach.

Kendall's lips twitched. She quickly typed a reply.

> He does look worried. I'm fine. Back at the resort. Just
> gotta get the bride home. Wish me luck.

His reply was quick.

> Do you need luck? Or a hand?

She smiled. Brody James. Always offering to help.

> I'm good. Jeep's acting up, but we can walk it. Not far.

She pocketed her phone, climbed out of the Jeep, and rounded the hood to begin the process of getting Charlotte vertical again. She opened the passenger door and unbuckled her, before giving her a gentle shake. "Charlotte."

Charlotte groaned and burrowed deeper into the seat.

"C'mon, Char. Work with me here."

She grabbed Charlotte's hands, trying to use them to pull her upright, but she was as floppy as a puppet. After several minutes of unsuccessful Charlotte wrangling, she stood back and grumbled, "You're not helping."

"Need a hand?"

As Brody approached, Kendall turned to look over her shoulder at him, her lips twitching and her blue eyes wry. "I should have known you wouldn't be able to resist a damsel in distress."

"Is that what you are?" Brody asked, coming to her side at the Jeep. Charlotte appeared to be fast asleep in the passenger seat, wearing a hot pink dress and a white glittery sash with BRIDE written on it. There was a fake tiara tangled in her hair and scarlet lipstick in a kiss mark on one cheek.

Brody had wondered if he was being ridiculous when he'd immediately crated Banner, thrown on some clothes, and jogged down to see if Kendall needed help after getting her text, but now he was glad he'd come.

"You wanna take one arm, I'll take the other?" he offered.

"Yeah, good idea," Kendall said. "That's probably more dignified than my plan to throw her over your shoulder."

"That's another option," Brody agreed, but they were already each taking one arm and levering Charlotte out of the Jeep—which was a lot harder than it looked. He'd thought being three-quarters asleep would make her pliant, but instead she was slippery as hell.

Together they managed to get the extremely floppy-when-drunk bride into the back seat of Brody's truck, and Kendall gave him directions for the short drive up the road to the NetZero Village condo complex where Charlotte and George lived.

"Does your dad mind that you seem to have stolen his truck?" Kendall asked as he drove. "I think after three weeks it stops being borrowing if you never bring it back."

"I actually bought it off him."

Kendall glanced over sharply. "Really? When?"

"About a week ago. Seemed like I ought to have my own ride if I was going to stick around." He'd always liked the truck. It had been instinct to offer to buy it off his dad. It just felt right.

"What did your parents think when you told them your knee wasn't hurt?" Kendall asked.

Brody felt his face heating, but luckily the darkness hid any evidence of his embarrassment. "I still haven't told them."

"Why not? Don't you have dinner with them every week?"

"Yeah, but...it's hard to explain." It wasn't that he didn't want to tell them. It was more that he didn't want to disappoint them.

"Just there." Kendall pointed him toward a parking lot beside a multistory cluster of condos, and Brody was grateful for the chance to focus on the task at hand.

He climbed out of the truck to help Kendall unload the bride-to-be from the back seat. Charlotte stirred this time as they tried to wrangle her out of the truck. She opened her eyes when they had her balanced on the edge of the seat and yelped, "Brody! You came to my party!"

She flung herself at him in a hug—which at least got her out of the truck without injuring herself, so he was calling it a win. "Hey, Charlotte," he said, awkwardly patting her on the back.

"I'm getting married!" she declared, lurching over to her best friend to hug her as well.

"I heard." He took her arm, and together he and Kendall managed to get her more or less balanced between them. They started toward her place, and Charlotte gazed up at him, smiling sleepily.

"I always liked you, Brody," she declared as they staggered along.

"Thank you."

"Third floor," Kendall grunted, steering them toward the stairs.

"You should come to my wedding," Charlotte slurred as she tried to spin around and sit down on the steps.

"No, no, no, up we go," Brody coaxed, keeping her from sitting down.

"Yes, you should," Charlotte insisted—but she was moving

upward, so she could argue with him all she wanted. "Kendall, tell him he should. I'm getting married!"

"So you said," Brody agreed as they reached the first landing.

"It's gonna be a great wedding. Kendall helped plan it, did you know? And you are gonna come. End of story."

Kendall caught Charlotte's flailing hand before it could smack her in the face. "Okay, come on, drunko."

"I'm not drunk. I'm the bride."

"I don't think those two things are mutually exclusive," Kendall said as they cleared the second landing.

Charlotte swung her bleary gaze back toward Brady as they started up the last flight. "Did Kendall tell you about her shoes yet?"

"Charlotte…" Kendall's voice had a distinct note of warning, but Brody couldn't figure out why.

"Her shoes for the wedding?"

"Her shoes for *you*. *Huge* shoes. Massive. Very very big."

"Uh…" He glanced over Charlotte's head at Kendall, who looked distinctly pained. "You got me shoes?"

"She's extremely drunk."

"I noticed."

Kendall's lips twitched. "Just ignore everything she says."

"No!" Charlotte declared, managing to swing free of Kendall's grasp—though they'd reached the top landing, so she didn't hurt herself. "I will not be ignored! I am the *bride*."

"Yes, you are," Kendall agreed, getting Charlotte moving toward her apartment door.

"And *you* are invited to my wedding," Charlotte insisted, stabbing one finger into Brody's chest. Then continuing to poke him repetitively, her attention focusing entirely on her finger.

"Where are your keys?" Kendall asked as they propped

Charlotte up beside her apartment door. She began searching Charlotte's coat pockets.

"I'm inviting you," Charlotte insisted. "Because I think you have shoes for Kendall. And you are good people."

"I'm sure Kendall has her own shoes."

"I *know*. That's what I just *said*."

"Ignore her," Kendall advised. "Char. Where are your keys?"

Under her winter coat she was wearing a sparkly pink dress and a sash reading BRIDE, but neither of them seemed to have pockets.

"In my purse," Charlotte said, as if the answer was obvious.

Kendall closed her eyes on a groan. *"Crap."*

"Is it back in your Jeep?" Brody asked. "Should I run and get it?"

Kendall shook her head, opening her eyes. "I haven't seen it since karaoke. It could be on the bus. We might have left it at the drag club…"

Brody cringed sympathetically. "Okay…does anyone else have a key?"

"George. But he's staying at the inn with his folks for a few nights—he and Charlotte thought it would be more romantic if they were apart before the wedding—and it's one in the morning. He might not even answer his phone and…crap. I don't think I even have his number. Charlotte is always our go-between and her phone is in her purse." She turned her attention on her extremely drunk friend. "Honey, where did you leave your purse? Do you remember?"

Charlotte just blinked at her, and looked around. "Are we at my place?"

Kendall stepped back, reaching for her phone. "I'm calling the bus company. Maybe someone is still there." She hung up almost immediately. "Straight to voicemail." She glanced at the time on her phone. "I bet the drag club is still open."

They were, and the background noise had Kendall shouting with one hand over her mouth in an attempt not to wake Charlotte's neighbors.

"The bride!" Brody heard someone yell through the phone. "We knew you'd call! You left your clutch, honey!"

Kendall didn't bother correcting them that she was the maid of honor. She quickly worked out logistics—asking how late they were open and where she should go when she arrived—and hung up the phone.

"They have it," she said to Brody, stating the obvious. "It's about a forty-minute drive, but they're open for another hour. If you can help me get her into my room at the resort—and if you don't mind me borrowing your truck—"

"Don't be ridiculous. I'll drive you."

"Seriously? Brody, it's the middle of the night."

"Yeah, but I'm invested now. And I have to do something to earn my wedding invite."

Kendall winced. "I don't think she really meant—"

"I know. I was kidding. But I want to help."

Kendall shook her head, the frown line between her brows deepening. "I am never going to be able to repay you, am I?"

"No repayment necessary. I like this. Come on," he coaxed, reaching for Charlotte, who was somehow snoring while standing upright, slumped against the wall. "Let's get her settled."

Chapter Twenty

They didn't end up stashing Charlotte in Kendall's room after all. They loaded her back into the truck to take her to the resort—and she promptly curled up on the bench seat in the back of the extended cab and fell asleep. Since Charlotte was too drunk to care where she slept, and Kendall was worried if they spent too much time trying to get her up the elevator to her suite they'd miss their window at the drag club, they ended up driving toward the club with an extremely drunk bride snoring loudly in the back seat.

"Are you okay not being Kev's best man?" Kendall asked after they'd been driving for a while and the silence started to get to her. Charlotte had been entirely too gushy about Brody and Kendall's "shoes," so she wanted to do everything she could to distract him from that part of the conversation.

Brody grimaced. "I can't really blame him. We haven't talked much lately. Even since I've been back. He couldn't figure out why I was staying here."

He's not the only one, Kendall thought, but kept her mouth shut. Even if he was retiring—which she still didn't quite buy—there was no reason for him to stay in Pine Hollow.

"We didn't really talk about it," Brody said, something almost evasive on his face. "It was mostly about his fiancée—I think your parents left me alone with him in the hopes that I would talk some sense into him."

"And did you?"

"Actually, I'm not sure it's such a terrible match. She sounds pretty amazing. Driven and compassionate. She could be really good for Kev."

"Wow. What did he say to you to get you on board so fast?"

"Nothing. He just…I don't know. I think he's in love. And he seems really sure. I know it's fast, but maybe that's just what happens when it's right."

Kendall huffed out a soft breath. "Brody James, closet romantic."

"If you hadn't had to run off for the bachelorette party, you would have seen. He knows what he wants," Brody marveled. "I kind of envy that."

"Yeah," Kendall agreed. They both fell silent for a while, each lost in their own thoughts as they sped down the highway toward the drag club.

"It feels a little ridiculous to be thirty and have no idea what you want to do with your life," he said after a moment.

"You've already done a lot."

"I guess."

"You're not the only one trying to figure out who you want to be when you grow up." Kendall stared out the window. Magda and Charlotte had reminded her that avoiding risks wasn't making her happy—but she didn't know what *would*. Which risks to take. That was a whole new conundrum.

Charlotte stirred suddenly in the back seat, sat up, and demanded, "Are we getting burgers?"

"It's almost two in the morning," Kendall reminded her.

"I want burgers, and I am the bride, so my word is law," Charlotte declared—before flopping back down onto the bench seat and passing out again.

Kendall glanced over to find Brody pressing his lips together, barely suppressing a smile. "Like you've never been drunk."

"She's adorable," Brody said, allowing Kendall to lower her hackles. Charlotte might be over the top, but Kendall would happily fight anyone who made fun of her. "I just have a hard time picturing you as best buddies with the I-love-everyone-and-everything-let's-cover-it-in-glitter type. I feel like there must be a story there."

"Not much of one. We've been friends since before I met you. Magda was super shy—I don't think she spoke for the entire first month of kindergarten. I was this mouthy little brat who kept getting in trouble because I would say anything that popped into my head. And Charlotte was the one who grabbed both of us—literally—on the playground one day and declared that we were going to be her best friends forever. Like she could make it happen through sheer force of will. And she did. I know they would do *anything* for me. And I can't think of a single thing I wouldn't do for them."

"Like driving to a drag club in the middle of the night?"

"Nah. This is nothing. Though I do appreciate the company."

"My pleasure."

He really did seem to mean it. He *wanted* to help. Kendall

eyed him in the darkness. "I still can't quite figure you out, Brody James."

"Oh?"

"I know Oskar's death hit you hard, but you don't have to atone for it. You weren't responsible." His jaw worked, but he didn't glance toward her. "And you don't have to be the nicest man on the face of the planet and help Steph and me and the resort to prove something. You don't have anything to prove."

"I know," he insisted. "That's not why I'm doing it."

"So why?" She asked the question that had been bugging her ever since he came back.

"I don't know," he admitted, glancing over at her. "It's like you were saying, though—about figuring out who we want to be when we grow up. If I'm not skiing, I don't know if I want to be a sportscaster or a coach or a freaking toothpaste model again. But I know what kind of person I want to be. And I want to be the one people call when they need help. The one they know they can rely on."

He paused, and she waited as he seemed to be searching for the right words to explain.

"It's like—Charlotte decided you were going to be best friends when you were five years old, and then she spent a lifetime proving you could trust her. I haven't done that. But I want to prove that Steph can trust me. And my parents. And Kev... and you..."

"I do," she said—and she meant it. But she also believed he would leave. That at some point a switch would flip and he would go back to his regular life.

"My training team was great, but we were always so focused on winning. I didn't have anyone who needed me for anything but skiing. I think that's what I realized in Zermatt. And I wanted…I don't know. Maybe it's like you said. I wanted to be the hero. And I used to think the hero was the one who won the race. But now I'm thinking that's just physics."

"But don't you miss it?" Kendall whispered. "That feeling when everything just clicks into place and you aren't even thinking anymore, you're just flying. That flow. That perfect quiet place in the middle of the race when you know you're *on*."

"Honestly, it hasn't felt like that in a while," Brody admitted. "It becomes a battle. You're fighting for every turn. Always chasing that sweet spot, trying to find that perfect line. Never satisfied. Training and studying the course and overanalyzing every choice. It was work. Long before Switzerland."

He sounded tired, and for the first time, Kendall started to wonder if he might actually be done with skiing for good. If he might actually retire.

"That's the club," she said, grateful for the distraction. "Just there on the right."

Brody pulled into the parking lot—right as Charlotte bolted awake again. "Bacon burger. Extra pickles."

"I'll just run in and grab the purse," Kendall offered. "I won't be a second."

"Sounds good," Brody agreed.

"And get extra fries!" Charlotte called as Kendall leapt out of the truck.

Kendall was in and out—the drag queens recognized her and handed her the purse with many insistences that she and her friends had to come back for another show soon. She jogged back to the parking lot, and she couldn't have been gone for more than three minutes when she opened the truck door—to the distinct sound of Charlotte crooning "Let's Get It On" from the back seat.

"Kendall!" Charlotte bellowed, cutting off mid-verse. "I was just telling Brody that you guys need to get it on."

Kendall groaned and set Charlotte's purse on the seat. "I'm so sorry about her," she told Brody as she climbed in.

"She has very strong opinions," he said, no longer trying to pretend he wasn't laughing. "Particularly about our shoes, for some reason."

"She likes fashion." Kendall calmly pretended she had no idea what that could possibly mean.

Charlotte then began singing "Let's Get It On" again— and Brody was too busy laughing to read anything into it. Thank God.

Charlotte passed out again about halfway back to Pine Hollow—after working her way a capella through what she described as her "sexytime playlist."

When she was finally silent again, Brody flipped on the radio, flicking through stations until he found one that wasn't mostly static as they twisted through the mountains. A woman with a sultry voice was crooning "Baby, I'm Yours," but Kendall stared out the window and staunchly pretended that she felt absolutely nothing romantic for the man driving the vehicle.

"Is she always such a persistent matchmaker?" Brody asked fifteen minutes later as they drew close to Pine Hollow.

"She's a meddler. It's kind of her thing."

"And the shoes? Is that like a Cinderella thing?"

"Not quite," Kendall said.

Brody pulled into the parking lot closest to Charlotte's condo and parked the truck alongside the bank of mailboxes—as close as he could get to the stairs up to Charlotte's place. Charlotte was snoring softly in the back seat, and neither Kendall nor Brody moved to get out of the truck.

"Thank you," Kendall murmured. "I really appreciate you doing this tonight."

"I like doing things for you."

Kendall knew that was just Brody and his quest to be needed, but she felt a flush of warmth all the same. She liked having him here. Far more than she should.

She had put herself in a box over these last several years, and while she certainly didn't need a man to break her out of it, he had helped her see that she wanted to. It wasn't just about reclaiming her daring, about leaping into frozen lakes and confessing things she'd kept buried. It was about figuring out who she was…and realizing that it was okay to let go of who she'd been. She hadn't known who she was without skiing, but neither did he. And they were figuring it out together.

She held his gaze, that vivid awareness between them waking up, the one that she'd felt last night. Her skin was suddenly tingly and tight. Her breath a little shallow.

"Brody…"

Charlotte lurched up in the back seat. "French fries! Make sure you get french fries."

"I should probably get her inside," Kendall said, reluctant to leave the cab of the truck and leave this moment behind.

"Probably," Brody agreed—though he made no move to get out either.

Charlotte was fumbling with the controls on the rear door and managed to get the window lowered several inches, letting a cold blast of air into the cab. "I'd like to order some french fries!" she demanded of the mailboxes. "And a bacon cheeseburger. Extra pickles!"

"She knows what she wants," Brody said. "I'm just glad I

came down. Who knows who she would have been trying to hook you up with all night if I hadn't been here."

Maybe she was feeling daring. Maybe it was the fact of Charlotte as the world's drunkest chaperone that made her feel safe telling him anything. But Kendall suddenly heard herself admitting, "She wouldn't have tried to hook me up with just anyone. She's been trying to get me to jump you ever since you got back."

Brody's eyebrows flew up. "Has she?"

"She knows I had a crush on you in high school."

He swallowed, something she couldn't read moving across his face. "You did?"

And suddenly Kendall found herself admitting more. "Do you remember when we played truth or dare? Not when we were kids, and not with Kev and the giggle brigade, but just you and me in high school? That one night?"

"I…" He shook his head. "I don't. I wish I did."

She nodded. It probably hadn't meant anything to him, but she'd been reliving that moment for months afterward. "I wanted so badly to dare you to kiss me, but I chickened out. Too scared."

"Kendall Walsh? Scared?" he said, a rasp behind the lightness of his voice. "Never."

"Always," she corrected softly. "But I used to love the rush of doing something that scared me. Haven't done that in a while." She watched him steadily as that tension kept twisting and tangling in the air. And that exciting fear grabbed her stomach.

"Kendall Walsh," he said softly, "are you flirting with me?"

"I don't flirt with employees."

"They flirt with you," he said.

"And I shut it down. I'm the boss. I can't do that."

He nodded, but his eyes held hers. "I'm not really a typical employee, though."

"You aren't," she acknowledged, her blood rushing faster.

"So it wouldn't really be breaking any rules…"

"No," she agreed.

"Excuse me!" Charlotte yelled. "I asked for french fries!"

Kendall tore her eyes off Brody—and saw Charlotte had managed to get her upper body through the gap in the window and was now stuck, hanging half out of the car, bellowing her drive-thru order at the mailboxes. "Oh crap," Kendall muttered, quickly unbuckling herself and scrambling around to the back seat before Charlotte could hurt herself.

"Hold on, honey," Kendall said as she lowered the window the rest of the way, one arm wrapped around Charlotte to keep her from tumbling out. Brody had jumped out of the car and was standing waiting to catch Charlotte if she tipped the wrong direction.

"They aren't listening to me," Charlotte complained, allowing Kendall to reel her back inside. Brody then opened the door.

"Don't let her out. She's done something with her shoes," Kendall said quickly, searching the floorboards.

"Maybe that's what she was going on about," Brody said, blocking the opening with his body, though Charlotte made no effort to leap out now, instead wrapping herself around Kendall's arm.

"I love you."

"I love you too," Kendall assured her, finally finding the heels wedged underneath the front passenger seat. She put them on Charlotte's feet, but when Brody scooped her up to carry her to her apartment, the shoes dropped to the snow. Kendall gathered them up—along with the reclaimed purse, and they made their way toward Charlotte's building.

"George carried me like a maiden on the moors once," Charlotte commented, wagging her feet. "Kendall, you should make Brody carry you like a maiden on the moors. It's very nice." She patted his chest. "He's very muscly."

"I'll keep that in mind."

"You guys should have sex," Charlotte declared. She waved one arm magnanimously. "Just get it out of your system. All that rippling sexual tension. You ripple," she informed Brody. "Or maybe Kendall ripples. There's rippling."

"She's not going to remember any of this, is she?" Brody asked as he climbed the steps.

"I doubt it."

"I'm getting maaaaarried." Charlotte sighed, settling happily into Brody's grasp.

Kendall reached the apartment door then and used Charlotte's keys to unlock it. She flipped on the light, and Brody carried Charlotte inside. Normally the dogs would be rushing to greet her, but thankfully tonight George had them at the inn with him because they'd all suspected Charlotte might want to go a little haywire at her bachelorette.

Kendall met Brody's eyes as he straightened from settling Charlotte on the couch. "Do you mind keeping Banner for the rest of the night? I'd kinda like to stay here and keep an eye on Charlotte. She doesn't usually get hangovers, but I think this one might be a doozy."

"Yeah, of course. Are you good? Can I bring you anything?"

She shook her head. "You've done more than enough."

"When are you going to accept that I like doing things for you?" he asked, the words heavy with meaning.

He held her gaze and her breath grew short.

"Rippling!" Charlotte declared from the couch, waving her arms. "Bang it out, lovebirds."

Brody glanced over at Charlotte, grinning, but Kendall's face flamed as she ushered him toward the door. "Thank you for everything."

"Kiss him!" Charlotte shouted, leaning over the arm of the couch to watch them.

"I'll see you tomorrow," Brody said, and Kendall nodded.

"Yep. You bet."

She shut the door between them before she could be tempted to do something epically stupid. Like kiss him.

He was still Kevin's best friend. He was still her interim resort manager. He was still helping her fix up the lodge. And he was still going to leave as soon as he worked through all of the things that had made him leave the tour.

All of which meant she needed to keep her wits about her. Keep her senses. And *not* as Charlotte had so eagerly pointed out *jump him*.

"Chicken," Charlotte accused as Kendall grabbed her hands to pull her up and guide her toward the bedroom.

She wasn't wrong. But Kendall was still working her way up to that big a risk.

Charlotte Jane Rodriguez

&

George Patrick Leneghan

*Invite you to
celebrate with them
as they tie the knot!*

♡

February 3rd at 3 o'clock
St. John's Church
Pine Hollow, Vermont

Merriment to follow at the
Pine Hollow Mountain Resort

Chapter Twenty-One

Brody had never crashed a wedding before.

He'd never thought he would, but Kendall was avoiding him and Charlotte had repeatedly invited him, so this might not even technically count as crashing. Though she probably didn't remember inviting him, or anything else from her bachelorette night, so yeah. Crashing it was.

The resort was holding the reception, so he could always pretend he was only checking on the staff as a manager, while wearing his nicest suit.

He just needed to see Kendall.

He couldn't stop thinking about her—and wondering what would have happened if Charlotte hadn't been hanging out the window in the back seat when Kendall had admitted she used to want to dare him to kiss her. Did she still want that? Did he? The memory kept circling, but he hadn't seen her since he'd left her at Charlotte's apartment.

He knew she was busy. It was Charlotte's wedding weekend, and with the rehearsal dinner and preparations for the reception at the resort, she had a lot consuming her time—but he had the definite sense that she was avoiding him. She'd even sent one of the ski instructors to pick up Banner from him on the morning after the bachelorette party, when she could easily have swung by and gotten him herself.

There were still fumes in the old lodge as the floors were being refinished, so she was just down the hall. It would have been easy for her to drop by. But he hadn't seen her in two days. So here he was, crashing a wedding.

The ballroom was bursting with color and sound when Brody arrived partway through the reception. It was the same room where Charlotte's sister had married his cousin less than a month earlier, but it could not have looked more different.

Instead of creams and muted pastels, each table was covered with a bright floral arrangement and a table runner in a different cheerful shade—teals and pinks and oranges and yellows. There was a buffet set up along one wall, instead of the three-course dinner, and a balloon arch over the door.

He knew, from talking to Kendall, that this wedding had a much smaller guest list than the last one, but the noise level was substantially higher—everyone moving and laughing and speaking loudly over one another. There was no head table, and every member of the bridal party wore a differing vibrant shade, a rainbow of colors, rather than the coordinated elegance of Anne and Bailey's wedding—which made it harder to spot Kendall in the crowd.

Brody searched the press of people, smiling and nodding to the guests. He recognized several of them, either as resort guests or locals from Pine Hollow he'd met in recent weeks, but he didn't stop to talk to anyone. He needed to find Kendall before anyone realized he wasn't supposed to be here.

But instead of Kendall, he nearly ran into the bride.

"Brody!"

"Charlotte." There were pink and teal ringlets mixed in with her dark brown hair, matching the ribbons streaming from the bouquet she was clutching. "You look beautiful. Sorry for crashing your reception."

"Oh, no, Kendall told me I invited you. Multiple times, apparently. I'm glad you made it!" She beamed and thrust the bouquet at him. "Take this, will you?"

He took the flowers, uncertain. "Uh…"

"Just put it next to the cake. There's a spot. People keep wanting pictures of me with it—because it's awesome—but George and I have to do our first dance now. You don't mind, do you? Enjoy the reception! Ask Kendall to dance! But if you upset her, I'll kneecap you with a ski pole."

She patted his arm and was gone before he had a chance to answer, leaving him standing there marveling at her cheerful bloodthirst and holding a giant bouquet of brightly colored flowers.

"You ask me if there'll come a time, when I grow tired of you…"

Kendall watched Charlotte and George sway in the middle of the dance floor as Magda's nephew Dylan gently crooned "Never My Love" into the microphone.

For months, Charlotte had been agonizing over what their first song should be—and whether it should involve an elaborately choreographed routine. But then George had stepped in and said he knew exactly what they should dance to. He'd insisted he wanted to surprise her on the day, so Charlotte hadn't had any idea what he was planning.

As they swayed in the middle of the dance floor, George

mouthed the lyrics to his bride, Charlotte cried happy tears for the fifth time today, and Kendall even got a little choked up herself.

He'd picked the perfect song.

Charlotte had always worried that she would be too much. She'd never let herself be truly herself in her previous relationships, but George knew her, through and through, and he held her as if she was the most precious thing in the world as they danced.

Kendall swallowed hard. Charlotte was *so happy*. And Kendall's happiness for her felt too big to fit inside her chest, pressing up against her throat and the backs of her eyes. But there was something whispering beneath it.

Envy.

Kendall had always been independent, even during that brief window when she was married. She'd always taken care of herself. Standing on her own two feet.

But that also meant she'd never really let herself be vulnerable with another person, the way Charlotte was with George. She'd never taken that risk. And maybe, just maybe, she was missing out on something by keeping the walls around herself so high.

She'd just been so *angry* for so long. At herself, mostly. At her body for letting her down. She'd built those walls, built that distance, to keep all that anger contained. But they had also kept her from letting any of it go.

Maybe it was time to let go. To stop holding on to the dreams she'd already lost. And the anger over losing them. But if she stopped being angry, she wasn't sure what she would feel. And she was a little afraid of what that might be.

As the song changed and Charlotte and George began

dancing with their parents, Kendall slipped away, stepping out onto the veranda. No one else was crazy enough to be out here in the cold without a jacket, but Kendall wrapped her arms around herself and stood facing the mountain.

God, she loved that mountain. It felt like a piece of her soul. But also a reminder that she'd once been more. And if she wasn't angry at what she'd lost, if she let herself stop clinging to that, the sadness crept in to fill the space her anger had claimed for all these years.

She didn't know how long she stood there, staring at the mountain and feeling her feelings. She didn't let herself do that very often. She was shivering and seconds from going back inside when a suit jacket draped her shoulders, enveloping her in warmth and a familiar scent.

"Trying to freeze yourself?" Brody asked softly.

"Just thinking," she replied.

"Care to think somewhere warmer?"

"No." She glanced up at him. "We can go in, but I think I'm done thinking for the night."

"Should I be worried?"

She shook her head, taking his arm, and together they slipped back into the ballroom. Once inside the warmth of the room, Kendall quickly shed Brody's jacket and handed it back to him.

"I didn't think you'd come," she said as he put the jacket back on and adjusted his cuffs. The man did look incredible in a suit.

"Charlotte did invite me. Very enthusiastically. And she knows I'm here. In fact, she told me I should ask you to dance. I wouldn't want to disappoint the bride." He held out his hand, palm up. "Care to dance, Speed Demon?"

This time the old nickname made her smile slightly. "I'm not much of a dancer."

"Maybe you never had the right partner. C'mon. Just hold on to me and sway."

Relenting, Kendall set her hand on his open palm, and let him lead her onto the dance floor.

Dylan was singing "Dive" now, sounding like the second coming of Ed Sheeran, with George's band backing him up. It was ridiculously romantic, and Kendall frowned slightly as Brody settled her into his arms.

Her hand found the muscle of his shoulder. His hand slid around her back, coaxing her closer, until she was almost brushing the front of his expensive suit. His other hand gently cupped hers—and as they began to sway it was that hand that had her breath going short. His thumb was slowly stroking her forefinger, up and down. She didn't know what should be so erotic about that tiny little motion, but she was suddenly excruciatingly aware of every inch of her skin. And every inch of his.

Of course he'd be good at this too. The man had been on *Dancing with the Freaking Stars*.

She wasn't looking at him, focused on his shoulder, right in front of her face, as Dylan sang the obnoxiously romantic song. But then Brody bent his head, his breath making the hairs that had slipped free of her updo shiver as he spoke close to her ear.

"Truth or dare?"

"No." She shook her head, a quick, tiny jerk. "No dares at my best friend's wedding. Absolutely not."

"I guess it's truth then." He paused for a moment, as if trying to think of a good one. "What does 'shoes' mean?"

Her face flamed, and she focused intently on the shoulder seam of his suit jacket. "Different question." She may have already admitted her teenage crush, but he didn't need to know the full extent of it.

"Technically against the rules, but I'll allow it this once." He paused again, and she looked up at him. Tactical error. As soon as her eyes met his, he asked, "Why didn't you dare me to kiss you?"

She flushed warmer. "I was sixteen—"

"Not back then. The other night."

She looked into his eyes, and met the challenge in them with one of her own. "Did you want me to?"

"Yes."

The answer was so simple, her jaw fell loose. "Oh."

"Unless you don't want that anymore."

Goosebumps broke out on her arms. A sudden whisper of possibility making her breath go shallow. "Truth or dare?" she whispered.

His smile kicked up on one side. "Dare."

He was daring her to dare him. And Kendall had never been able to resist a good dare. But she didn't want him to see how badly she wanted this. She narrowed her eyes as she met the challenge. "Fine. I'll dare you. But you better be a good kisser, Brody James."

He chuckled, the sound deliciously wicked. "Only one way to find out."

She held his eyes, so close to hers, and so incredibly familiar. "I dare you," she whispered.

Brody smiled, his gaze dropping to her lips. He lowered his head right as the song was ending, his lips settling softly, perfectly over hers.

It should have been tepid—he barely kissed her—but every atom in her body woke up and came to attention as he pressed his lips softly against hers for two seconds and then released the pressure to sigh against her lips. It should *not* have been as freaking hot as it was. And she should *not* have been weak at the knees from one brief, closed-mouth, barely-a-hello of a kiss.

But her stupid knees weren't listening and had decided to be decidedly weak indeed.

The emcee began speaking, and Kendall realized she really needed to pay attention to those words, but her ears seemed to be blocking out every sound that wasn't Brody. Then the words penetrated and she sighed, rocking back on her heels—when she hadn't even realized she'd gone up on tiptoe.

"They're cutting the cake. I should be there."

"Right," Brody murmured, putting slightly more distance between them.

"Um…" What did you say to the man who had just given you a heart attack with a two-second peck on the mouth? "I'll, uh, see you round."

He blinked. "Okay."

She patted his chest. "Okay."

Telling her wobbly knees to get with the program and buck up, she straightened her spine and walked off the dance floor, toward the crowd that had formed around the wedding cake. The urge to look back was strong, but she forced herself to keep walking. Until she couldn't quite resist one little peek over her shoulder.

He was watching her walk away.

She ducked her head, tucking a stray curl back behind her ear. And managed not to smile until she'd turned back to face the wedding party. Brody freaking James just kissed her. Holy crap.

She could have brought him with her. There was no reason

he couldn't stand beside her while Charlotte and George mashed cake into one another's faces. But she'd retreated, needing the space to breathe. To think about what she wanted.

It was one thing to have a crush. It was another to chase it. To see if it could be something real. Brody had existed in the safe place of the unattainable for so long that she needed a second to process the reality that *this could happen*.

And she didn't want to spend the entire wedding focused on Brody. This was Charlotte's moment, and she wanted to be here for Charlotte.

At least that's what she told herself as she walked away.

Brody hadn't really felt like a wedding crasher when he first walked into the wedding. He'd been a man on a mission. Find Kendall. But as she slipped into the crowd clustered around the little dais where the wedding cake was on display, he was suddenly acutely aware that he didn't really know anyone else here.

And they all knew him.

"Hey. You're Brody James, right?" a man with a cellphone in one hand asked.

Over the last few weeks, people had started gawking a little less around the resort—the staff all knew him now, and even some of the skiers had gotten used to having him around—but he still had to play *the* Brody James from time to time.

"I am," he confirmed. "Did you want a selfie?"

The man shook his head, pocketing the phone he'd been holding. "No, thanks. I just wanna know your intentions." He had curly auburn hair and an easy smile that suddenly had an edge to it.

Brody blinked. "I'm sorry?"

"I'm Mac. Friend of the groom. Also, friend of the bride's

older sister—which means I grew up looking out for Charlotte. And Kendall," he added meaningfully.

Brody felt his face heating. "Right." That kiss had been a little more public than he'd planned—but he hadn't been thinking. He'd been in a bubble with Kendall, caught up in the music and the dare.

"You're lucky it's me interrogating you and not Levi. He's married to Charlotte's sister. Chief of police. Very intimidating. You were a few years behind us in school—you went to Woodland, right?"

"Yeah, that's right."

"But you partied here. With Kevin. Had quite a reputation too."

Brody's face heated. "I was a kid."

Mac smiled. "I know. We all do stupid shit when we're kids. I'm not gonna hold that against you. But I still wanna know what your intentions are."

Brody didn't know how to answer that. He hadn't really *had* intentions. He hadn't been thinking more than one step ahead the entire time he'd been back. Everything had been instinct. At first, he'd just wanted to help Steph. Help Kendall. Just put one foot in front of the other and do the next good thing.

He hadn't planned to kiss her. He'd come here tonight because he needed her to stop avoiding him. He needed to see her and make sure they were okay. And he'd wanted more of that feeling he got when they were together.

But then they'd been dancing, and he'd been holding her, and he hadn't been able to think why they'd never done this before. The kiss had been the most natural thing in the world. The result of some inevitable progression he hadn't even been aware they were on.

But he didn't know what his intentions were.

Mac read the uncertainty on his face. "Maybe that's something you should figure out," he advised. "Before you lead anyone on."

"Yeah," Brody murmured as Mac jerked his chin in farewell and moved away to join the rest of the wedding guests.

He didn't want to lead Kendall on, but he didn't know what he wanted next. He couldn't just hook up with her without consequences. With all the ways their lives were tangled together, it would have repercussions. It would have *meaning*.

And he might...he was realizing he might want that. He might want something real. With Kendall Walsh.

Chapter Twenty-Two

I'm sorry, were you seriously *making out* with Brody on the dance floor? And how did I miss it?" Charlotte demanded, appearing out of the blue and cornering Kendall near the bar.

Kendall had been eyeing the champagne bottles in the chiller, surreptitiously checking to make sure the supply was holding up to demand. She wasn't technically working tonight, but she couldn't seem to stop herself from checking to make sure everything was perfect.

"We weren't making out." She turned away from the bar so she could pretend for Charlotte that she hadn't been in work mode. "It was one kiss. More of a peck. It barely happened."

"You really kissed him?" Charlotte squealed. "Kendall! Was it good?"

"No comment."

"Oh my God. It was so good. It's all over your face. You're welcome, by the way." Charlotte bounced, the brightly colored curls that had been added to her hair springing up. "I am the world's best matchmaker."

"It was a dare. Don't make it a thing."

"The guy you've had a crush on since puberty kissed you. It's a thing," Charlotte insisted. "The only question is if you want more of that thing."

She did. She absolutely did. But she was also thinking about how irresponsible it felt to want him. They were working together. He was her brother's best friend. He was leaving—at some point—and she was still shackled to this resort until she could get it back on good financial footing.

A relationship would never last. But Kendall had never been emotional about sex. She didn't need to be madly in love to enjoy herself.

"If I wanted more of that thing—and I'm not saying I do," she amended quickly when Charlotte squeaked excitedly. "If I did, it would just be like you said—a get-it-out-of-our-system thing. Don't get all excited and picture us riding off into the sunset together. That isn't happening."

"Even if he's kind of perfect for you?"

Kendall frowned repressively. "You barely know him."

"I know he drove halfway across the state to help you get my purse back. I know how he looks at you. And I know how you are when you're with him."

Kendall refused to ask how he looked at her. She did *not* need Charlotte's romantic propaganda. "Don't you have a bouquet to throw?"

"I do. And you better not try to avoid catching it."

"I'm not scared of a bunch of flowers. It's just a superstition."

"My best friend isn't scared of anything. Even love." Charlotte grabbed her hand suddenly, squeezing tight. "Have I said thank you enough? Like a million times? Because you've been so amazing. You know that? Everything's been perfect. You moved it all up on the fly. Your toast was wonderful. And you haven't made me feel like a bridezilla once, even though I have been repeatedly ridiculous."

Kendall's frown darkened. "I hate that term. It's so insulting. As if a woman wanting to have a beautiful wedding is like a monster crushing Tokyo. You haven't even been that ridiculous."

There had been one moment, earlier, when Charlotte had freaked out a little before the wedding ceremony. She'd suddenly worried that since George's sisters were standing up with him as his groom's people, it would be too much of a chickfest at the altar. Kendall and Magda had talked her down, assuring a panicking Charlotte that it would not, in fact, look like George was marrying a harem.

But that had been the only hysterical blip in what had otherwise been a remarkably smooth day. Charlotte was just so *happy* to be marrying George. From the second the ceremony had started, she'd been glowing.

"I'm just happy you're happy," Kendall said.

"I am." She squeezed Kendall's hand harder. "And promise me you'll grab the chance for your own happiness. For me?"

"Go throw some flowers," Kendall said—but she was smiling.

Charlotte grinned and bounced off, bubbling over with joy. She'd always been expressive, and it was good to see her like this. Kendall had never been so demonstrative…but she hadn't realized how much her loved ones had noticed her unhappiness. She'd been too busy ignoring it herself. Pushing it down and just putting one foot in front of the other and doing what needed to be done.

These last few weeks had been different. *She* felt different.

Maybe it was finally having the chance to do something meaningful for the resort. Maybe it was not having to deal with as many of the day-to-day headaches of running it. But maybe it was something else. Some*one* else.

Brody had woken her up. And she didn't want to go back to sleep.

She scanned the room, but she didn't see him. She hadn't seen him since the kiss.

Had he left? She checked her phone, but there were no messages from him.

The singles were called to the dance floor, and Kendall easily caught the bouquet—she pretty much had to, after Charlotte dared her to. After that, it wasn't long before Charlotte and George made their getaway amid a hail of bubbles.

From that point on, it was just the DJ providing love songs for those who wanted to keep dancing. Kendall might have stayed, but she didn't see Brody anywhere, and there wasn't anyone else she wanted to sway with. She couldn't believe he'd just left after their kiss—though she hadn't exactly given him much encouragement.

With one final glance to make sure everything was still going smoothly, she slipped out of the ballroom and immediately bent to take off her heels. She was still staying in a room upstairs—the fumes should be cleared out of the lodge by tomorrow, but she'd realized she didn't want Banner's claws scratching up the new floors, so she was going to have to figure out where she wanted to live sooner rather than later.

Kendall headed toward the elevators, high heels in one hand, bouquet in the other, with the clutch with her phone and room key dangling from her wrist. God, she was tired. She'd been in go-mode for the last three days, and now that there was nothing she needed to do for twenty-four hours, all she wanted to do was sleep for twenty-three of them.

But then she turned the corner, saw the elevators ahead of her—and the man leaning against the wall in front of them, idly scrolling on his phone.

Kendall stopped in her tracks, her exhaustion retreating on a tide of adrenaline.

Brody must have sensed something, because he glanced up, straightening and shoving his phone into his pocket as soon as he saw her. "Hey."

"Hey," she replied, continuing toward him. "You left."

He watched her approach, his hands deep in his pockets in front of the elevator doors. "Being a wedding crasher felt kind of weird," he admitted. "And I didn't want to crowd you. Heard your speech, though."

"Yeah?" She hadn't thought it was anything special. Just a few words about how happy she was for them and how glad she was Charlotte had found someone who loved her as she deserved. She'd kept it brief.

"Good speech," Brody said. "Very you."

She didn't know what he meant by that, but she was nearly to the elevators now.

He nodded to the flowers in her hand. "You caught the bouquet?"

"Yeah, well. Charlotte dared me." She reached past him to push the up button with the hand holding her shoes. "You lying in wait for me?"

"Thought I'd see if you wanted to head out to the hot tub. Unwind a bit."

She was still exhausted…but she wasn't nearly as eager for the night to end as she had been a few minutes ago. She didn't have to worry about Banner—she hadn't known how late the festivities would go, so she'd arranged before the wedding for him to spend the night with Michelle, who ran the ski school. And the hot tub did sound amazing.

"I could be persuaded." The elevator doors opened and she stepped inside. "I need to get my suit."

"I don't have mine either," he said, stepping in beside her as she pushed the button for their floor and the doors started to close.

The elevator hummed upward, and Kendall glanced sideways up at Brody. Damn, the man looked good in a suit. If he didn't go back to skiing, he could have a lucrative career as a model.

And she would go back to pining for him from afar, just like Charlotte had accused her.

Another missed opportunity.

In that moment, she realized she didn't want to go to the hot tub. She didn't want to flirt in the moonlight with the safety of knowing they might be interrupted, so they couldn't let things go too far.

Kendall didn't want safe. Not tonight. She wanted to remember what it felt like to be the girl who ran right into the jaws of whatever scared her, just to prove she could.

She wanted to do what Charlotte had been goading her to do for weeks and bang Brody James right out of her system. Because the last thing she needed in her life was one more shoulda-coulda-woulda regret.

"Truth or dare?"

Brody had been looking straight ahead, but at that, his head turned sharply toward her and she could swear she actually saw his pupils dilate, his eyes going dark. A slow, wicked smile curved his lips before he murmured, "Dare."

The elevator binged, and Kendall smiled as the doors opened on their floor. "Walk me to my room?"

"Is that the dare?"

She simply smiled and stepped out of the elevator, heading left, knowing he wouldn't be able to resist the challenge to follow. Their rooms were on opposite ends of the same floor—his all the way to the right, hers at the end of the hall to the left.

Brody fell into step beside her.

"I propose a new game," she said casually as she strolled down the hall, swinging her shoes. "A sort of modified truth or dare. For the next thirty minutes, we both have to answer every question we're asked truthfully. So if, for example, I were to say 'Do you like it when I do this?' or 'Do you want more?' you would have to answer honestly."

Brody made a small noise in his throat.

Kendall stopped at her room, dropping her shoes and handing the bouquet to him so she could unzip her clutch to get her key. But she didn't turn to her door. Not yet.

She looked up at him, at his extremely intent eyes. "And for the next thirty minutes, every dare is only a request. There's no penalty if you don't want to do what you're dared to do. So if I, just hypothetically, were to dare you to kiss me again, you would be under no obligation to do so. Unless you wanted to."

Those extremely intent blue eyes locked on hers, Brody stepped forward, crowding her against the door. His hand holding the bouquet braced on the door above her head as he leaned in. "And if I want to?"

She rested her head against the door as she smiled up at him, watching him from beneath her lashes. "Then I dare you to find out what happens next."

Brody leaned down slowly, deliciously dragging out the moment, until his lips were a breath away from hers. "I think I like this game," he murmured against her mouth, before sinking into a kiss.

Just like the last time, it started as a slow, soft press and hold of his lips, almost a prelude to a kiss—one beat. Two. He lifted his head just enough for her to sigh against his lips—then his free hand cupped her face, he tilted his head, and his mouth slanted hard over hers.

Kendall grabbed his suit coat, clutching him to her as she arched between him and the door. That first kiss was just a spark, but now the fuse was lit and he pressed into her, his lips devouring hers. The heady scent of the bouquet pressed to the door beside her head was nothing next to the dizzying rush of *him*.

The man was a *good* kisser. Not because he was aggressive—which he could be—but because he seemed to know exactly when not to be. When to pull back. When to tempt. When to tease. When to deny her just enough to make her desperate before he gave her exactly what she was desperate for.

It was a game. And God, she loved this game.

The warning *bing* of the elevator down the hall had him jerking back sharply. Her hand was still fisted on his jacket, so she nearly stumbled after him as he took a step away. They both looked toward the elevator, breathing hard, but no one came out. Then his burning eyes were back on her.

"Maybe we should move this inside," Kendall murmured. She'd dropped her keycard at some point, and they both glanced down at the carpet where it had landed.

Brody sank to one knee, grabbing the card—and glanced down the hall to make sure they were still alone before he stood, wrapping the arm still holding the bouquet under her ass and lifting her off her feet in the same motion as he claimed her mouth again. A moment later, the door beeped and opened against her back—

She had to respect a man who could multitask, unlocking the door and driving her crazy at the same time.

She could feel the bouquet against her hip as he carried her across the threshold and kicked the door shut. Kendall lifted her head with the click. It was dark, but not so dark that she couldn't see the look on his face. "Truth or dare?" she whispered.

Brody smiled wickedly, white teeth flashing. "With you? *Dare me.*"

Chapter Twenty-Three

Brody stared at the ceiling with that heavy post-sex feeling saturating his body. "I will never think of truth or dare the same way again."

Kendall hummed, one finger tracing the Olympic rings tattoo on his rib cage. "It always had the potential to be a dirty game. Don't tell me you never realized that."

He shifted his arm tighter around her. They were lying in her bed together, the glow of the ski lifts lighting up the mountain outside. "Are you saying you play grown-up truth or dare often?"

"Never have," she admitted. "But the possibilities are endless."

"Probably not something we should share with your brother." His fingers trailed down her spine, feeling the sudden tension in it when he added, "He warned me to stay away from you."

Kendall levered herself up, the frown line between her brows intense. "I'm sorry, what? When was this?" she demanded.

"When he came up here to tell us about his engagement. He didn't want you getting hurt."

"Like it's any of his damn business. I'm an adult. He has no right to interfere with my sex life." She flopped back against him, restless with irritation. "Bad enough he stole my best friend when I was eleven. Now, what? He thinks I'm going to use sex to steal you back?"

"I'm pretty sure that isn't what he thinks. And I am capable of being friends with both of you. No one stole anything."

"You know what I mean," Kendall grumped. "When we were kids, you came to see *me*. To ski with me. I was the one you told stuff. Then you turned twelve, grew five inches, and you and Kevin were too busy bro-ing out to have me around."

He hadn't remembered it quite that way, but she probably wasn't wrong. "I was a teenage boy. We're all idiots."

"It just sucked to be left behind. I was so mad at Kevin. And you. You were so different with him."

"I thought you had a crush on me." He flexed the arm beneath his head, wagging his eyebrows lecherously to get her to roll her eyes.

"Don't get excited, egomaniac. That was later. I was mad for months. But then I entered my own idiotic teen years and decided to pine for someone unattainable for a while."

"Who says I was unattainable? How do you know I didn't always have a thing for you?"

Kendall snorted. "Because you didn't."

Honesty forced him to admit, "Okay, you're right, I didn't. I was kind of terrified of you in high school. You were faster than me. And you never cooed at me and massaged my ego like all the other girls I knew."

"I was honest with you."

"You were always glaring at me," he said, earning a glare. "And making me feel like I was never quite doing enough to earn your respect—which I'm sure made me better. But I liked the girls who were easy on me. Not the ones who challenged me." He played with a lock of her hair, twirling it around his fingers. "Like I said. Young and stupid."

"So you don't want me to marvel at what a big, strong man you are now?"

"I mean I wouldn't *mind*," he said, laughing when she socked him in the side. "Nah. I'm realizing the challenge can be a lot more fun."

She humphed and settled back against him, yawning. It had been a long day, and he'd already kept her up later than she'd probably planned.

He ran his fingers over the tattoo on her shoulder she'd gotten when she was seventeen. A little devil on skis. He'd found three tattoos tonight. All from before she stopped racing.

"You never got any more ink."

"It was supposed to be the rings," she said, her voice holding a strange note as she ran her fingers again over the Olympic rings on his ribs. "My next tat. I'd picked out the spot. I was going to get it as soon as I won the trials."

"Shit," he murmured. "And you never…"

"I never wanted to get another one after that," she murmured drowsily, shifting against him.

Her eyes were closed now, and he thought she might have fallen asleep when she stopped talking, until she sighed and mumbled, "I used to be so free. But maybe that's just life. Maybe we grow out of that."

"Maybe we don't have to," he said softly.

He wasn't sure she'd even heard him as she went on sleepily. "I had so much to prove," she whispered. "I had to *show every-*

one. I had to be faster than Kev. Faster than all the boys. And then I wasn't." She sighed, her breath gusting out against his chest. "My dad barely looks at me anymore. That feels like my fault too."

"It isn't your fault," Brody insisted. "None of it was ever your fault."

Kendall sighed softly, but the next sound from her was a soft, breathy snore.

"It wasn't your fault," he said again, even though she was asleep. He just needed her to hear the words, even if only her subconscious was listening.

He settled back onto the pillows, his arm still wrapped around Kendall. Banner was spending the night with one of the ski instructors, so it was just the two of them in her room, the only light coming from the reflection off the snow of the mountain outside the windows.

A sense of peace seemed to fill the room, and Brody had never felt quite so certain that he was exactly where he needed to be.

He'd been stuck in the temporary since he got back, but maybe it was time to start looking forward. To start building something here. With Kendall. Maybe *this* was what real happiness felt like. This bone-deep contented *ease.*

Now he just had to figure out how to hold on to this feeling.

Someone was smothering her.

Kendall shoved at the arms and legs tangled around her like a boa constrictor, twisting and pushing until the heavy form grunted and rolled away from her. Released from confinement, she scooted farther away, draping herself over the edge of the bed with one arm and leg dangling off the side, and sighed with relief.

She woke up that way—half on, half off the bed, as far as she could get from Brody as possible.

She'd never liked people touching her while she slept. Cuddling after sex was one thing, but once she was ready to fall asleep, she always pushed her lovers away. She couldn't believe she'd actually fallen asleep wrapped up with Brody last night. She must have been even more exhausted than she thought.

Sunlight—and Brody's snores—filled the room. Neither of them had bothered to shut the drapes last night. It must be after nine, because as she squinted against the sun, she could see chair five running already, carrying skiers up the mountain.

Kendall rolled the rest of the way out of bed, landing on her feet and making a beeline for the shower. She stood under the hot spray, washing away the smell of sex and questionable decisions.

She didn't regret last night. Not for a second. But the whole morning-after thing wasn't something she was looking forward to navigating. This was supposed to be simple. Bang it out of their systems. Dealing with manly feelings first thing in the morning was definitely not on her to-do list. She had too much else to accomplish.

She couldn't believe Kev had tried to interfere. Like she needed a big strong man to protect her from her feelings. Kendall was fully capable of having sex without getting all twitterpated, thank you very much, and the absolute last person who should be making decisions on her love life was her brother—whose relationships prior to this just-add-water instant engagement tended to last a grand total of three weeks. She couldn't believe Brody wasn't as horrified by the idea of that wedding as she was.

Her thoughts swirled as the soap swirled down the drain. Kev was obviously out of his depth, but he was going to crash and burn on his own.

And in the meantime, she would be seeing Brody. If he was interested in keeping this going, she saw no reason to stop. She was a big girl. She knew he'd be leaving soon, and she wasn't going to be attached when he did. Kendall didn't do attached.

But last night had been fun. It had been a release—in more ways than one—after the stress of the last few weeks. It wasn't just the sex—though that had been pretty damn spectacular. Their chemistry certainly didn't disappoint. Or maybe that was simply what happened when sexual tension had been building up for over a decade.

Kendall shut off the water and worked out a plan for the day as she dried off. Charlotte's wedding had gone beautifully—and if there had been any hitches behind the scenes, Kendall hadn't heard about them. Charlotte and George were now off on their two day mini-moon, and Kendall had arranged to take today off, but there was still so much to do at the old lodge, and only a few weeks left before Steph's wedding.

She wanted to check on the floors, make sure they looked all right after the last sealant had been applied. Then she needed to schedule the chandelier install with the electrician, paint the back rooms, confirm with the tile guy, and get started finding the furnishings they would need.

The style of the lodge was so different from the ballroom that she didn't want to use the tables they had there—and she wanted, down the road, to be able to host events in both locations simultaneously. So she needed more tables and chairs. Hopefully in a rustic style. And hopefully cheap. Which could mean used or mismatched—depending on what she could find on her budget. She had the information for a few chair and table rental places as a fallback, but it would be more cost-effective in the long run if she got the stuff she needed while her dad was still blinded by Brody's awesomeness.

Brody was still snoring when Kendall stepped out of the bathroom and quickly got dressed. She mentally ran through her to-do list. Pick up Banner. Call the electrician. Look for tables and chairs—there was a flea market in Barnard this weekend. And an estate sale at a farmhouse near Burlington—

"Where are you going?"

Kendall turned toward the bed, her keys in one hand. "You're awake," she said, in a fit of obviousness. He was half-sitting up in bed, the sheet dipping over his washboard abs.

"You're sneaking out."

She rolled her eyes. "I'd hardly call this sneaking. You're the one who sleeps like the dead."

"You kick, you know that? Woke me up twice. I'm gonna be bruised."

"I don't like people smothering me while I'm sleeping. You give me space, and I won't have to kick you."

"Noted," Brody said, and then gave her a little smile—and Kendall felt the stupid, dippy urge to smile back at him. Just because he was smiling and it was cute and she felt good.

"I have to pick up Banner," she said instead. "And I wanna look for tables, chairs, stuff for the lodge."

"I thought you had today off."

"I do. I just want to get a jump on things."

"You want company?"

It was a knee-jerk impulse to say no—she had this, she could manage on her own. She always managed on her own. But he looked so freaking hopeful that she found herself asking instead, skeptically, "You really want to go to an estate sale and a flea market with me?"

"If we find something, we can fit more in my truck than your Jeep."

She couldn't argue with that logic, and she kind of liked having him around. He was useful for lifting heavy things, if nothing else. "Yeah, okay." He smiled as if she'd given him a gift, rather than signed him up for a day of digging through dusty furniture. "You really like flea markets, huh?"

"Never been to one," he admitted, shrugging into the button-down shirt she'd helped him remove the night before. Then he crossed the room, grabbed the nape of her neck, and bent his head to press one of those quick, lethal kisses on her lips. "I really like *you*."

He turned away, grabbing his jacket and his shoes—as casual as if everyone just said things like that, first thing in the morning.

"Yeah, okay," she muttered, her face flushing. Kendall didn't get flustered, but something about Brody James still flustered her. And she kind of liked it.

Chapter Twenty-Four

The estate sale was a bust, but they struck gold on the tables at the flea market. They still only had about half as many as they needed, and there were no chairs—which would be problematic at a wedding—but it was a start.

And Brody enjoyed himself entirely too much.

They talked, mostly about wedding logistics and the lodge, as they drove from Pine Hollow to Burlington to Barnard, with Banner riding with his head out the window and his jowls flapping. Brody was more and more convinced Kendall was going to wind up keeping Banner as a foster fail, but she was still insisting he was only temporarily hers. Even as she bought him puppy treats and praised him for being the best boy when he behaved at the flea market.

On the way back, Kendall cuddled the sleeping dog and talked about where she and Banner might live next—and Brody found himself wondering the same thing. He'd spent most of his career bouncing from hotel to hotel, but he didn't want to live in hotel rooms forever. He'd sold his condo in Aspen because he felt like he was never there, but now he liked the idea of finding a place to settle down and build a life. There were some nice places not far from the resort…

He'd never really thought about life after skiing. Even this last month, he'd been distracting himself, keeping busy. Doing everything he could *not* to think about what came next. Last night, after the dance with Kendall, something had clicked and he'd started thinking about the future differently. Even before their game of adult truth or dare.

For the last month, he'd rejected even the idea of returning to competition, but he hadn't let himself think about what came next either. Too freaking scared to really face a life without skiing. But last night while he'd waited for Kendall outside the wedding, he'd downloaded a book on retirement to his phone and read part of it. It had been vaguely horrifying—talking about the statistical likelihood of dying within a year of early retirement—but it had helped Brody realize he didn't want to stop working, even if he transitioned to a new career.

The trick would be figuring out what that could be. His reps always talked about commentating or being a spokesperson of some kind, when they talked about his eventual retirement from the sport, but none of that appealed to him.

He wanted to do something active. To see his impact. So it felt like he was moving toward something rather than walking away from the biggest thing he would ever do.

His next step, he realized, was going to have to be telling his family. He'd been putting off talking to them, avoiding the topic, but if he wasn't going back, he was going to have to face their disappointment at some point.

Steph was coming up for the weekend after Valentine's Day, bringing her dress and taking care of some things for the wedding. He could tell them then. It was better to do it in person, he rationalized. Which gave him some time to work up to it.

And in the meantime, there was Kendall.

"I wish there was a better way to get people from the parking lot to the old lodge," she said that evening as she lay sprawled out on the floor beside the coffee table in his hotel room, hanging on to one end of Banner's tug-of-war toy as he whipped his head back and forth.

Even with Brody's truck, they'd had to make two trips to pick up all the tables they'd found at the flea market, and the sun had been setting by the time they crammed the final load into the storage unit. After they'd finished, they'd both been starving, and he'd lured her back to his hotel room with the promise of grilled cheese sandwiches.

Neither he nor Kendall had ever learned to cook, but grilled cheese was the one thing he could make really well. Even in a hotel room with no real kitchen. His mother had gotten him a tiny panini press when he'd first started touring, and he'd pretty much lived off of grilled cheese and grilled peanut butter and jelly.

Kendall had been openly skeptical of his claims of panini prowess, and he was ridiculously determined to impress her.

They hadn't talked about last night. If he'd expected her to be gushy and affectionate, he would have been wildly disappointed, but he knew Kendall too well to have expected anything like that. She still frowned at him with that groove between her eyebrows and was openly baffled when he offered to help her with things.

It was sort of comforting that nothing had changed. He wouldn't have known what to do if Kendall had suddenly started batting her eyelashes at him.

"We have ATVs to bring people who can't walk the forest trail," she continued in between mock growls with Banner, while Brody monitored the panini press. "But I'm not sure bouncing along in an ATV in her wedding dress is what Steph envisioned, you know?"

"I'm sure she'll understand that you didn't have a horse-drawn carriage on call," he said, watching the sandwiches for the perfect level of cheesy ooze.

"What did you say?"

At the sharpness in her voice, he glanced over his shoulder. Kendall had gone still, her eyes wide. "I said Steph will understand—"

"No, the carriage." Her smile flashed. "God, why didn't I think of that? You're a genius."

"Obviously," he agreed, though he still had no idea what she was talking about. "You have a carriage stashed somewhere I don't know about?"

"Magda's uncle does." Kendall sat up, releasing Banner's tug-of-war toy and making the dog roll backward at the sudden shift of momentum. "A horse-drawn sleigh. He uses it to give tourists rides through the town square at Christmastime. I'm sure we could hire him for the day. I can't believe I didn't think of it."

"Well, you are allergic to all things romantic." Her stomach growled loudly. "And possibly faint from hunger. Here." He plated the first sandwich, setting it on the coffee table with a flourish.

"Thanks." She picked up one half, eyeing him dubiously. "You sure this is safe to eat?"

"You're going to eat those words," he taunted as Kendall took her first bite—and instantly closed her eyes with a groan of bliss.

Brody grinned smugly, feeling a ridiculous surge of satisfaction. She wasn't the first woman he'd made grilled cheese for in his hotel room, but Kendall would never massage his ego, like most of those other women, so her appreciation was exponentially more gratifying.

"Okay, this is freaking amazing," she acknowledged.

Brody bowed and turned back to the next sandwich in the press—while Banner belly-crawled toward Kendall with big ole puppy dog eyes, begging for some cheese, even though he'd already had his dinner.

Another appreciative groan sounded behind him. "What is that? Garlic? There's something else."

"You can't expect a master to reveal his secrets. I want you to keep coming back for more."

"Are you trying to seduce me with grilled cheese, Brody James?"

He met her eyes over his shoulder, hoping it was working. She'd been hands-off all day, and he was definitely hoping for a hands-on night. "You complaining?"

"No," she said, waving a hand magnanimously. "Feel free to use all your wiles."

He grinned. "Wiles, huh?" He turned back to remove his own sandwich before it burned.

"Charlotte has started reading a lot of romance," Kendall explained. "It's a bonding thing with George's sisters, but apparently there are a lot of wiles being employed."

"Good to know." Brody plated his first sandwich and slid the next one into the press, closing it. "You ever going to tell me what shoes really are?"

"Nope."

He grinned as he took a seat on the floor across from her

at the coffee table, and Banner wiggled around to see if there would be grilled cheese scraps coming from both sides.

Kendall was engrossed in her sandwich, and for a moment, Brody just watched her, drinking in the open enjoyment on her face—until she caught him looking. Her eyes narrowed.

"This is your thing, isn't it? So what's your next move? After you soften them up with gourmet grilled cheese?"

He arched his brows. "I'm not sure I have any other moves. The grilled cheese is pretty much it. You really think it's that good?"

"Undeniably panty dropping. Which I'm sure you've heard before."

"Yeah, but when you say it, it counts."

She met his eyes for a beat, then pulled a face, grumbling, "Women make things too easy on you. You just flex your muscles and they flock around you."

"Yeah, kind of." He couldn't disagree with that. "Except you."

"I am exceptional." She finished off half of her sandwich. "And so is this. If the whole world-class athlete thing doesn't work out, you can always open a grilled cheese food truck. Lure women in with comfort food."

Something tightened in his chest at the mention of what came next, but he forced his voice to stay light. "I've heard worse ideas. I'm not sure how much longer 'wanna look at my Olympic medals' is going to work."

"I doubt that one ever gets old. You'll be using it in your retirement home. Wooing all the little old ladies." She glanced around the room, taking in the standard-issue hotel suite he'd done nothing to personalize. "Where do you keep them? Your medals?"

"My mom has most of them. She has a whole trophy room."

And what would she say if there were no more trophies coming? He finished half of his sandwich, which suddenly didn't taste quite so satisfying. "I don't know what she's going to think when I'm not Brody James anymore."

"Hey." Kendall gave him a knock-it-off look. "Don't play all sad and pitiable. You'll still be Brody James. And you don't have to retire. You can always go back. When you're ready. Though with as little as you've been skiing, your conditioning must be shot to shit."

"You wanna help me work out?" he deflected with a challenge. "Ski with me?"

"Ha. Nice try."

He stood to check on the next sandwich in the panini press. "I know you think it's burnout, but I really am done," he said, unsure which one of them he was trying to convince. "Though apparently retirement is more hazardous than I thought. Did you know death rates spike in the first year after you retire? Insurance companies have done studies."

Kendall rolled her eyes. "You aren't going to die if you retire."

"Yeah. But it kind of feels like it."

"So don't retire. Are you really not at all tempted to go back?"

"Not even a little," he said—though something twinged in his chest at the words. He cut the final grilled cheese into pieces and carried it back to her, sliding one section onto her plate, and sitting down opposite her.

She toyed with the sandwich, eyeing him. "If you didn't love it, you wouldn't have done it so long," she said softly.

"I did love it," he admitted. "I can't explain it. I just need to be something else now."

"You're going to have to tell your family eventually."

"I will," he insisted. "I just…I want to have a plan, and I don't have one yet." He was still holding the same sandwich triangle, not taking a bite. He looked down at the oozing cheese as he admitted, "I'm scared to tell my parents. I'm thirty years old, and I'm still afraid of disappointing them."

"That's only because you never have," Kendall said. "But I doubt they'll be disappointed. Regardless of what you decide to do. They love you. And you're still an Olympian, Brody. Most people never get that."

"I know. Poor Brody, his life is so perfect."

"I didn't say that." She reached one leg under the table, gently bumping his knee with her shin. Banner squirmed excitedly at the movement, snuffling for stray grilled cheese.

"I don't know what I want to do," he admitted. "My reps think I should become a commentator, but that just feels so pointless."

"I don't know about that," Kendall argued. "You could change the way they talk about things. Stop glorifying the pain. Acknowledge that we aren't all machines or comeback stories. You could be really good."

"I guess. But I think I'd rather do something more direct. Be able to see the impact I have." He shifted a little, almost nervously. "I've thought about doing something with the mental health stuff—but other people smarter than me are already doing that. Michael Phelps is out there trying to normalize therapy—"

"That doesn't mean there isn't space for you to help too. If that's what you want to do. You'd be a good coach," Kendall suggested. "You're a good teacher. You always have been. And you could prioritize the mental health stuff with your students. Establish a program or something."

"Maybe." He glanced out the window to their left, where the lights of the ski lifts illuminated the mountain. "Do you think you'll ever leave the resort?"

"I don't know." He could feel her pull in on herself, even though she didn't move away. "I keep thinking we'll hit some point when it'll get easier. When the resort will be solidly in the black and I can take some time off and think about myself for a minute. When I can figure out what I would want to do if I didn't *have* to be doing this. But we never seem to get there. I'm starting to wonder if this is just what life is. Constantly chasing a goalpost that keeps moving out of reach."

"It might not ever be the right time. You might just need to get away, take a vacation."

"Yeah, maybe." She dragged a fingernail through the crumbs on her plate. "Or maybe after Steph's wedding is a wild success and the old lodge starts raking in money hand-over-fist, I'll be able to do whatever I want. Get it all running and hand it off to someone else."

He let his skepticism show. "You think you can actually trust someone else to run it the way you want? Don't think I haven't noticed you looking over my shoulder this month."

She met his eyes, fighting a smile. "You're new. I'm overseeing. It's my job."

"Uh-huh."

"There are plenty of people out there who want to run weddings, and I would gladly hand them off. That was never me."

Brody feigned shock. "*No.* I thought you loved the weddings."

She kicked him. Hard. "It was just the first thing I got my dad to say yes to." She glanced over her shoulder toward the mountain. "In a perfect world, we'd run the lifts for mountain bikers in the summer, maybe even have motocross weekends. Set up a ninja course or a few zip lines. If my dad wanted to go all corporate, we could even do team-building adventure retreats—with climbing and rappelling to build trust and team spirit. Paintball—couldn't see you see the mountain as one giant paintball course in the summer?"

"That'd be great. Why haven't you done any of that?"

"Because my father doesn't listen to me. He just says 'I'll think about it' and then does whatever Kev suggests off the top of his head with no research or experience to back it up."

"I'm sure your dad—"

"Why are you always sure?" she cut in. "He's been telling me what to do since I was eight years old, when he realized I was his best shot at continuing the skiing dynasty. He has always thought he knew the right way to do everything, and that didn't change just because I stopped being his little golden girl. He only listens to Kevin, because he's successful now. The cult of victory. No wonder my mom left."

"He and Laurie seem very happy."

"Because she never says no to him. She *loves* doing stuff his way."

"I thought you loved Laurie."

"I do. She's great. But she's always his wife first and my step-mom second. And whenever I really want to push for one of my ideas, she looks at him and echoes whatever he says. So he acts like, 'Oh look, you've been outvoted, Kendall, this is a democracy,' when it was just his puppet confirming whatever he hath proclaimed."

"Have you thought about leaving?"

"I told you there's no time—"

"I don't mean a vacation. I mean leaving. Quitting your job."

She huffed, unamused. "You say that like it's only a job. Like it's not four generations of family legacy and two hundred thousand dollars of medical debt. Money that was siphoned out of the resort—"

"Did you tell your dad to do that? Did you ask him to?"

"Of course not."

"Then it was his choice. Not yours. And you shouldn't be trapped here because of his choices."

Kendall breathed out, shaking her head. "It isn't that simple."

"Maybe it is." She leaned back, like she was going to get up, like she was going to leave, and Brody reached quickly across the table, catching her wrist. "I'm sorry."

Kendall stopped, staring at his hand rather than his face. "It's complicated."

"I know. I'm sorry." He shifted his grip, tangling their fingers together—relieved when she didn't pull away. "I shouldn't be telling you what to do about your dad. Especially when I'm scared to even tell my parents the real reason I left the tour."

She met his eyes then. "They aren't going to care, Brody. You'll still be you."

He nodded, but her assurance didn't make it past the surface. Maybe because *he* didn't know who he would be without skiing. He wasn't sure he'd ever known who he was, ever thought about it, always thinking of the next race instead.

"Do you want me to come with you? When you tell them?"

He met her eyes in surprise, instant relief flooding through him at the idea of telling them with Kendall standing beside him, but he shook his head automatically. "I can't ask you—"

"You aren't asking. I'm offering. Isn't that what you always say?" she teased lightly. "After all the stuff you've done for me these last few weeks, I think I can do that much for you."

He smiled slightly. "Thank you."

"We're friends, aren't we?"

"Is that all we are?" He gave her his most over-the-top sexy look as he came up on his knees, using their linked hands to draw her toward him.

Kendall fought a smile as she let him reel her in. "There might be benefits," she admitted, smiling as he kissed her.

He wanted more than that. He was starting to realize he might want a lot more than that. But with Kendall, he would take whatever he could get. Because with Kendall he was starting to suspect he would always want more.

Chapter Twenty-Five

Ten days later, Kendall was forced to acknowledge there might be a slight hitch in her plan to bang Brody out of her system.

He was just so damn *likeable*. And she was finding that she liked him more the more time she spent with him. That *never* happened. Kendall wasn't a people person. There were very few humans she actually wanted to spend long periods of time with and even fewer who didn't get on her nerves with accumulated time, but Brody kept growing on her, making her smile more, even as they spent a ridiculous amount of time together, working on the lodge.

It was just so *easy*. Everything with Brody felt so natural. And she felt like herself again, in a way she hadn't in forever.

Not that it meant anything. She still didn't believe he was staying. But right now, things were going well.

The chandelier was in. The bathroom tile would go in next week. They had all the tables they needed now, though the chairs were proving more problematic—at least within her budget. This week, Brody had started reaching out to rummage sales and antique dealers in other states, when he wasn't making sure the resort ran more smoothly than it ever had.

Her father was over the moon—about the resort. He didn't know about the new "benefits" situation between Kendall and Brody. They'd been very careful not to let any of the resort staff see them together. Kendall hadn't even told Magda and Charlotte that she and Brody were hooking up, but that was only because she'd been too busy to see them. She wasn't *hiding* it necessarily. Hardly worth hiding. Just a silly little fling.

Though it didn't feel like a fling anymore. Or a pure sex relationship. Somehow they felt like a partnership. A couple. Which was disorienting in part because Kendall was realizing she'd never been part of a couple before. Even when she was married.

It was sort of nice.

Too nice. She needed to keep things casual.

So she did what any anti-romantic would do when Valentine's Day suddenly arrived and she'd accidentally found herself as part of a couple.

She took him ax throwing.

It was actually Charlotte's idea. Or Charlotte's sister's friend's. Apparently Elinor's friend Deenie and her husband had a whole Valentine's slasher movie ritual, and they'd decided to take it up a notch this year by adding ax throwing. Since her husband was in a poker group with Elinor's and Charlotte's husbands, and they'd all wanted to try it, it had quickly become a group Valentine's activity.

And since Kendall was desperately looking for something to occupy Brody so he didn't go all romantic on her, she'd jumped on the bandwagon as well.

There were already half a dozen couples at the ax-throwing

place when Kendall and Brody arrived. Plus Magda and Mac, who had both decided to join the group without dates. Kendall had her doubts about Mac and Mags being in a room with that many sharp objects, but so far they seemed to be staying on opposite sides of the big old barn that had been converted into an ax-throwing range.

Kendall headed toward Charlotte, hoping that would feel the least date-like. Brody trailed behind her, pausing to trade handshakes and backslaps with those he'd met before—and thankfully not trying to hold her hand.

"Hey! You made it!" Charlotte gushed, grabbing her in a hug.

"Did you think I wouldn't?"

"I had my doubts. You've been so busy with the resort. I haven't seen your face since my wedding." Her gaze slid past Kendall to land on Brody. "Unless it isn't the resort that's keeping you tied up."

"Don't be ridiculous," Kendall said—but she must have blushed or given something away because Charlotte's eyes flared wide.

"Oh my God, you did it. You totally jumped him!"

"Jesus, Char. A little louder next time."

"Is it a secret?" Charlotte asked—but at least she lowered her voice to an excited whisper. "Are you having a secret relationship?"

"It's not a relationship, and it's not secret. I just don't feel the need to advertise it all over town. Everyone was gossiping about me with Jamie after one date."

"So you're trying not to let on that you have a thing for Brody by making him your Valentine?"

Kendall glared at Charlotte. "He's not my Valentine. Mags is here. Mac's here. No one's accusing them of dating."

"Because we're too busy taking bets on which one of them gets 'accidentally' axed by the other. No one would ever believe Mac and Mags were a thing. But you and Brody on the other hand…"

"Are also not a thing," she said firmly.

Charlotte sighed. "You can't blame a girl for hoping. I just want you to be happy. Was it good at least?"

"No comment."

"Ooooh." Charlotte bounced. "Did you test out his endurance? Would you give him the gold?"

"Shut up," Kendall said, laughing, as Brody finally finished slapping everyone on the back and made his way to her side.

"Hey, Charlotte," he said, giving her a little half-hug in greeting. Apparently carrying someone drunk across a condo complex forged a bond. "So how's this work? We just chuck axes at the wall?"

"Pretty much. There's a dude who's going to give us a tutorial, and then we take turns trying to hit the targets. We've all put in an extra twenty bucks, and the closest team wins the pot. Though from what I hear, you don't have any trouble hitting the right spot."

"Oh my God," Kendall groaned. "Ignore her. I've told her nothing."

Charlotte grinned, unrepentant. "Can't blame a girl for trying. Now if you two lovebirds will excuse me, I see my husband beckoning." She beamed, bouncing a little. "I love saying that. I wonder how long it takes for that to stop being so fun to say."

She bounded off, leaving Kendall to face Brody's amused grin and raised eyebrows. "I hit the spot, huh?"

"I didn't even admit that we were, you know. She just figured it out."

"Are we not supposed to be admitting it?"

Kendall squirmed. "I just…there's a lot of gossip in this town, okay?"

"So we're platonic ax-throwing friends?"

She pursed her lips, fighting a smile at the twinkle in his eyes. Why was he so damn *cute*? "For all they know I only brought you because you're athletic and I want to win."

"I should have known. Using me for my muscles."

"Always."

The instructor called for their attention then to give a demonstration on the correct throwing technique.

As he was speaking, Brody leaned closer, with that glint in his eyes, and whispered, "How about a little side bet? Just to make things interesting, since we're clearly going to wipe the floor with these other teams."

God, she loved it when he challenged her. "What did you have in mind?"

"Whoever gets closer gets to pick their prize."

"Nope. Stakes beforehand or no bet."

"Fair enough," he acknowledged. "If I win, you go skiing with me."

Kendall opened her mouth to say no, an instinctive refusal, but then reconsidered. She had no intention of losing. And the idea of getting whatever she wanted from Brody was incredibly tempting. She looked up into his eyes, neither of them paying any attention to the instructor as he detailed the correct release point.

"If I win," she murmured, thinking as she spoke. What did she really want from him? "You make a video calling us the best resort you've ever skied at—and you do it shirtless."

Brody released a snort of laughter—then held up a hand in apology when several other couples glanced their way. "Sorry," he chuckled. Then he looked down at her. "Deal."

Kendall tried not to look too smug. She'd been taught from an early age to be a gracious winner.

Brody looked equally confident that he'd just won.

Until they took their first throws.

His flew straight and hard—right into the ground ten feet in front of him.

Kendall's lodged into the board about two inches to the left of the bull's-eye. Nearly perfect.

Brody gaped at her, and she just shrugged, smiling sweetly.

"You never asked if I'd done this before."

"You realize this means war," he said, grinning.

Kendall just laughed.

"I should never have invited you," Charlotte grumbled, an hour later, when the final throws were being measured. Though the measuring was just a formality to determine second through seventh place.

Kendall and Brody had destroyed the competition. He'd had a few wild throws, but once he'd found his release point, he'd been annoyingly good at it.

Annoying, because with his last throw he'd managed to land a perfect dead-center bull's-eye—winning both the pot for their team, and the side bet she'd had a lock on until that moment.

"Though I'm not sure how either of you managed to hit the target," Charlotte continued grousing. "What with the way you were giggling and flirting while we were learning how to throw."

"Excuse me." Kendall bristled. "There was no giggling. I do not giggle."

"Oh, I definitely heard a giggle. *Multiple* giggles. You could not *stop* giggling at that man."

"Lies. Slander."

Charlotte just grinned. "It's good to see you smile for a change."

"I have not been that depressing," Kendall protested.

"No, but have you been happy? As happy as you are now?"

"Who says I'm happy?"

"That silly smile says it," Magda said, joining their conversation. "And it's really good to see."

"I am not silly. And I do not giggle. Where is this coming from?"

"From Brody, by the look of things," Charlotte said with a leer.

"Please stop," Kendall groaned. "We're just having a little fun."

Charlotte lifted her wine in a toast. "To fun."

"May I someday have some of that kind of fun too," Magda agreed, clinking her glass to Charlotte's.

"Yeah, why are we not giving Mags a hard time about *her* love life?"

"Because I don't have one?" Mags suggested.

"Because Magda is focused on becoming a social media darling so she can get on *Cake-Off*," Charlotte corrected. "Did you see the last post? We've already more than quadrupled her interactions. It's happening. I can feel it. And maybe you'll meet the love of your life on *Cake-Off*," Charlotte told Magda. "They do say the way to a man's heart is through his stomach."

Kendall nodded sagely. "It's true. I learned that from *Alien*."

Magda snorted. "I don't think that's what that saying means."

"No?" Kendall feigned confusion. "I must be doing it wrong."

"I'm using that line on your next post," Charlotte told Magda, tapping a note into her phone. "*The way...heart...learned... Alien.*"

"Very Valentinesy," Magda said. "I approve."

Kendall began to respond, but Brody started toward them then and she lost her train of thought as she watched him approach, a smile automatically curving her lips. Charlotte coughed out *"Giggler,"* and Kendall shot her a glare before greeting Brody with a sunny smile as Charlotte and Mags drifted away. "Hey."

"It's official," he announced. "We won. Technically, *I* won."

"Ugh. No one likes a sore winner, Brody."

He arched his eyebrows in exaggerated innocence. "Am I not allowed to enjoy my victory?"

"Of course. With humility and grace."

"I seem to remember you crowing in my face every time you beat me in a race."

Kendall batted her eyes innocently. "I have no memory of that."

"Oh really?" Movement near the door caught his attention, and he nodded toward the exit. "Come on, Amnesia Girl. They're throwing us out."

Kendall realized the movement was everyone gathering up their things and leaving. "Are they closing this early?"

"Brett wants to get home to his wife. Apparently it's Valentine's Day."

"Brett?"

"The owner. We were talking about what it takes to run one of these."

"Your next career?"

"Maybe. I am incredibly good at it. As evidenced by my win."

She rolled her eyes at his exaggerated cockiness and grabbed her bag.

Out in the parking lot, most of their group lingered, still talking, even though it had started to snow.

Brody tipped his head back, taking in the big, puffy flakes, and she saw something on his face—that skier's look—as he mumbled, "Fresh powder tomorrow." Something in her throat squeezed, but she ignored it as they joined the rest of the group.

Most of the other couples were draped around one another, all lovey-dovey—though she supposed that made sense. It was Valentine's Day. Brody, thank goodness, didn't try for public affection. He stood beside her, chatting with Mac and George, but other than occasionally bumping her arm, there was no contact.

Preoccupied with her own thoughts, Kendall watched the group as Brody made friends with everyone. No wonder she liked him. *Everyone* liked him. He was curious about everything and always the first to volunteer to help. Also charming and funny and smart. What wasn't to like?

Levi and Elinor were the first to announce they were heading home and break off from the group, which seemed to be the signal for everyone else to start trickling toward their cars in pairs.

Brody bumped her arm. "Should we go release Banner from puppy jail?"

"Yeah," Kendall agreed.

She was halfway across the parking lot with him before she realized he'd taken her hand. It was so natural, holding hands with Brody. She glanced around, self-conscious, but no one was paying them any attention. Even Charlotte, the incurable meddler, was distracted by her own Valentine.

Brody released her hand when they reached the truck. He didn't try to open her door for her, just moved to the driver's side—and she smiled a little. She hated when men tried to open her car door—she knew it was a whole chivalry thing, but the idea that she couldn't get herself in and out of a vehicle without assistance drove her up the wall. Brody never treated her like she was delicate. He was always ready and willing to help her, but he never assumed she needed his help to function.

He *got* her.

And she liked him way too much.

Because she got him too. She knew him. And she knew someday soon, he would leave.

Lately, he'd started talking about what he might do with his life after skiing. Every day he seemed to have a new career idea, but he still hadn't told anyone else he was retiring—not his family, not his training team—and until he did, he still had one foot back in that world.

She *knew* this was temporary, but her stupid heart didn't seem to be getting the message, letting him charm his way past all her defenses. Part of her would just as soon he decide to leave already—so the other shoe would drop.

She glanced over at him as he put the truck in gear. Keeping her tone casual, she said, "I hear there's a World Cup competition coming up in Lake Placid. Right after Steph's wedding." It was why Steph had picked the weekend she did to get married. She'd figured her brother would already be only a couple of hours away, getting ready to compete.

Brody glanced over at her, his brow furrowed. "I know."

His old life would only be a couple hours away. After they were done with the renovation. After he would have no reason left to stay.

"It'd be easy to drop by. Visit your old life."

Brody didn't even react as he pulled out onto the road. "I'm good right here."

"Don't you even wonder what it would feel like? Could be good for closure at least. Clarity."

He looked over at her, frowning, before the road conditions and the thickening snowfall called his attention back to the road. "Do you want me to go back?"

No. She wanted him to stay. But…"I would have if I could," she said softly. "I don't want you to regret walking away. And I do think if you were really done with it, you would have told your family by now."

"I will," he insisted. "This weekend. Steph's going to be here."

"Okay. Good," Kendall murmured, unsure how she felt.

"You still coming with?" he asked.

"I'll be there," she promised. "But you won't need me, Brody."

"Don't be so sure," he said. "You're my shoes."

Her lips twitched. "Nope. Not how it's used. Totally wrong."

"I'll figure it out one of these days." He grinned, turning his attention back to the road, and she studied his movie-star profile.

He needed to tell his family. Then his parents would talk some sense into him. He would see what he was giving up. And then he would leave and she would get on with her life.

She couldn't follow him. Even if the resort had been thriving, she couldn't go back to the World Cup tour as a girlfriend. Not when she'd once been a star.

Kendall watched him drive, her chest tight.

The last ten days had been fun, but reality was always waiting to smack you in the face—and she was ready for it to just hit her already. She had learned she could recover from anything, but the waiting…the waiting was the worst.

Chapter Twenty-Six

His parents had staged an intervention.

Brody had expected that he and Kendall would be walking into a perfectly normal family dinner—perhaps with the focus heavily on wedding stuff for Steph, since the big day was only two weeks away. He'd figured when there was a lull in the wedding talk, he'd find a way to work into the conversation that his knee was actually fine and he was thinking of making his break from skiing a permanent one.

He was completely unprepared to walk into his parents' living room and find himself in the middle of a shrine to his own career.

His mother had emptied the trophy room. Medals and framed newspaper clippings decorated every possible surface. Even the television was running a highlight reel of his greatest hits.

Brody ground to a stop, Kendall bumping into his back when she didn't stop as quickly. His parents and his sister were all lined up on the couch facing him—along with Valeria and his agent, Reg. He stared from his ex to his parents to his agent, trying to figure out what the hell he'd just walked into.

"What's going on?"

"Brody," his mother said, standing and taking the lead with a rehearsed, studied calm. "We're all very worried about you."

"What?"

Kendall made a small sound behind him. "Maybe I should…"

Brody's hand shot out, grabbing hers before she could go anywhere, though he didn't take his eyes off his family. "I'm fine," he reassured them.

"You haven't really been yourself," his sister said, her expression almost apologetic, like she wasn't quite sure she wanted to be there.

"You haven't been training," his dad added. "If you need to see specialists for your knee—"

"I'm *fine*," he insisted. "My knee is fine."

"You've missed three competitions," Valeria said. "Your World Cup ranking is dropping."

"Why do you care what my ranking is?" Brody demanded. "You broke up with me in a text."

Valeria's eyes flared, and she opened her mouth to defend herself—but his agent stepped in, rising to his feet and holding out his hands in a calming gesture. "We all care about you, buddy. We've been patient, but it's been over a month now. Rumors of your retirement have started to leak. It's going to start affecting endorsement offers if you don't get back out there. The tour is coming to the US soon. It could be a way to ease back in—"

He ignored Reg, focusing on his parents. "I was coming here to talk to you about this. I don't know if I want to get back out there. I think I might be done." His mom made a small shocked sound, her hand flying to her mouth—and Kendall's hand tightened reflexively on his.

"Brody…" He looked at his mom—and his resolve wavered. She looked so crushed. How could he tell her he'd had a freaking existential crisis and thrown his career away without a backward glance?

"At least get a second opinion on your knee," Valeria encouraged, rising to her feet.

"Why are you here?" Brody snapped, knowing he was being a dick, but feeling incapable of reeling himself in with all of them ambushing him. "You dumped me the second you realized I wasn't going to be getting headlines anymore."

"Brody," Kendall said softly—and shame tried to claw its way up his throat, but he swallowed it down hard.

"I don't need an intervention, or whatever this is. I'm retiring. And I'm happy about it." Mostly. "End of story."

"So you're just going to work at a ski resort for the rest of your life?" his father asked. "No offense, Kendall."

"None taken," Kendall assured him.

"I don't know what I'm going to do. I'm figuring it out, but I'm not going back. I don't want to compete anymore."

"But *why?*" his mother asked softly.

"I don't know!" His voice boomed, echoing in the room—instantly chased by a rush of guilt. He'd never yelled at his mother in his life.

Kendall said his name again, softly, and he met her eyes, reminded of why he'd come. He'd had a whole plan of how he was going to explain this to his parents, but then he'd walked in and seen the pressure to be *the* Brody James again and something instinctive and defensive had kicked in. He felt like he needed to fight for his right *not* to do something he'd always wanted to do before. Like he was fighting for his freaking life.

It was fear.

Fear of being Oskar? Fear of something else? Of them not loving him anymore if he stopped? He'd always been shit at the self-analysis stuff. How did people do this?

He looked back at his parents, pleading with him, trying to understand.

"I wasn't happy," he said finally. "I felt really alone. I built my entire life around being the best, but I don't want skiing to be all I am. After what happened to Oskar, I needed...*family*. Home. Balance. Maybe I'll want to go back to the tour someday. Maybe I'll be ready for that once I have some sort of foundation here, but right now, I just need to be focused on this. On *being here*. Because I haven't been here for years. I've missed Thanksgivings and Christmases because it was too far to fly home and risk jet lag messing up my next race. I trained all year round, and when I wasn't, I was still trying to be the great Brody James. I taught you to count me out of all your decisions. And you went along. Everyone was giving me space to chase my dreams—so no one was there. It was like we all agreed that skiing was the most important thing in the world, and it took me ten years to realize it wasn't. That I don't care if I win anymore." The last words felt violently wrong and he shook his head. "I mean obviously I want to win. I love winning. But there's more to life, right? I want to get some of that."

Silence reigned for a moment after he finished the speech he hadn't intended to make. Reg stared at him, piercing and pensive, but his sister watched their parents.

After a moment, his mother said, "Why didn't you tell us?"

"I didn't want to disappoint you," Brody admitted, his

throat tight. He waved at the paraphernalia around them. "I know how much all this means to you."

"Brody Adam James," his mother scolded, standing and approaching him. "I'm proud of *you*. Of the man you are. I don't need trophies for that."

He released Kendall's hand—only realizing he was still holding on to her like a lifeline when he had to let her go to hug his mother. His mom squeezed him hard, but the tension inside him wouldn't unknot. Above his mom's head, he could see Valeria watching them, her lips pursed tight.

God, he'd messed that up.

He met her eyes as he pulled away from his mother. "We should talk."

Kendall seemed to immediately sense what he needed. She turned to his sister and his parents. "We put in the chandelier this week. Would you like to see the latest photos?"

As Kendall distracted his family, Brody followed Valeria onto the front porch. His ex took a position standing at one end, and he leaned against the opposite railing.

"I didn't care about the headlines," she said softly—and his guilt over how badly he'd handled things rose up. Not just today, but pretty much since the beginning of their relationship.

"I know," he said. "I shouldn't have thrown that at you. I shouldn't have done a lot of things. I'm sorry, Valeria."

She nodded slightly, watching him. She was gorgeous, and distant—and he realized he'd liked those things about her. There had been safety in being with someone so contained and aloof. He'd told himself she didn't need him—so he'd never let himself need her.

"Why didn't you say you were lonely?" she asked.

"I'm not sure I knew I was," he said, knowing he owed

her more of an explanation. "I was pretty good at ignoring my feelings—so completely focused on my goal, telling myself it was all that mattered. But that's no excuse for ignoring yours."

"That was shitty," she said, her accent somehow making the word sound elegant.

"I told myself we were using each other, that it was more an alliance or a flirtation than a relationship, so I didn't have to feel bad for pulling away."

She looked away, pressing her lips tight as she nodded. "Even if we were, it didn't feel good that I only learned you'd left the continent because your coach called to find if I knew what was wrong."

He winced. "I'm sorry. I wasn't thinking clearly."

"But you weren't thinking of me."

"No," he confirmed.

She nodded. "I deserve someone who thinks of me."

"You do," he agreed. "I'm sorry I was kind of a shitty boyfriend."

She hummed in her throat. "I let you be. Until I thought you were going to break up with me, so I broke up with you first."

"Why did you come?" he asked.

"I don't know. To call you an asshole to your face? To see if maybe you changed your mind and wanted to grovel for a few weeks? I would have let you grovel, I think. I did like you."

"I liked you too. I'm sorry, Valeria."

"Hmm." She glanced toward the house. "She's pretty. Your blond girl."

"I'm not sure she's mine." Kendall was so independent, it was hard to imagine her as anyone's. Kind of like Valeria.

"She is," Valeria confirmed, as if it was fact. "Try not to

break her heart." She straightened then, moving toward the driveway and the rental car he'd assumed was his sister's. "Ciao, Brody."

"Ciao, Valeria."

The front door opened then, and his agent emerged. "You need some time to think," Reg said before he could speak. "I get it. I won't say anything to anyone. It's not a good time to announce anyway. We'll keep our options open and talk more."

"Reg…"

"Nope. You're still reacting. I wouldn't be doing my job if I let you make a hasty decision now that would affect your future. We'll talk later."

Brody stared after them, not moving from the porch as Reg and Valeria drove away. Dreading going back inside to face his family. His mother had said she would still be proud, but what else was she supposed to say?

The front door opened again.

"That didn't quite go as planned," Kendall said lightly as she moved to stand beside him at the railing. "That your first intervention?"

"It's not yours?"

Kendall shrugged. "Charlotte's an obsessive meddler. She throws pseudo-interventions all the time. Usually with really good snacks, though. And the results aren't always terrible. That's how I got Banner." She bumped her shoulder against his. "You okay?"

He wasn't sure how to answer that.

"I feel like I'm letting everyone down. Like when there are all these people who want you to do something, you need a better reason than *I don't feel like it* to walk away."

"You said it. You weren't happy."

"Is that enough?"

"It's your life, Brody. You're the one who has to live it. You aren't hurting anyone by retiring—"

"Except my agent's ten percent."

"He's got other clients. And you can refer all the superstars you coach to him, if you decide to go in that direction. Or you can go back to the tour, like you said. Once you're ready. But you don't have to explain yourself to anyone. You don't owe it to your parents or your agent or anyone else."

"I miss racing," he said softly. "I do. I just don't want that to be all I am."

"So find the middle, all-or-nothing Brody James. Find your balance."

He studied her eyes. *She* was his balance. Kendall made him feel centered in a way nothing else had in the last few months—but the front door opened before he could say the words out loud.

"Is it safe to come out?" Steph asked. "Are you pissed at me?"

Brody sighed. "I'm not mad. But a little warning would have been nice. What the hell was that?"

"That was Mom being convinced you *needed* us and something was catastrophically wrong. She's the one who called in Reg and Valeria." She folded her arms, glaring at him. "Why didn't you just tell us you wanted to retire?"

"Like it's so easy? You all couldn't wait for me to go back. I was going to let everyone down."

Steph rolled her eyes. "God, Brody, stop trying to be so perfect. You don't have to be Mr. Olympics for us to love you. How shallow do you think we are?"

"I don't. I'm just not used to not knowing what I want." Or

how he felt. This whole self-reflection thing was a lot. It was so much easier to just dogmatically chase perfection.

"Come inside. Mom's frantically hiding all your trophies. Now that you've told her you want to come home and settle down, she's going to be setting you up with every single woman in a twenty-mile radius. At least that will get her off me and Frankie having kids for a while."

"Oh…well…" Brody glanced at Kendall, realizing he hadn't indicated they were *together*, but Kendall was already pushing away from the railing and smiling at Steph.

"I can hear the giggling now," Kendall said. "He could never resist a giggler."

Brody frowned, and followed them inside. He would figure out later why Kendall was playing it off like they weren't together. Right now, he had enough to worry about just convincing his family he knew what he was doing. Not to mention convincing himself.

Kendall was quiet as they drove back to the resort that night, but so was Brody. She leaned against the door of the truck, letting her eyes close and pretending to sleep.

He'd said as they were getting into the car that he probably should have talked to his parents weeks ago, and she'd agreed without any censure. She completely understood avoiding the messy emotional stuff. Like right now, when she was chickening out and pretending to sleep.

He'd actually told them.

Yes, he hadn't really had a choice because they'd ambushed him, but he could have folded in the face of their concern, and he hadn't. He'd come right out and told the most important people in his life that he was retiring from skiing.

She'd told herself these last few weeks that she was just getting him out of her system. And when that had proven to be impossible, she'd told herself it was temporary, so no matter what she felt, it was safe because he was going back to his life, even if he didn't know it yet.

But what if he stayed?

The idea scared her a little. It was pressure she hadn't been ready for.

There was so much more *weight* on the idea of them than there had been a few hours ago—and it scared the crap out of her.

Of course, he still might go back to racing. He'd said he missed it. The words had nearly made her flinch, but they weren't the part that was making her feign sleep.

If he was staying…if this was real…then she had to think about the future. She had to think about what she actually wanted. And if she wanted him in it.

Kendall had always kept it light when the future came up—or strategically avoided the topic by changing the subject to talk about the lodge. Talking about the lodge was safe. Thinking about Brody sticking around for good? As if it might actually happen? *There be monsters.*

"Why didn't you want my family to know we've been seeing each other?" Brody asked softly as they neared the resort, proving he hadn't bought her sleeping routine—and dropping a hand grenade in the middle of her desire to avoid that subject.

"I figured you didn't want your mom getting carried away."

"Yeah. That's probably smart," Brody acknowledged, and she almost thought that would be the end of it, but then he kept talking. "But we're good, right?"

"Of course."

"Truth?" he asked—and she looked over at him, meeting his eyes for a moment before he had to look back to the road.

Thank God her phone buzzed at that moment, because she wasn't sure what she would have said to him. She glanced down, opening the incoming text.

"Oh, shit."

"Shit?" Brody asked, glancing over at her as he drove.

"It's the tile guy. He's in the hospital." Which was terrible news, but she felt a rush of calm that they had a crisis to deal with that had nothing to do with *feelings*.

"Armand? Is he okay?"

"He's okay, but he broke five bones in his right hand."

"Oh, shit," Brody echoed.

Her thumbs raced as she texted back. "He's out of commission until after the wedding. Apparently he's already tried calling every other tiler he knows—he didn't want to disappoint the great Brody James—but none of them can fit us in. *Crap.* Why did we yank out the old tile already? We could've just left the bathrooms seventies and pretended it was retro."

Brody frowned, pulling into the staff lot at the resort. "If he has a broken hand, how is he texting you?"

"It's his wife," Kendall explained, holding up her phone. "She sent a picture of his hand."

Brody winced as he caught sight of the screen—and the metal pins holding the poor guy's bones in place. "Ouch." He threw the truck into park. "Okay. Maybe we can fly someone in—"

"Without destroying the budget? We can barely afford *chairs*."

"What if we did it?"

Kendall scoffed. "You know how to lay tile?"

"I know how to google. And I bet Armand would coach us on FaceTime if we begged for help."

Kendall shook her head, her thoughts still racing. "I wonder if any of the other contractors do tile on the side."

"Kendall," Brody said—and the serious note in his voice caught her attention. She glanced over and his eyes held hers, steadily. "We've got this."

Somehow, looking in his eyes, she believed him. They were a team. She didn't want to think about the twinge in her chest or what that might mean. All the feelings crap could wait. All that mattered right now was the wedding. The lodge. Just focus on that. Everything else would be fine.

"Okay. Let's lay some freaking tile."

Chapter Twenty-Seven

O h, that is *sexy*."

Kendall glanced over her shoulder. Normally she would love to hear those words from Brody in that awe-filled tone, but in this case…"You're talking about the tile, aren't you?"

Brody looked up from the corner he was scrubbing clean. They were wrapping up their tile adventure, putting the final touches on bathroom number two. Armand had been only too happy to be their FaceTime tile coach. He'd still been a little loopy on pain meds, but with his help—and that of half a dozen YouTube tutorials—Kendall and Brody had managed to do a damn fine job of retiling the bathrooms.

Brody, as it turned out, was a freaking tile savant. And his enthusiasm for the project was absurdly adorable.

"In my defense," he said. "It is incredibly sexy tile."

Kendall smothered a laugh. She'd expected the project to be a chore, but Brody's enthusiasm had made that impossible. He took a ridiculous amount of pleasure when the cuts lined up just right, celebrating every step of the way.

After his third "*Yeah*, baby!" following a particularly satisfying placement, Kendall had given up trying to hold back her laughter. He was just so *proud* of himself—and his zeal was infectious.

When they'd finished the first bathroom, wiping off the excess grout, they'd FaceTimed Armand again, and he confirmed that he couldn't have done it any better. Even if he was lying, Kendall had to agree that the place looked fantastic.

Brody had somehow talked her dad into letting Michelle cover his managerial duties for the week. The head of the ski school was the one Kendall had been trying to get her dad to consider for the manager position full-time, so it was a win on multiple levels. Banner had been underfoot and poking his nose into everything on the first day, but on day two the ski school borrowed him for the morning to distract kids from their nerves, and then Laurie had volunteered to take him for the rest of the week—which meant Kendall and Brody were free to concentrate on the tile job without canine help. The work had gone much faster after that.

"You, however, are also incredibly sexy," Brody said now, coming up behind her. She'd been cleaning up their materials, as they were nearly done with the second bathroom. He kissed the side of her neck, sliding his arms around her, and Kendall tilted her head.

"As sexy as tile?"

"I mean, let's not get carried away."

Kendall huffed out a laugh, turning at his coaxing and letting him press her into the wall for a kiss.

"I am a tile god," Brody said against her lips and Kendall laughed.

"I don't know about deification…"

"A *god*," he insisted, kissing her again—and she couldn't argue with that.

Until he bumped a pile of fragments, making them clatter. "Out," she urged, coming up for air. "Not on the tile."

Never stopping the kiss, Brody staggered with her into the hallway, pinning her against the wall between the two bathrooms. His hands were working their way under her shirt, and her hands were on his belt when they both heard a cheerful "Hello! Anyone home?"

Kendall jerked away from him, frantically straightening her clothes at the sound of her stepmother's voice. Brody tried to reel her back. "What if we pretend we aren't here?" he whispered.

"She's bringing back Banner," Kendall said—right as the dog appeared at the end of the hallway, dragging Laurie with him in his eagerness to get to them.

"Oh! There you are!" Her stepmother beamed. "How's the tile going?"

"Good." Kendall slapped on a smile, and crouched to greet the dog, who went into contortions of joy, even though he'd only been away from her for a few hours. "Hello, chaos monster. I think we're almost done."

"No almost. We are done," Brody corrected, opening the door to the second bathroom to show Laurie.

"Really?" Kendall stood up, keeping Banner from lunging in to investigate the new tile. Sure enough, that final corner was complete. She'd been too distracted by Brody to notice.

They'd done it. They'd finished.

A strange feeling settled on her chest.

"It looks wonderful," Laurie praised. "I'm so proud of you both." She looked up and down the hallway. "What else do you have left to do?"

And that was when Kendall realized what the strange feeling in her chest was. A vague sort of disappointment, which didn't make any sense, because they'd done it. They were done.

"I think that's it," she said aloud. The plumber had come in yesterday to install the fixtures, working around them while they were applying the grout. Today had been mostly cleanup, scrubbing away the excess, and making it shine. "It's just décor now."

The finishing touches needed to be put in place and the main space decorated—Kendall wanted to wrap twinkle lights around the exposed rafters, and Steph had asked for white bunting to drape from the railings—but it was still eight days before the wedding and the tile was the last major renovation project.

They'd actually done it. They'd finished early. And miraculously under budget.

The hearth had been cleaned, windows resealed, and floors refinished, along with the long wooden slab of a bar. The bathrooms had been retiled, the heater serviced, and the back rooms spruced up so they were simple but elegant.

The tables would need to be set up, along with the handmade chairs that would be delivered on Monday—the ones that would have broken the budget if Brody hadn't been able to negotiate a discount. Without dropping his famous name once. Then all that would be missing would be the centerpieces and floral arrangements that would arrive on the day of the wedding.

"You two make a good team," Laurie said, something glinting in her eyes.

Kendall flushed. "Brody was very dedicated."

Laurie hummed…and Kendall moved with Banner toward the main room, taking everything in.

There was still a lot of work to do. Setting up the tables and arranging the loft—Steph wanted it to be a photo area where guests could pose with silly props—and the back rooms would need a few finishing touches, now that the paint had finished drying, but other than that, it really was done.

"I feel like lightning is going to strike and burn the whole thing down. Or a pipe will burst and flood it all. Some natural disaster to take it all away," Kendall admitted. It looked too perfect. Whenever everything was going too well, she was braced for it to come crashing down around her.

Just like with Brody.

"Nothing is going to happen," Laurie assured her.

"I won't allow it," Brody added.

"Just enjoy your accomplishment," Laurie urged. "You two should take the rest of the day off. The ski school asked if they could have Banner again this afternoon—I was just coming by to make sure that was all right. You should go have fun. You've definitely earned it"

"Thanks, Laurie."

After her stepmom left with Banner, they finished cleaning up—and then found themselves standing in the middle of the main room, both frowning as they took it all in.

"It feels weird, doesn't it?" Brody said finally. "Sort of anticlimactic. What do we do now?"

That was exactly what she'd been asking herself. What would he do now that he didn't have a reason to be here anymore?

They'd hired him to be the resort manager, but he'd spent nearly as much time helping her with the renovations as he had taking care of staffing—though he hadn't shirked his duties there. He was just so much *better* at the people stuff than Kendall was. Which was galling, but also comforting. She'd been able to accept that the resort was in good hands and focus on the wedding stuff. She'd expected the last seven weeks to be the most stressful of her life, but instead she'd enjoyed herself.

She'd enjoyed him. And after next weekend, his sister's wedding would be over. This goal that they'd been working toward. Things would go back to normal at the resort. And he would realize he was wasting his time here.

Brody looked down from his contemplation of the loft and caught her watching him. "We should celebrate. Champagne?"

Kendall met his eyes, a sudden impulse taking hold. "I have a better idea."

"Oh yeah?"

That old familiar feeling of daring dug in. "I believe I still owe you a ski date."

Brody's eyes lit, but his expression remained cautious. "Are you sure? We can always change the bet."

Kendall frowned.

He would let her. He would let her back out of it.

And she would never be able to look herself in the eye again.

She didn't really want her first time putting on skis in over two years to be in front of Brody James, but she needed to do this. If only to prove to herself that she could. To prove that her past didn't have any power over her anymore. That she'd really moved on.

"No. Let's go."

"Yeah?"

"Right now. Let's do it."

A smile split across his face like she'd given him a Christmas present. "Okay."

It was two in the afternoon. The lifts would all be busy. The rumors would start flying immediately—both because Brody

James was skiing in public and because everyone on the resort knew that Kendall didn't ski anymore. Her muscles were already tired from scrubbing excess grout off the tiles all morning, and this was probably going to be a disaster. But she didn't care.

She needed to prove to herself that she wasn't scared of the mountain. She needed to accept who she was now and stop being so scared of not being who she'd been.

"Give me half an hour." She'd need at least that long to get ready. Her skis hadn't been waxed in two years. She'd only kept a couple pairs and they'd been gathering dust in the family ski locker. It would probably take her an hour to gather up all her stuff and get her gear ready—but if she was rushing, she wasn't thinking and she didn't want to give her brain time to second-guess.

Brody grinned. "Can't wait."

The line for chair four was as long as it got. It was a Friday afternoon and the conditions were perfect. Fresh powder, no wind, and a crystal-blue sky. When Brody was a teenager, he'd skipped school on a couple days like today, because the mountain had been calling him and he'd needed to be on the slopes. But he hadn't been this stoked for an afternoon of skiing in a while.

It had felt good, clicking his boots into his bindings with that familiar heavy *thunk*. They weren't as tight as they would be on a race day, but that sound still resonated with something inside him like a tuning fork being struck.

He and Kendall both kept their goggles down as they shuffled inch by inch toward the front of the line, which made it easier to avoid recognition—though the lift operator immediately recognized them both, his eyes widening as they slid into place and waited to board.

"Have a good run," Marco said, and Brody could feel him watching them even after he and Kendall had been whooshed up the mountain on a chair dangling from a cable.

"You okay with the safety bar?" Kendall asked, reaching behind her to bring it over their heads. It dropped into place, and Brody lifted one ski to prop on the footrest, leaving the other to dangle as Kendall propped up both of hers.

There was a slight breeze, amplified by the movement of the chair, and Brody tipped his face up to it, feeling that familiar cold wind against his face. He inhaled deeply. God, he'd missed this.

He hadn't thought, when he challenged Kendall to come skiing with him, that it would mean him getting back on the mountain again too. He'd only been thinking about Kendall. About how much they'd both loved this, before life happened.

He glanced over to find her glowering at the hill like it had done something to piss her off. She caught him watching her, and her perma-frown deepened.

"It's not going to be like it was," she grumbled. "I'm not like I was. You'll have to slow down for me."

And God, she would hate that. His throat squeezed, but he kept his voice light. "I don't care if you're fast, Kendall. We can ski the bunny hill, if you want." She'd propped her goggles on top of her head, and he met her eyes. "You used to love it before you were the best, remember?"

She arched a brow. "That can't be right. I was always the best."

He grinned at her show of arrogance, but then he sobered, thinking back to those first daredevil days. "Do you remember when we were kids?" he asked. "How we always used to try to time the chairlifts at the end of the day to get one last run?"

Kendall smiled at the memory. "It was a skill. You had to be at the top of the lift when the chairs stopped running. For the maximum time on the mountain."

"Bonus points if you were the absolute last rider up before they shut it all down." He looked up at the familiar mountain. "We couldn't get enough. Remember how that felt?"

"We were kids," she reminded him.

"We knew what we wanted." He missed that feeling. Knowing what he was meant to do.

He'd been trying to figure it out, these last couple weeks. Everywhere they'd gone, he'd talked to people. Asking about everything from ax throwing to running a microbrewery or being a physical therapist, working in construction or running a diner—but nothing really fit. They all felt like hobbies. Like escapes from his real life. Nothing that would fill the hole skiing left in his life.

He realized he was incredibly privileged. Most people didn't get to pick their careers based on passion and whim, but the freedom wasn't helping his decision. It only seemed to be making it harder. It was almost a letdown that the renovations on the old lodge were over. Obviously he'd wanted it to be ready in time, but the project had given him purpose.

They reached the top of the mountain and glided off the chairlift, taking the gradual turn to the left and pausing to adjust their gear where the trail split. A black diamond to the right. An easier blue square to the left.

There never would have been a question which way they went down before, but things were different now. Brody looked over at Kendall and tried to read her eyes, barely visible through her goggles.

"Is this safe for you?" he asked, feeling stupid for not asking sooner. "Getting hurt isn't worth it for a bet."

"I'm not here because of the bet," Kendall said, gripping her poles. "I'll be sore, but I'll be all right." She tipped her head challengingly. "Will you?"

His heart began to pound as her teeth flashed in a grin—then she shoved off, dropping onto a run that was definitely not a bunny hill—and Brody dropped in behind her. Always chasing that blond braid.

She was fast—not world-class fast, but she could still move. Brody's smile grew as he tightened his tuck and picked up speed. Wind whipped past him, and something clicked into place—he'd *missed* this. The feel of the snow, his muscles responding before he even had time to think, all reaction and instinct and adrenaline.

Life was freaking *perfect*—

Until she went down.

For a second Brody's heart felt like it stopped beating. *"Kendall!"*

Kendall groaned—ninety-five percent irritation and five percent pain—as she levered herself up from where she'd smashed into a mogul. She'd gotten cocky after the first couple turns, feeling pretty good, if not flawless, and then she'd caught an edge. Like a freaking rookie.

Brody was suddenly there in a spray of snow, his face hovering over hers. "Kendall! Are you all right? Where does it hurt?"

"My ego, mostly." She poked at him gently with her pole. "Gimme some space so I can get up."

"It isn't your back?"

"Brody, I'm fine."

The worry eased from his face, and he shifted to give her room. "You look good."

"You mean before I ate it?"

His smile flashed. "You said you hadn't skied in a while. I didn't know what to expect."

"Me either," she muttered, digging snow out of her cuffs. Though she should have known the first run was going to be a nightmare. She was in good shape, but she hadn't used her muscles in this way in years.

She nodded down the hill. "Let's go."

"You sure?"

"Lead the way, Brody."

She saw the hesitation on his face. It was easier to babysit her if he was above her—he'd be able to see if she fell, wouldn't have to climb back up to help her if she went down—but she had no intention of going down again. And after a moment, Brody gave a little nod and shoved off. He was purposefully going slow—which pissed her off—but was probably smart.

Nothing felt right.

She wasn't magically amazing. A miracle hadn't occurred and instantly returned her to the peak of her career. She was awkward and rusty, but she wasn't about to give up. When they made it down—so much slower than she wanted and two almost-falls later—she looked over at Brody and demanded, "Let's go again."

And it got better.

Halfway through the second run, she started to catch her rhythm and it stopped being work. She stopped fighting her own instincts and started to trust herself again—and it actually felt *good*.

She still wasn't fast. Brody had to be reining himself in every second to avoid racing ahead of her, but as they zigged down the runs she'd known her entire life, it stopped being a competition.

She stopped racing him—or racing the idea of herself—and started to have fun. She'd always wanted to be fast—but she used to want that because it was so much more *fun* to feel the wind in her face and the freedom of it.

As they rode the chairlift up the mountain for the fifth time, she looked over at Brody and admitted, "You were right."

"Of course I was," he agreed. "What was I right about?"

"I did love skiing before I was good."

"You're still good."

"Yeah," she agreed, because she was. She was still one of the best skiers on the mountain on any given day, but she wasn't *great*. She'd lost greatness. And she'd never wanted to let that go. But *fun* didn't care if she was great. And she was starting to think that enjoying life might actually be better than being great at it.

"Thanks for getting me out here," she said.

"Likewise."

He leaned back into his corner of the chair, perfectly relaxed as he stared up at the mountain—and Kendall's heart squeezed hard. He looked so much himself in that moment. This was who he was. How could he give it up? She kept waiting for that moment when something was going to pull him back, like a rubber band snapping.

"I've missed this. A lot," he murmured, and she fought the panic those words inspired.

"You could have been doing this all along," she reminded him, flicking the season pass attached to his jacket. "Most of our employees only work here because of the mountain privileges."

"I know. But I made skiing all I was for so long that I thought if I didn't completely walk away, I'd never have room to be anything else."

"All-or-nothing Brody James."

He glanced over, smiling. "You're one to talk."

"I'm working on it," Kendall said.

"Me too."

Balance. It was such a tricky concept. That tightrope between what she wanted and what she could have.

It was a risk, letting him dig himself a little deeper into her heart when part of her still felt like this was going to go down in flames the second he went back to his real life.

But she wasn't ready to let go either.

When he took her gloved hand, she felt his grip squeezing a little tighter around her heart.

She would hold on…just a little longer.

Together with their families

Stephanie May James

and

Franklin Grant Kealey

Request the pleasure of your company
as they say "I Do!"

Saturday, the second of March

Five o'clock in the evening
Trinity Church
Woodland, Vermont

Followed by dinner & dancing
at Windsor Mountain Chalet

Chapter Twenty-Eight

Brody was dancing with the flower girl.

Kendall leaned against the wall, back in her black pant-suit, and watched to make sure everything was running smoothly—which it was. The reception had been going for a lit-tle over an hour now. The horse-drawn sleighs—courtesy of Len Miller, who did carriage rides at Christmastime and hayrides in the summer for the tourists in Pine Hollow—had been perfect to bring the guests who didn't want to walk the forest path to the reception in their finery. Kendall had gotten a few shots for the resort website, including some of the bride and groom in the sleigh as they arrived at the venue.

The old lodge looked magnificent.

Twinkle lights wrapped the exposed rafters—which had taken Kendall and Brody an entire day teetering at the top of ladders. White bunting artfully draped the polished log banis-ters. A mix-and-match set of wooden tables decorated with white flowers and evergreen boughs encircled the dance floor, where the newly refinished floors shone to perfection. The overall effect was rustic elegance with warmth and character—exactly what Stephanie had been hoping for.

Dinner had gone off perfectly—the catering company had complained about the size of the kitchen, but if that was the worst thing that happened all night, Kendall would take it. The toasts had been surprisingly succinct—apparently Steph had sent out guidelines and time limits, and those toasting the bride and groom had actually stuck to them. Everything had been—shockingly—right on schedule when Steph and Frankie took the floor for their first dance to "All of Me."

And now Brody was dancing with the four-year-old flower girl.

Kendall was working tonight, but Brody was in full brother-of-the-bride festive mode. As he should be. Something shifted and tugged in her chest, watching him there, twirling the little girl in the poofy white dress.

He'd be such a great dad. There was something about seeing him with that little girl that made her feel all squishy inside in a way that was frankly terrifying. Kendall didn't do squishy.

Steph wove toward her, and Kendall jerked to attention as she realized she'd been gawping at Brody too long. Had she missed something? Was something wrong?

"Steph! Hi." She flashed her most professional smile. "What can I do for you?"

Steph had opted for simple lines rather than the opulence of Charlotte's gown, but she looked just as beautiful—and just as happy. Though her eyes were more calculating than glowing at the moment.

"Are you secretly dating my brother?"

Kendall flushed. "I wouldn't—ah—I wouldn't say secretly."

Steph's smile grew positively massive. "I knew it! Why

haven't you guys said anything? He acted like he didn't want to bring a date."

"I didn't want to come as his date. I wanted to focus on making sure everything ran smoothly for you."

"And it's been wonderful, thank you. But I think you can take time off for a dance or two. You've definitely earned it. This place…" She looked up at the lights. "It's magical. I don't know how you did it."

"Brody did a lot."

"Yeah." Steph eyed Kendall. "I wonder what got into him."

Kendall shook her head, refusing the credit. "He really wanted to do this for you."

But now that it was over, he had no real reason to stay.

"I'm not sure that's all it was about," Steph said. "He's really changed these last couple of months, and I think you had a lot to do with that."

"I wouldn't say that."

"I would. My brother has always been a good guy. He's got a huge heart. But skiing was the only thing he ever really *worked* for. The only thing he seemed to care about. Everything else was the easy way. But you never took it easy on him. You didn't give him a free pass just because he was Brody James. And I think it was really good for him to have to work for something for a change."

"I don't know about that." Brody had been the one who decided he wanted to help. He'd been as dedicated as she was to finishing the lodge.

"I do. Now go dance. Bride's orders."

"I'll consider it," Kendall promised and Steph pointed toward the dance floor insistently before moving to hug an approaching friend.

The song ended, and Brody bowed elaborately to the flower girl, who tackle-hugged his legs and then raced off. He straightened, a smile lingering on his face, and caught Kendall watching him. His smile shifted, aiming right at her, and he made a little chin jerk gesture toward the dance floor, his eyebrows arching upward.

Kendall bit her lip and nodded. Bride's orders, after all.

He met her halfway, catching her hand and tugging her with him onto the dance floor.

"Hi," he murmured as she stepped into his arms, her hand resting on the pad of his shoulder. The man always looked unfairly good in a suit, and he'd taken off his jacket again—just like at Anne and Bailey's wedding—and rolled up the sleeves of his dress shirt to show off his forearms.

"Hi," she said back.

Steph and Frank had hired a DJ instead of a band, and the next song was a slow one. Nearby Steph and her groom were swaying. Kendall ducked her head, and Brody's hand shifted on the small of her back, pulling her a little closer.

"Your last dance partner had some pretty impressive moves," she said, when the feeling of the song got to be a little too much.

"She was very into the twirling. Though she didn't care for the song. She kept asking Alexa to change it to Beyoncé. I tried to explain that Alexa wasn't here, but she seemed very certain that Alexa was a magic wishing fairy who was *everywhere* and I was a little slow because I didn't know that."

Kendall's lips twitched. "She sounds very knowledgeable," she said, keeping her tone light while inside she was starting to spiral.

She used to think they were so alike—both racing headlong into life, neither knowing how to stop—but now she could only see their differences. Brody had left the tour to build himself a new life—and she'd been clinging to her old life as hard as she could, incapable of letting it go. She was working on that—on being who she was now rather than a regret-filled echo of her past, but she didn't really know what she wanted yet—and she refused to be the girl who defined herself by her relationship.

But she wanted him to be happy. She *needed* that, on some level.

The song ended while she was tangled up with things that suddenly felt entirely too real.

"I want to make a toast!" Stephanie declared, standing on the stairs to the loft and holding a champagne glass aloft. "You all got to make your toasts earlier, now it's my turn."

Kendall stepped out of Brody's arms and looked toward Steph as everyone laughed and scrambled for glasses.

"I want to thank my wonderful family and wonderful friends and all of you wonderful people for making this day so...*wonderful*," Steph said, and everyone chuckled. "I especially need to thank my baby brother and Kendall Walsh, who stepped in to save the day when we lost our original reception venue." She tilted her glass in their direction. "You're awesome. And I don't know what I would have done without you." Then she turned to look at the man standing just below her. "But this toast is really to my new husband."

An *awwww* rippled through the room.

"When I met Frank, he was the last person I would have expected to fall madly in love with. He was just that annoying guy at work who sent way too many memos."

The crowd chuckled, and Steph smiled fondly at her groom.

"I wasn't looking for love. In fact, I'd pretty much given up on the whole idea. But then I went to the company Memorial

Day picnic. It was held at this lake with games and activities set up along the shore. That lake was *freezing* cold. No one wanted to go in there. And it was all fun and games until a huge gust of wind comes up and blows this little kid's dinosaur toy into the lake. The kid is losing it—he's only three or four years old, and he's inconsolable. Everyone's trying to distract him, offering him ice cream and promising to replace the toy—and Frank just grabs a kayak and starts paddling."

A little cheer moved through the crowd, but Steph shook her head. "Oh, no, it wasn't that easy. The wind kept blowing the toy farther and farther out, but Frank kept going. He must have paddled for half an hour, chasing that ridiculous little dinosaur all over the lake. But he got it. He puts it in the kayak and starts back—and as soon as he has it, everyone on the shore lets out this big cheer. And when Frank realizes he has an audience, he gets all flustered—and capsizes the kayak."

A sympathetic groan from the wedding guests had Frank grinning and shaking his head.

"He was drenched in icy lake water, trying to get back into a kayak that was rocking like crazy and being blown around by the wind—but he never let go of that dinosaur. And when he came out of the water, he was embarrassed that everyone had been watching him, and smiling through his chattering teeth, and I remember thinking, 'That is one of the good ones.'"

Steph met her groom's eyes, her own smile a little teary. "So I got him a towel and a cup of coffee. And I never looked back. So I just want to say thank you to that gust of wind, that kid and his dinosaur, and all the little twists of fate that got me here, marrying the best man I've ever met, who will practically drown himself in a freezing lake to make a kid smile. To Frankie."

The guests all echoed, "To Frankie!"

Kendall glanced up at Brody—the best man *she* had ever met—and her heart gave a little lurch. "I need to—go check on—" She didn't bother finishing the sentence, waving vaguely toward the kitchen area and slipping away before he could ask her for anything else. Like another dance. Or her entire freaking heart.

She was so in love with Brody James.

Which was incredibly inconvenient.

At some point, he was going to go back to being a rock-star ski god, and she couldn't go with him. She had managed for years, living in proximity to her dream, but to tag along after him like some kind of lift bunny instead of being the one on the slopes? That might crush her.

She ducked into the back rooms, veering past the kitchen, where the catering staff were cleaning up from dinner, and into the room she'd set up as the bride's sanctuary, since the other room was currently being used as a coat check area. The room wasn't frilly. She'd kept the rustic theme going back here, with a few of Alan's pieces providing romantic accents.

She sank down onto the sectional with the crisp new slipcover and reminded herself that much worse things had happened to her in her life than falling stupidly in love with a truly good man.

"You okay?" that good man asked a moment later, appearing in the doorway.

"They seem really happy," Kendall murmured.

Brody smiled, glancing over his shoulder back toward the main room. "Yeah. They do."

"You should go back to the tour."

Brody's head snapped around so fast she was surprised he didn't sprain something. "What?"

She hadn't meant to blurt that out, but now that she'd said it, it felt right. "You did what you came to do. You were the hero of Steph's wedding. But you belong on the slopes."

"I can ski here."

"You're a racer, Brody. Just like me. It would kill a piece of you to stop."

"You think that's all I am? A racer?"

"Stop it," she snapped at the edge in his voice. "You know that's not what I think. You're good at everything. You're a better manager than I am. You got this reno done faster—and cheaper—than I would have been able to do it. You can even lay tile *perfectly*. You can be whatever you want, but I know you, Brody. I know you love it. And I don't want you to make a decision based on fear or something else that you're going to regret for the rest of your life."

"It's not fear."

"Are you going to be happy with the way you left the tour if you never go back? Is that how you want to go out?"

"Maybe I do," he said curtly. "Maybe I'm sick of chasing gold. Maybe I just want to be with someone who doesn't give a shit if I'm the best. I thought you of all people would understand that."

"Don't do that. I don't want you to go back to being Mr. Ski God so I'll love you. I want you to go back for you. Because you need this."

"I think it's my call what I need."

"You ran away from your life!"

"And you didn't?"

"Hey…"

Both of them froze as a new voice spoke from the doorway. One of the servers stood there, looking uncertain.

Kendall quickly slapped what she hoped was a professional expression on her face. "Angie. Sorry. Is everything all right? Did you need me?"

"Um…" Angie's gaze flicked back and forth between Brody and Kendall. "The bride asked me to, um, find you two. She's about to throw the bouquet. She said I was supposed to tell you that she'll know if you don't try your hardest to catch it."

Kendall glanced at Brody. "We'll be right there. Thank you."

Angie retreated and Kendall took a deep breath, forcing herself toward calm. "I'm sorry," she said without looking at Brody. "It's none of my business what you decide to do."

"I think technically as both my boss and my girlfriend, my plans do affect you. I just didn't realize you were counting down the seconds until I left."

Her heart tried to trip over the word *girlfriend*, but Kendall kept her face calm. "I'm not. I don't want you to…" She caught the words, taking another breath. She would not allow herself to ask him to stay. "Even when I was my most jealous of you, I was always happy that you were doing what we always said we were going to do. I only want you to be sure. Before you walk away. I didn't get the chance to leave the sport the way I wanted. And I would never forgive myself, as your friend, if I was part of the reason you gave it up before you were really ready." She didn't want him to stay for her. She'd break up with him before she let that happen.

Brody's Adam's apple worked as he swallowed. "Okay."

She didn't know what that meant. Was he going back? Was he not mad at her anymore?

"We should go before Steph sends someone else after us."

"Right," Kendall agreed. But she stopped him with a hand

on his arm before he'd gotten more than two steps. "Are we okay?"

"Yeah," he murmured—but the light was out of his face, and Kendall felt like the worst sort of jerk for putting that look on his face at his sister's wedding.

"Brody…"

A pale echo of his usual sunny smile appeared. "I'm good, Kendall," he said. "I'm just realizing you're right, and I didn't want you to be."

Her heart stuttered. He was going back. He was leaving. It was what she'd just been badgering him to do, so why did her throat close and moisture suddenly prick at the back of her eyes? "Oh."

He caught her hand, gently tugging her back toward the main room. "Come on. You have some flowers to catch."

"Right," she murmured, trailing after him—and trying to escape the feeling that everything was coming to an end.

Chapter Twenty-Nine

Kendall caught the bouquet, but then Brody had known she would. There weren't that many single women at his sister's wedding, and Kendall had never met a competition she didn't want to win. But he had a hard time smiling when his sister smirked at him after Kendall snagged the flowers out of the air.

Steph was clearly thinking riding-off-into-the-sunset thoughts, but Brody's thoughts were on a much different track.

Kendall was right. His job here was done. He could keep managing the resort, but without the renovation and the weddings to plan, Kendall didn't really *need* him anymore. Especially since she'd been hinting that she wanted Michelle to take over when he left. He was almost in the way here.

And he had his own life to get back to.

She was right about that too. He had run away. That was never how he'd envisioned going out. These last few weeks, he'd told himself that he was trusting his instincts, that it was simply time to retire—but even if he was going to leave the sport, running away after a bad training run left a bad taste in his mouth.

And he missed it. Since he and Kendall had gone skiing last week, he'd found himself back up on the mountain every day. He wasn't sure he wanted to go back to competing, but he needed to at least consider it. To try. To revisit his old life and be *sure*, before he did anything else.

And that old life was only a few hours away. Lake Placid.

He could go tomorrow.

Not to compete—his conditioning was shot right now—but he could at least face his demons.

"Brody, my boy!"

Brody turned, surprised to find Kendall's dad hovering at the edges of the reception. Mr. Walsh didn't make a habit of attending the events, but there he was. "Mr. Walsh."

"Kurt, remember." He clapped Brody on the shoulder. "I had to come by and see for myself. Incredible what you managed to do with the place."

"It was all Kendall's vision."

"Of course," Mr. Walsh said, but the words were a little too glib.

Brody recalled all the times Kendall had said her dad didn't listen to her ideas. Maybe he just needed a nudge.

"She has a lot of amazing ideas for the resort," he said. "If you ask me, she's spot on, and you need to be trying to suck in adventurers, not business types. You don't want to compete with conference hotels close to major airports when you could be capitalizing on what you already have here—a great mountain. It's all about attracting the extreme sports addicts and nature lovers who can't get enough. The ones who will come back again and again—winter or summer. Build that loyalty."

Mr. Walsh grinned, still clasping Brody's shoulder and

giving him an affectionate shake. "You've got good instincts, young man. I think the resort business is in your blood."

"It's not me. It's all Kendall."

"You're too modest. None of this happened until you got here."

Brody had no idea how to tactfully point out that Mr. Walsh hadn't *let* anything happen until Brody got there—and then Kendall saved him by joining them.

"Dad. Is everything okay? What are you doing here?"

"Just came by to check on my investment."

"Did you see the numbers I sent you? We came in under budget. And we've already had several inquiries on the website."

"We'll talk about it tomorrow," her father promised. "Good work," he said, but he was looking at Brody when he said it, giving him one last squeeze on the shoulder before nodding to Kendall and heading back out the way he'd come.

Irritation flashed across Kendall's face.

"I told him it was all you," Brody said, trying to make it better. "He knows."

She shook her head. "It doesn't matter. You should enjoy the wedding. You've earned it."

The dancing continued behind her, and Brody knew she was right, but things felt off between them, and he didn't want to leave them that way—and a few minutes ago, his phone had buzzed with a text he'd been waiting for. Perfect timing.

"I have a surprise for you."

Her perma-frown deepened. "I'm really not in the mood for surprises, Brody."

"Please? Trust me. It's a good surprise."

She glanced over her shoulder, checking to make sure everything was going smoothly. The bartenders were keeping up—and at this point in the night, that was all her staff needed to do. She turned back to Brody. "Does it involve a public spectacle? Because I'm definitely not that girl."

"Nope. Just you and me. It's outside."

"Yeah, okay," she begrudged.

He caught her hand, the one that wasn't still holding the bouquet she'd caught, and led her out through the front door.

The railings on the porch were wrapped with white twinkle lights, and more lined the eaves of the building. That had been their last project, getting ready for the reception yesterday.

A pool of light from the floodlights illuminated the area directly in front of the lodge, where the sleigh had loaded and unloaded all night. Len and his horse were there now, but Brody just waved and guided Kendall past them. What he wanted to show her was up the hill, in the darkness outside the bright glow of the floodlight.

"These shoes aren't designed for snow," she grumbled—and Brody turned and swept her up into his arms, carrying her up the hill. Kendall snorted as he crunched through the snow, muttering something that sounded like "maiden on the moors."

Then what they were walking toward became visible—at first only an outline in the moonlight as their eyes adjusted. He knew the moment Kendall spotted it, her spine going stiff. She jerked a little more upright, then her gaze snapped to him, studying his face. "What is that? How did that get here?"

"Alan brought it," Brody explained. "I was hoping it'd arrive before the wedding—in time for Steph to get some photos in front of it—but Alan didn't finish it until today. I think he was prioritizing the projects you'd asked him for, for the back rooms. But when I talked to him this morning, I mentioned this was a surprise for you, and I think that lit a fire under him.

He insisted on bringing it down tonight and setting it up." He set her back on her feet, nervously watching her face. "Do you like it?"

Kendall frowned, always hard to read, and stared at her surprise.

It was the rusty old lift chair. Or it had been. Brody had gathered up all the pieces of the chair after it broke, driving them up to Alan and asking if they could be salvaged—and the artist had gone one better. He'd transformed them. It was still, very obviously, an old ski liftchair, but now it was also a freestanding glider—and a work of art.

Alan had welded on other bits of salvage that Kendall had brought him from the resort over the years, somehow shaping it all so it gave the impression of flames rising up the overhead bar.

"He called it *Fire and Ice*," Brody said, watching Kendall in the moonlight. "But I like to think of it as the Phoenix."

"It's…it's really good," Kendall said. The words weren't gushy, but she had to clear her throat, choked up, and Brody felt a glow of satisfaction seeping deep into his chest.

"Shall we?" He extended a hand toward the glider, and Kendall sat down beside him.

The cushions were cold, and neither of them was dressed for the outdoors, so Brody pulled her close, tugging her snugly against his side and wrapping both arms around her to give her as much of his warmth as he could. She set on his lap the flowers she'd caught and put her head on his shoulder.

They glided gently back and forth, both staring up at the mountain.

"I'm sorry about earlier," he murmured after a moment.

"So am I. I shouldn't have pushed—"

"No. You were right. I ran away, and I've been hiding here

ever since. Telling myself that I'm moving forward because I'm trying something different, when I'm really refusing to look too closely at why I ran."

"There's always sports therapists."

"Yeah. I should probably get one of those."

She nodded slightly. "So you're going back."

"I don't know." He rubbed her bare arms. "You could come with me."

She shook her head against his chest. "I can't."

"Why not? If you feel so trapped here, let's go. Let's get away."

"I owe him."

"What?" Brody challenged. "What do you owe him? Your entire life?"

She pulled away. "It's cold. We should go inside."

"Kendall."

She had stood up, but she turned to face him. "I can't trail after you and be your cheering section, Brody. I know things aren't ideal with my dad, but this is my home. This is who I am now."

"Are you happy?" he asked, echoing the question he'd asked her in the hot tub, months ago.

She met his eyes, repeating her original response, but this time the words were soft, aching. "Are you?"

And he realized, in perhaps the worst moment to figure it out, that he wanted to be the one who made her happy. He was in love with her.

On some subconscious level, he'd probably been in love with her for weeks. Every wild idea he'd come up with for his future life, every possible iteration of Brody without skiing—they'd all included Kendall by his side. He'd simply known that if he was going to be happy, she was the one thing that wasn't negotiable.

He loved her. He loved her perma-frown and the flash of excitement in her eyes when he challenged her. He loved the thrill of victory he got when he made her crack a smile, and the way she always told him exactly what she thought and never what she thought he wanted to hear.

She would always drive him crazy. They would always be sparking off one another like flint and steel—and he wouldn't have it any other way.

"I am," he said finally. "I love you, Kendall."

Her eyes flared wide. Her expression was almost horrified— but this was Kendall, and he knew better than to take that personally. "I…" She wet her lips, a thousand thoughts racing behind her eyes. "I have to go check on the wedding."

Not an ideal response, but not necessarily a problem. "Okay."

She started back toward the lodge, but only made it a few feet before she stopped, her heels sinking deep into the snow. She froze for a beat, then turned around. "I really like you, Brody," she said. "I lo—" She stopped short of saying it. "I really…do. Like you."

He couldn't stop his smile. She was so freaking gone for him. Kendall Walsh might hate the mushy feelings stuff, but he knew her. "Okay," he said, because saying *I love you too* would only set her off on a rant about how she hadn't said *that*.

His smile made her glower. Which only made him grin more.

"Cocky asshole," she muttered, turning and stomping back toward the lodge. Her heels pierced the snow, so with every step she dropped down into it, up to her calves.

"I can carry you back," he offered.

She casually flipped him off over her shoulder without looking back—and Brody laughed.

"I love you, Kendall Walsh!" he shouted.

He was a little surprised she didn't turn and fire the bouquet at his face like a fastball. Instead, she shook her head, still not looking back, and muttered to herself as she stomped away.

His arms were freezing where he'd rolled up his sleeves, and his dress shoes had not been designed for tromping through snow. His socks were wet, and it was too damn cold to be standing outside grinning like an idiot at the love of his life. But right now, there was no place he'd rather be.

Chapter Thirty

B rody James was in love with her.

Kendall's brain spun with that single thought on repeat as she walked along the icy sidewalk on her way to pick up Banner from Michelle. She'd stopped off at her room long enough to change into boots and grab a hoodie and a heavier jacket, since the temperature had dropped and her little blazer hadn't been cutting it.

The ski instructor lived in the old condos across the road from the resort. The complex had seen better days, but it was walking distance from the mountain. Kendall had considered getting a place there herself, now that the old lodge was being put to better use.

She couldn't picture Brody there.

Brody, who was in love with her. Though that might have been the wedding talking. People got carried away by romantic stuff at weddings.

But he hadn't seemed carried away. He'd seemed...happy. And she'd been happy. But she'd also been spinning. They'd *just* talked about him going back to the tour. He'd mentioned her leaving the resort—as if it was that simple. As if she could simply walk away.

She knocked on Michelle's door, her thoughts and emotions still an awkward stew beneath the surface. She heard Banner bark inside, rushing toward the door, and her lips quirked up. He was such a chaos monster, the adorable little pest.

Kendall immediately dropped to her knees to greet the furry little ball of chaos as soon as Michelle opened the door. "Hey, Trouble."

"Hey." The surprise on Michelle's face reminded Kendall that she'd forgotten to text that she was on her way.

"Sorry," Kendall said while Banner squirmed and tried to lick every inch of her face. "I should have let you know I was coming." Michelle waved her inside, and Kendall herded the dog's wiggling form with her. After she shut the door, she grimaced apologetically. "I promise I won't just show up unannounced again."

"It's fine," Michelle assured her. "But I would have told you not to make the trip. I'm happy to keep him tonight. In fact, I wanted to talk to you. About Banner."

Kendall winced, the dog still trying to lick every inch of visible skin. "Oh God, did he get your cellphone? I'll replace it—"

"No, nothing like that." Michelle looked uncomfortable. Which was unusual enough that Kendall's attention sharpened.

"Whatever he did, I'll pay for it—"

"Actually, I wanted to ask if you were adopting him."

Kendall shook her head as understanding hit. "No. I promise. I'm just fostering. I know I've relied on you a lot in the last few weeks, but Ally is going to find the perfect family for him, and in the meantime I won't be nearly as busy with the old lodge, so I won't have to ask you to watch him so much—"

"No, I like doing it," Michelle said. "In fact, I like it so much that if you aren't going to keep him, I thought I might."

Kendall blinked. "What?"

"Obviously, if you want him, I don't want to steal your dog, but if he's not yours, I've been thinking it's kind of nice, having him around."

Kendall was not an emotional person. So there was absolutely no excuse for her sudden and inexplicable urge to cry. "Right," she said, trying to keep all the chaos swirling around inside her beneath the surface. "That's…yeah."

"So I thought, if you don't mind, I could keep him tonight. Maybe keep him for a few days. As like, a test run?"

"He doesn't have his stuff here," Kendall protested. "And Ally has to vet all the adoption applications. You'd need to go through her."

"Of course. But maybe I could just keep him tonight. I did it when you had that other wedding."

The night she'd hooked up with Brody.

Kendall nodded, feeling like her stupid emotions were taking over, but trying to keep them off the controls for a few more minutes. "Yeah. Sure."

"I'll talk to Ally tomorrow," Michelle promised. "I just wanted to check with you first."

"I appreciate that."

Michelle frowned slightly, studying her. "Are you sure this is okay?"

Kendall forced her most composed expression onto her face, even going for a little smile. "I'm sure," she insisted. "You two have fun."

Then she crouched down, cuddling the dog, stroking his ears, telling him he was a good baby, telling him to be good for Michelle—and feeling like her heart was going to break right there on the spot when she walked out the door and he tried to come with her.

She heard a little whine, right as the door closed—as if he couldn't understand why she was leaving him behind—and all the things she'd been pushing down rose up.

It was too much. Tonight was too much. So she did the only thing she could think of. She texted Magda and Charlotte.

I have shoes. Help?

And because they were the best friends in the history of friends, they came.

"Brody told me he loves me," Kendall confessed as soon as her friends arrived at her hotel room—thankfully at the same time, because she wasn't sure she could have waited for them both to get there.

"That's good, isn't it?" Magda said as she perched on the bed. "Unless you don't feel the same…"

"He fixed my chair," Kendall blurted nonsensically.

"Okay…" Charlotte said, exchanging a glance with Magda.

Kendall didn't talk about the emotional stuff—which explained why she was so bad at it. She would support her friends and be tough love for them when they needed a wake-up call, but when it came to delving into her own feelings, she was much happier on the surface, snarking and keeping all the real stuff at bay. But she couldn't do that tonight.

"Is that his hoodie?" Magda asked.

Kendall looked down at herself. She hadn't even realized that when she grabbed a hoodie to go fetch Banner, she'd instinctively reached for the one that she'd stolen from Brody.

"Michelle wants to adopt Banner," she blurted out.

Magda blinked. "I'm not following."

Because Kendall was awful at this part. She paced as Charlotte and Magda watched her. "She's been watching him for me—when Brody can't and he can't be with me—but when I went to pick him up tonight, she asked if I was keeping him, and when I said I wasn't, she said she wanted to—"

"Which made you realize that you really want to keep Banner and Brody and you're completely in love with both of them? In different ways, of course."

Kendall sighed, relieved to have Charlotte state it so clearly. "Yeah. Pretty much."

Charlotte waved a hand like a queen granting clemency. "So you keep them both. Problem solved."

Except it wasn't that simple.

Was it?

"I told Brody he needed to go back to competing or he would regret it for the rest of his life, and I'm pretty sure he agreed with me, but I can't be that girl who follows her boyfriend from one ski resort to the next all winter long. Maybe if I hadn't wanted it for myself, I could do it, but..."

"So you do the long-distance thing during the season," Charlotte said. "He'll probably only compete for a few more years before he retires for real."

"And until then I do what? Wait for him here? Organizing weddings and stuck in the same place I've been for the last six years?"

"Do you not want to be in the same place?" Magda asked gently.

"I don't know what I want," Kendall said. "I thought I did. I thought I just wanted this place to be in the black again. I thought I wanted breathing room and a chance to prove to my dad that I was right—but I've done that. The wedding section of the website has only been up for a couple weeks, and already I'm getting calls. Two brides have already asked to reserve the old lodge for weddings this summer. I thought I was going to stay here and do this—and yes, it would suck when Brody went back to his regular life, but I was fine with that. Or I thought I was. But then Brody said he was leaving and Michelle wanted to take my dog and I realized I hadn't wanted to get attached to Banner because deep down I've been treating this as a phase and I never wanted to stay—but I can't leave the resort and I can't go with Brody—"

"Why can't you leave the resort?" Magda asked.

"Because of my dad? Because I owe him? Because I don't know how to do anything else?"

"Okay, that's just ridiculous," Charlotte said. "You can do anything. I've seen you. You didn't know anything about construction and you renovated that lodge in less than two months, and it looks freaking amazing."

"I just don't want to fail again," Kendall said.

"There it is," Charlotte agreed, pointing at her nose.

"But what if you don't?" Magda asked softly. "What would you do if you knew you wouldn't fail?"

"I don't know," Kendall admitted. Her failure had been so massive, so life-changing, that she'd lived the last six years in instinctive fear of something like that happening again. She'd squashed down her wants in favor of needs. Nothing had felt like a choice. It was all simply what needed to be done.

The resort had been safe. Even her frustrations had been familiar. She'd buried herself. Until Brody had shown up to remind her of who she used to be. And she'd realized that part of that person was still inside her.

She wasn't the same. She'd never be the girl who had started that run at the Olympic trials. But she might actually like herself better now. She and Brody would have been awful together when they were younger. Neither of them had known how to slow down, or when to quit. But now...

Balance.

It had taken her a long time to come to terms with everything. She'd been clinging to her regret, holding on to it even as she pantomimed moving on with her life. But these last couple months, something in her had let go.

She sank down between her friends on the bed. "Brody asked me earlier if I was happy, and the thing is, these last few weeks, I have been. I haven't been some stress zombie. I've *enjoyed* things again. And I don't think all of that was Banner. Or even Brody. I think it was just me, remembering what it feels like to...live."

Charlotte wrapped her arms around her. "Welcome back to the land of the living."

"But I still don't know what to do," Kendall said. "I don't want to leave the resort—not when things are just starting to go well—especially before I even know what I want or where I would be going. I don't want to go straight from living my life for my dad to living my life for Brody, but I also don't want to lose him. If he goes back to the tour and I don't see him for months at a time—"

"The season's almost over this year, isn't it?" Magda asked. "Don't borrow trouble."

"And talk to him," Charlotte insisted. "Isn't that what you told me when I was being ridiculous and self-sabotaging?"

"I'm much better at giving advice than taking it."

"Who isn't?" Magda said. "But you've got this. You already know he's wild about you. I'm pretty sure you can figure out the rest."

Chapter Thirty-One

Kendall's fist landed on Brody's hotel room door a little too hard. She hadn't meant to knock quite so loudly at quarter to one in the morning, but her nerves seemed to have short-circuited her control over the strength of her arm.

Charlotte and Magda had gone home fifteen minutes ago—after Charlotte had made her promise she was going to adopt Banner and have dozens of puppy play dates with their dogs. Kendall had planned to wait until morning to sort out her life—no good decisions were made after midnight—but there was one thing she'd needed to say to Brody or she'd never be able to sleep.

She stood in the hallway, barefoot, still wearing her black pantsuit and his hoodie. Her hair had long since fallen out of her French twist and was now loose and chaotic.

She was just starting to wonder if he was already asleep when the door suddenly opened.

Brody stood there, wiping a hand across his face like he was still half asleep, wearing a T-shirt and a pair of boxers. "Hey," he said, his voice scratchy. "You okay? I texted you after you picked up Banner, but when I didn't hear from you, I figured you'd fallen asleep."

"I didn't pick up Banner. I love you too," she blurted. "I just needed to tell you that. 'Cuz I didn't say it earlier."

The biggest, dopiest grin spread slowly across his face. He braced one arm against the doorframe, his bicep bulging. "I mean, I kind of figured," he said.

"You *figured*?" She glared at him. "Never mind. I take it back."

She started to turn on her heel, but Brody caught her arm, reeling her in. "Nope. No take-backs." He pulled her into his arms, still with that ridiculously smug grin. "You love me."

"I'm rethinking my life choices."

He grinned at her grumbling. Then he slid his hands into her hair, cupping her neck, and those laughing blue eyes sobered as they gazed into hers. "Truth: I am crazy about you."

She was slightly mollified by the naked feeling behind the words—okay, completely gooey for it. Her freaking knees were melting. "Likewise."

"And I dare you," he said, lowering his head to whisper the words against her lips, "never to stop."

She overslept.

Apparently that was what happened when a knot that you'd been holding tight inside yourself for half your life suddenly released.

That's what it had felt like, last night.

She'd been a coiled spring, winding tighter and tighter, year after year, and last night after she'd told Brody she loved him and he'd pulled her into his room and they'd hooked up—only it hadn't been hooking up, it had been making love, and when she climaxed, it was like that spring had suddenly released all the pent-up tension of her entire life.

She'd never felt anything like that. Of course, she wasn't sure she'd ever actually "made love" before. Sex had been fun and athletic and a total rush when it was good—but it had never been that. It had never been Brody and the look in his eyes and the clench of his jaw and the lines of strain on his neck and her loving every fucking cell of his body and him loving hers—and the relief of it, the release, had been intense.

She'd slept like the dead, the best sleep of possibly her entire life, and hadn't stirred until the sun was fully up and blasting over the mountain and through the window.

Brody was gone. For all she knew, he'd tried to wake her, but she didn't mind the absence. She kind of liked waking up alone, but knowing he had been beside her. She stretched and arched in the soft sheets, sighing happily. Her body felt rested and *soft* in a way she never remembered feeling before, but also limber and loose and ready to face the world. No wonder people were so dippy about love. This was freaking amazing.

She rolled out of bed and padded to the shower, singing one of the songs from the wedding last night to herself as she started her day.

It was Sunday and she was off, but she needed to go pick up Banner.

She would apologize to Michelle. She would offer to buy her any dog she wanted, but Kendall couldn't give up the little chaos monster. He was *her* trouble baby.

Some of her lovely relaxation evaporated as she swung by her room to get clean clothes and headed toward Michelle's condo, running the upcoming conversation through her head and dreading it.

But when she explained everything to Michelle, the ski instructor was all smiles.

"I completely understand. He really is your dog," Michelle said, watching Banner climbing all over Kendall in his joy at her arrival. "And, if I'm honest, I've been second-guessing a little. He ate the remote last night—and I really can't afford to replace my phone if he gets hold of it. And then this morning, with the promotion, I started thinking about the longer hours, and I really want to prove I can do this job right and not be distracted, so maybe this isn't the best time for me to be adopting, you know?"

Kendall blinked, looking up from Banner's contortions of joy. "Promotion?"

"Your dad called me himself. I guess Brody recommended me. Though I know none of this would be happening if not for all you've done for me—"

"They're making you resort manager." The job Kendall had been lobbying for her to get since last summer.

"Interim," Michelle clarified. "It's a trial thing. You don't think I'm too young, do you?"

"I think you're going to be amazing," Kendall assured her. She'd wanted this. She'd pulled for this. It was absolutely what was best for the resort—but her thoughts felt strangely jagged.

If Michelle was interim resort manager, then Brody was really leaving. But that wasn't what kept snagging at the edges of her brain. What made her heart beat loud in her ears.

She needed to talk to her father.

"You promoted Michelle Pham to resort manager?"

She found her father at the Sunday brunch buffet. He always ate there, believing it made him more approachable to the guests. He looked up from his eggs briefly before going back to his meal. "I thought you liked Michelle."

"I love Michelle. That's why I've been telling you to promote her since *July*. She was my first choice for the job."

"Then what are you upset about?" He smiled at a passing guest. "Sit down. You're making a scene."

Kendall yanked out the chair beside his and sat, knowing he wouldn't listen to her until she did.

Not that he ever listened to her. No matter what she did. No matter how she proved herself.

Her father stabbed a piece of sausage. "Brody told me this morning that he needs to go to Lake Placid, get back to competing, but he recommended Michelle to fill in for him. He's had his eye on her these last few weeks and he really thinks she has what it takes."

"*I* told you she has what it takes."

"And he agrees with you. He has a lot of great ideas. We talked this morning about ways to attract the adventurer clientele. Maybe even run the lifts for mountain bikers in the summers."

Which she had been begging him to do for *two years*.

Kendall just stared, her ears beginning to ring. "Are you kidding me right now? Am I being pranked? Is someone recording this?"

Her father frowned. "What are you talking about?"

"This is a joke, right? You're messing with me. You can't actually be this clueless."

Her father's expression darkened. "Kendall—"

She didn't let him get started on whatever scold he was about to deliver. "I can't do this anymore."

He sighed, turning back to his breakfast. "You're being childish—"

"It's like you can't even hear me when I talk. You act like everything Kevin says is genius—"

"Your brother has some good ideas."

"So do I!" Her father glanced around, uncomfortable with her volume. "You listen to Kevin. You listen to Brody, but when I speak, it's like I don't even exist. I have been the one here doing the work for years. I have been *killing* myself to make this resort profitable. I haven't had a *life* because I've been trying so hard for you, and you don't even *hear* me."

"Lower your voice."

"No. I never wanted this, but I have worked my *ass* off for you. I made a wedding venue out of a broken-down lodge and it's *gorgeous*. I turned us into a one-stop shop for bachelor and bachelorette adventures, weddings, and receptions. I made a plan to bring in more adventurers in the summers. I did that, not Brody, and you have never once said I did a good job."

His mouth twisted. "I'm sorry if I'm not praising you enough."

"I'm sorry too. I'm sorry I couldn't make it to the Olympics. I'm sorry I disappointed you. I wanted to pay you back—and make up for letting you down. I have been trying to apologize for getting hurt for the last six years, but I can't do that anymore. I'm sorry I'm not the golden child anymore. I'm sorry everything changed. I'm sorry I'm not who I used to be, but I'm finally thinking about who I *want* to be again—I'm finally looking around at what I want to change in my life and it's *this*. I love this resort. I love you, Dad. But I am *done*." She met his eyes, angry tears burning in hers. "I quit."

Her father shook his head, his expression indicating he was more annoyed by the disturbance than anything else. "I'm not going to indulge these dramatics."

She huffed out a soft, scoffing breath. She shouldn't have expected him to start listening to her now. "You don't have to. We're done here."

She stood and stalked out of the dining room, looking neither left nor right. She didn't want to know how many spectators had watched that scene. She didn't care to think about how much the staff would gossip or whether she'd disrupted a guest's vacation with her outburst.

That wasn't her problem anymore.

She'd been so convinced she'd failed him. So convinced, deep down, on a level she'd never wanted to admit, that the accident was her fault. That she should have been better. That she shouldn't have let it happen. That she should have been able to make it back. She'd been begging for forgiveness with every action for the last six years, trying to make it up to her father by running his resort, but it wasn't her fault.

It had happened. She'd probably never know why. The why didn't really matter anyway. She was never going to go back to who she'd been before. And she wasn't sure she'd want to if she could. She had a different kind of strength now. And now, finally, she had her balance.

Brody found her packing up her room while Banner bounded around, delighted by the frenzy of activity.

"There's a rumor going around that you told your dad to go to hell," he said after she'd opened the suite door.

Kendall moved back to the bed, shoving more clothes into her suitcase. "Not in so many words."

"You really quit?"

"I kind of lost it," she admitted. "He started gushing about how brilliant you were to suggest promoting Michelle and opening the lifts in the summer, and I saw red."

"I *told* him those were your ideas."

"I believe you," she said with feeling. "He just…honestly, I don't even know. I don't know what his problem is."

"I take it from the packing that you aren't regretting the decision."

"I feel like a one-hundred-eighty-two-room weight has been lifted off my shoulders," she said, feeling a little guilty for how true that was. "Maybe at some point I'll panic, but right now, I just feel *relieved*."

"You wanna come to Lake Placid?"

She paused in her packing, looking up at him. The question was mild. No pressure. And suddenly she did want to. The life she'd been pushing away, refusing to look at too closely, it was right there. And she wanted to immerse herself in it like a polar plunge. To see how it felt after all this time.

"Yeah. Let's go." She reached for a pair of jeans, shoving them into her suitcase. "You'd better pack. I'm not waiting around for you."

He smiled. "I could never keep up with you, Kendall Walsh."

Chapter Thirty-Two

The tour hadn't changed.

It was still the same buzz of activity. Still the sound of a dozen languages being spoken in every public area. In some of the European countries, there would be fans lined up trying to get autographs or selfies with their favorite athletes, but in the US, as he'd told his mother, alpine skiing wasn't as big a deal and the die-hard fans weren't as thick on the ground.

Brody still got recognized, though, as he and Kendall walked down the sidewalks of Lake Placid. Spectators and members of the World Cup community alike called out to him and welcomed him back, asking if he was skiing this week.

He dodged the questions, and Kendall stayed silent at his side as they made their way toward the chalet, where he'd arranged to meet with his team. He'd already tried asking her how she was doing, how it felt to be back, and she'd just shrugged, that frown line grooved between her eyebrows.

Banner zigged and zagged around them, trying to smell everything and forcing Kendall to keep him on a short leash so he didn't trip any passersby—and Brody was grateful for the distraction of the goofy dog.

He was incredibly nervous about what he'd decided to do.

His parents had come. They were there in the chalet when Kendall and Brody arrived, along with his agent. His coaches and trainer were the last to arrive. And then Brody had no excuse to keep up the small talk.

Kendall stood by the fireplace, keeping Banner entertained with a chew toy so he didn't start hunting for tasty cellphones. Brody took a seat, facing all the people who had supported him throughout his career, the people who had made him great, and said the words he'd been working up to all week.

"There's nothing wrong with my knee."

"That's great," one of his coaches said. "Did a doctor sign off on you competing this week?"

"There was never anything wrong with my knee," Brody clarified. "At least no more than usual."

His coach's mouth snapped shut—and his trainer, Alex, grimaced slightly, as if he'd known.

"I didn't know how to talk about what was going on with me, so I made up a reason that made sense. Something you all would accept. So I didn't have to admit the real problem was in my head." They all stared at him silently, but he made himself keep going. "I took Oskar's death a lot harder than I let myself acknowledge. I'd been so focused on beating him all those years that I never really looked around at my life, and when he was gone, I realized I had become an athlete and a brand and lost sight of who I was as anything else."

He slid a glance toward Kendall, who gave him a slight nod of encouragement. "I went back to Vermont to be with people who really knew me, and I realized I didn't actually have a life there to go back to. I needed to be home. To be something other than a skier for a while, to remember why I wanted it in the first place."

"And did you?" Reg asked. "Are you back? Or is this a thanks-for-the-memories speech?"

"I'm not entirely sure yet," he admitted. "I'm still figuring that part out. If I come back, it will be for next season. But I don't want skiing to be all that I am anymore. And maybe that means I won't be great. Maybe it has to be all you care about in order to be the best. But I want to be more than an Olympian. Even if that means I'm never an Olympian again. And I understand if you want to work with athletes who are more dedicated. Or younger." He grinned, trying to find some levity. "I'm getting old—especially my knees. The ride wasn't going to last much longer anyway. And if you're all pissed at me for bailing these last couple months, I get it. But if you're still willing to work with me, I'd really love to have you all on my team. And I promise to be more up-front in the future. No more running away."

All eyes turned to his head coach. Joe was a man of few words. He folded his arms, his eyes narrowed for a long moment before he nodded slowly. "Okay."

Brody smiled, relieved. "Okay."

They stayed for the competition. Brody had spoken one-on-one with each member of his team, and then he and Kendall headed up to the spectator section to watch the first event.

Banner was next to her, and Kendall kept half her focus on making sure he didn't bolt onto the course—which kept her from focusing too much on the racers themselves. It wasn't actually as painful as she'd thought it might be. She'd built it up in her head on the drive here, pretending for Brody that she was perfectly fine as she silently wondered what the hell she'd been thinking.

She'd blown up her entire life—quit her job, left her home, followed a guy back into a life that she'd always dreamed of but would now always be out of reach. She'd thought she'd be a mess, internally. But now that she was here…it wasn't so bad. It was just a competition. And she knew competitions.

The sound of cowbells jangling made her feel right at home. She recognized a few faces, and even more names. It was familiar and sort of exciting. She might not actually mind coming to the competitions when Brody went back to racing.

And she was pretty sure it was a *when* not an *if.*

He was rapt on each run, his body twitching and jumping as if he was skiing with them. She was six years and a thousand disappointments removed from this life, but it was still in him.

After one run when his entire body lurched forward as the racer crossed the finish line, Kendall leaned close to him. "You can't stand it, can you? You're dying to be up there."

Brody rocked back, pretending he hadn't been leaning in with all his might. "No, of course not."

She snorted. "You think I can't tell that the only reason you haven't already grabbed a pair of skis and tried to talk your way onto the start list is because you're out of shape and afraid of embarrassing yourself?"

"I wouldn't say *afraid.*"

Kendall smiled. God, she loved him so stupidly much. "It's okay if you want to go back, Brody. It's okay to love it. To miss it."

"I didn't realize how hard it was going to be to sit and watch," he admitted, then something shifted on his face. "Are you okay?"

"It's not hard for me. It's just scar tissue now. I've been borrowing trouble, as Magda likes to say. Making it bigger in my head than it needed to be."

"Are you sure? I don't want to torture you every time I have a race." He took her hand. "I love you more than winning."

"Oh my God, the cheesy romantic mush." Kendall rolled her eyes, grinning up at him. "I love you almost as much as winning."

A laugh burst out of him, and Kendall smiled again, linking her arm through his.

"And one of the things I love is that you can't stand being here and not racing. I wanna watch you win, Brody James. And yes, I'm probably gonna be a mess. I'll be worried about you every time you race—which seems like fair karmic payback for all the panic I gave poor Laurie as a teen."

"We don't have to decide now. Next season doesn't start until October."

"True," Kendall agreed. "Which raises an interesting question."

Another racer came into sight and Brody's body tensed, but he still asked, "What question?"

"What the hell do we do until then?"

Before we say "I do,"
we want to see you!

Please join us for a rehearsal dinner
honoring the marriage of

Alba

Regina Lopez

&

Kevin

Chandler Walsh

on Friday 5th April at 7pm

Villa Berulia
107 E. 34th St., New York, NY

Send all RSVPs by email to Kevin at
kwalsh@gscfinancial.com

Chapter Thirty-Three

Kendall wasn't sure she'd gone a full month without seeing her father in her entire life.

In the last few weeks, she'd kept up with Michelle, answering her questions and making sure her transition to manager—which was much more abrupt than any of them had intended—went smoothly. She corresponded with Laurie, who had emailed her a week after she left and started asking questions about the wedding and events coordination. Apparently the web form had been getting a lot of inquiries, and Laurie had decided it was time she took a more active role in the resort.

Kendall answered texts from nearly every employee at the resort—making sure she was okay and asking if she'd really thrown water in her father's face and stormed out of the restaurant. She assured everyone that she was well and ignored the legend of her dramatic exit as it continued to grow.

She had a group chat with Mags and Charlotte, both of whom she'd stopped off to see before she and Brody left town—but she hadn't said a word to her father. She hadn't even opened his emails or texts after the first one, which had told her to stop being childish. She might have taken his call, but he hadn't tried calling, and everyone else who was corresponding with her carefully avoided mentioning him. Even Laurie.

After the competition in Lake Placid, she and Brody had gone on vacation, her first since she stopped skiing. Kendall had wanted sun and sand but also wanted to bring Chaos Banner along and hadn't been sure how he would fare on a long plane ride, so they ended up driving all the way to Key West.

The road trip took over a week as they wended their way southward, slowed somewhat by their tendency to spot road signs and dare one another to check out the local attractions. When they finally made it as far as they could go without falling into the ocean, Brody found them a little condo a block from the beach, and they did absolutely nothing for ten days straight.

It was heaven—for the first four days. Then Kendall's brain had recharged enough that she started worrying about what she was going to do with the rest of her life.

She and Brody talked for hours about the future and what they wanted it to look like. They both still saw themselves in Pine Hollow, for at least part of the year. Kendall didn't want to start over, start a life anywhere else, and Brody loved the idea of Pine Hollow as his home base to live and train when he wasn't actively at competitions.

But Kendall wasn't sure she really wanted to be a wedding planner or go back to working at the resort. She didn't *hate* the weddings, but what she really loved was the adventure packages she'd been able to organize.

After about a week of sun and sand, Kendall realized she was daydreaming about starting her own business. Being her own boss. Maybe she could work out a partnership or a contract with the resort to provide packages for their guests, but she wanted this next thing to be *hers*.

By the time they started driving north again for Kev's wedding, she'd already started working up a business plan and researching small business loans.

She'd always been good with spreadsheets.

Brody volunteered to be her first employee—during the off-season, when he wasn't training.

She could think of a thousand reasons that was a terrible idea. Mixing business and pleasure was notoriously dicey. People would think it was his idea and give him all the credit. It would be an absolute *mess* if they ever broke up. And if the business failed, she didn't want one of them blaming the other.

But the last few months had proven they worked well together. And she couldn't think of anyone else she would rather crash and burn with.

They had a plan. One she felt hopeful and excited about for the first time in years.

But before they could go back to Pine Hollow, find a place to live, and get started on their next adventure, they had to go to her brother's wedding in New York.

Which meant coming face-to-face with her father at the rehearsal dinner.

Kendall had warned Kev that she and her dad weren't really speaking and promised not to make a scene in front of his new in-laws, but she had no idea what her father was thinking.

Which was new. She'd *always* known what her dad wanted from her—whether that was as a coach or a boss or a parent. Not knowing felt wrong. And entirely too nerve-wracking as she and Brody got dressed and headed to the dinner.

Brody had found a pet sitter for the evening, and they

dropped Banner off on their way. Then they walked hand in hand toward the restaurant Kev had picked for the rehearsal dinner. The noise of the city was foreign, but strangely comforting. Millions of people going about their lives—all of whom couldn't care less about Kendall and her personal drama.

"Do we need a safe word?" Brody asked as they neared the restaurant. "Something you say and I suddenly feign food poisoning to get us out of there?"

"Pumpernickel?" Kendall suggested.

"Probably best to pick something not food related. In case they have pumpernickel appetizers."

Kendall grinned at the ridiculousness of an Italian restaurant with pumpernickel hors d'oeuvres. "Machete?"

"Perfect."

They'd reached the restaurant, and he opened the door for her. The host directed them toward the private event dining room, and Kendall headed in that direction. Brody moved with her, his hand resting lightly on the small of her back.

They entered the room and a wall of laughter and loud talking hit them. Kevin's bride came from a large family—and they apparently all talked at full volume. Kendall didn't see her father, but she did see a dozen smiling faces, and some of her tension unknotted.

"Kendall! Brody! You're here!" Kevin shouted over the din as soon as he spotted them.

He hugged them both, looking almost giddy—and then smacked Brody on the shoulder. "I thought I told you to stay away from my sister."

"You told me not to break her heart. And I don't plan to."

Kev arched his eyebrows and looked at Kendall, who just shrugged. "He's completely obsessed with me."

Kevin snorted. "I know the feeling. Come on. You've gotta meet Alba."

He dragged them into the crowd in search of his bride to introduce them. After two minutes of conversation, Kendall could see why Kevin was so besotted—and she had a feeling she and her new sister-in-law were going to be good friends. When Kevin noticed Kendall glancing around, on alert for signs of her father, he squeezed her arm.

"Don't worry. Alba seated him all the way on the other side of the room," he assured her—and Kendall felt a stab of guilt.

"I'm sorry," she murmured. "I know you don't want drama at your wedding."

She appreciated the accommodation, because she really didn't want to spend the entire night defending her choices to her father—but she also hated that it was necessary. She was going to have to talk to him. Especially if she was heading back to Pine Hollow.

Kev shrugged. "You and Dad have been butting heads your entire life. It wouldn't be a family gathering without a few glares. And honestly? I'm proud of you for telling him to go to hell. It's about time."

"I didn't actually…" Kendall protested, but Kev was already being pulled away to greet more guests.

Kendall and Brody found their place cards and sat down to dinner shortly thereafter—and once everyone was seated, she immediately spotted her father and Laurie.

He hadn't seen her yet—his back was mostly to her—but Laurie had. She made a little fluttering wave with her fingers, which of course made her father turn to see who she was waving at. Kendall expected a glower or a disapproving frown. She expected the looks she used to get when she was a teenager who had misbehaved. But there was no *what do you have to say for yourself, young lady* glare. He looked…not sad exactly. Or remorseful. It was more restrained than that. Almost resigned.

Brody's hand closed over hers on the tablecloth, and she jerked.

"You okay?" he whispered. "Do we need to break out the machete?"

She shook her head, shooting him a grateful glance. "I'm good," she assured him as the woman on his other side leaned forward to ask how they knew the happy couple.

Kendall shoved all her feelings about her father into that convenient box on that shelf inside her head. She wouldn't leave them there forever, but right now, she needed to be focused on Kev and Alba and getting to know her new family. So for the next hour, that's exactly what she did.

She socialized. She smiled. She told embarrassing stories about her brother. And whenever she started to feel a little off-balance or overwhelmed, Brody would take her hand under the table or jump in with *his* most embarrassing Kev stories until her smile relaxed and became real again.

"You are so done dealing with people, aren't you?" Brody asked under his breath as their dessert plates were being cleared.

"Does it show?"

"Only to me."

The other guests were perfectly lovely people and Brody made everything fun, but Kendall wasn't a people person and was tired of being *on*. "I'm gonna find a bathroom. I'll be right back."

Brody nodded in acknowledgment, and she slipped away.

The main dining area was crowded, and Kendall bypassed it, and the bathrooms, heading instead toward the patio area that wasn't yet in use this early in the season. She stepped outside and took a deep breath, tipping her face up to the skyscrapers around her. She closed her eyes, breathing in and out again, the smells of the city thick around her.

Before she could open her eyes, a soft feminine voice spoke behind her. "Hello, sweetheart."

Kendall turned to face Laurie, unsurprised that she'd been followed. "Hey."

Her stepmother closed the distance between them, enfolding Kendall in her arms. She was barely five feet tall, several inches shorter than Kendall and built like a stiff breeze would knock her over, but she'd always given the best hugs.

"How are you?" Laurie asked, in her gentle way, as soon as they separated.

"I should be asking you that question. I've been on a beach for the last two weeks while you've been dealing with my mess."

"It wasn't a mess, and I've discovered I'm actually very good at wedding coordinating. I think I like it quite a lot."

"I'm glad."

"Though I would welcome a partner if you wanted to come back."

Kendall winced. "Brody and I are talking about coming back to Pine Hollow, but I don't think it's good for me to work for Dad anymore."

Laurie nodded, without an ounce of surprise on her face. "It's hard for him to admit when he's in the wrong. He knows it, if that helps. But that just makes him beat himself up. He pulls it all inside, mad at himself. He…well, it's not my place to say."

"I know. And I don't want you to feel like you're caught in the middle. I know you've gotta take his side."

"I don't have to do anything of the sort. Not when he's being an idiot," Laurie said, a twitch of amusement around her lips. "I know you don't think of me as a mother. You never wanted to let me in, even when you were thirteen. But I love you, and your brother. And I don't always take your father's side—even if I don't disagree with him in front of you. I learned long ago that countering him in public only makes him dig in—he's so stubborn. Kind of like someone else I know," she said, gently nudging Kendall's elbow. "But I work on him, behind the scenes. I talk up your ideas. I always thought of us as kind of a team." She grimaced. "But I can see how you wouldn't see that. I never really showed you. There were a lot of things I didn't want to say in front of you. I didn't want to negatively impact your relationship with your father, but I think I was too careful about that."

"It's all right—"

"It isn't," Laurie insisted. "Your father has his own apologies to make, but this is mine. I should have made sure you knew I was always behind you."

"I understood why you went along with him. He's your husband."

Laurie looked at her, then seemed to come to a decision. "I almost left him, after your accident."

Surprise sharpened her attention. "What?"

Laurie caught her hand. "We almost lost you. I couldn't bear the idea of you racing again. I made him promise that he wouldn't push you to go back, but he just kept pushing. We almost didn't come back from that."

Kendall didn't remember any of that, but she'd been in her own world then. "How did you?"

"You stopped. He stopped pushing for the comeback. And I felt like I could breathe again."

"I'm sorry," Kendall murmured. "I didn't know things were ever rocky between you two."

"Because I hid it from you. But I'm going to try not to do that anymore."

Kendall met her gentle eyes. "I still don't think I can work at the resort."

"I know. I hope you come back to Pine Hollow so we can see you, but I just want you to be happy, kiddo. That's all I've ever wanted. Happy and safe—but that's a lot to ask from a Walsh."

Kendall smiled. "Yeah. Safe wasn't really my priority."

"Got that from me."

Kendall spun at the deep voice. Her father stood at the entrance to the patio, his expression almost tentative.

"Kendall," he grunted.

"Dad."

Chapter Thirty-Four

Laurie crossed to her husband's side as Brody appeared behind him, looking ready to tackle Kendall's father if necessary.

Laurie frowned at her husband meaningfully and silent communication passed between them for several moments before Laurie made a little huffing sound and turned to face Kendall. "Your father has something he'd like to say to you," she announced.

Her father looked at Laurie like a petulant child being called on the carpet, but when she furrowed her eyebrows at him, he relented and spoke to Kendall's shoes.

"I'm sorry," he muttered.

He'd never said those words to her before. They were sort of revolutionary. Kendall wanted to forgive him, but something stopped her from letting him off the hook. "You can't even say that to my face."

He met her eyes briefly, but couldn't hold the contact, slanting his eyes to the side.

"Kurt," Laurie said gently, and he swallowed hard.

Kendall shook her head. "If I'm such a disappointment that you can't even look at me—"

"Don't say that," he snapped.

"What should I say?" Kendall challenged. "At first I thought I was imagining things, but you never *look* at me. What am I supposed to think?"

"It's not you," he growled. "I mean, it *is* you." Kendall scoffed. "It's my fault," he snapped. "I can't look at you without feeling sick because it was my fault."

He said it like it was some big confession, but Kendall shook her head, confused. "What was your fault?"

"The accident. Your accident. I'm the reason you got hurt."

Kendall snorted. "Because you taught me to ski?"

"Because I made you go. That morning. Of the trials."

"What?"

"You said your knees felt funny, and I didn't listen to you. I told you it was nerves and to ski as fast as you could. Push the course. Get every fraction of a second you could going into the slalom. I made you go, and you nearly died."

"Dad…"

"And then you didn't even remember. You didn't blame me, and I couldn't tell you it was my fault. So I put everything I had into getting you back out there. Getting your dream back for you. And when you couldn't compete anymore, I knew it was my fault. I was the only one who knew, but every time I looked at you, it was like you were judging me and blaming me. I wanted you at the resort. I wanted to help you get on your feet again. But you had all these ideas, all these things you wanted to change—telling me I was doing everything wrong. And I didn't want to hear it—I couldn't hear it from you. Every time I heard your voice, I felt guilty. So I just blocked it out."

Kendall stared at her father, her mouth hanging open. She hadn't seen any of that coming. She'd kind of assumed he was an incurable misogynist—and that might still be part of it—but the rest of it. All that stuff about her accident...

"It wasn't your fault."

They were words she hadn't been able to say to herself two months ago, let alone him. But now she had finally made peace with everything that had happened that day.

"You don't remember—"

"I don't need to. I know who I was, Dad. No force on earth was going to stop me from going down that hill as fast as I could. It was the Olympic trials. It was my *shot*. My knees were probably wobbly because it meant so much. But you didn't make me go. You couldn't have stopped me."

He shook his head. "I trained you to take risks. To push the envelope."

"You think I wouldn't have done that anyway? We take these risks over and over again, until they become normal. Until they stop feeling like risks. And we ride that knife's edge as long as we can. Until we fall. But I don't blame you, Dad. Not for that. But for freezing me out and pushing me away for six years— that's the part I need an apology for."

He swallowed hard, nodding.

"At first I didn't even notice," Kendall admitted. "I was totally wrapped up in mourning what I'd lost. The resort gave me something to do. It gave me purpose, and I was grateful to you for that. And I felt so guilty that you'd siphoned money from the resort into my recovery. I needed to make it up to you.

But it was like as soon as I stopped skiing, I stopped being your daughter and became an annoying employee."

"That was never my intention. I just didn't like feeling the way I felt every time I looked at you—"

"So you avoided me. And ignored me. And I got madder and madder and kept trying to prove myself and earn your love. And nothing ever worked."

"You don't have to—" Her father choked, his mouth twisting, and looked to the side. Moisture glistened in his eyes as he gritted out, "I am very sorry, Kendall. You have never had to earn anything. And I, ah…" He cleared his throat roughly. "I love you very much."

She pursed her lips to hold back her own emotion, nodding, before she composed herself enough to answer, "I love you too."

They were standing half a patio apart, but it was the closest to her father she'd felt in years.

"You two." Laurie sniffled, shaking her head and openly crying. "You're entirely too alike." Laurie walked forward, wrapping Kendall in a hug. She'd been holding herself rigid, but no one could stay rigid in the face of Laurie's warmth. She softened, and her chin wobbled all over again.

When Laurie pulled away, she looked up into Kendall's face. "I'm sorry too. I didn't know what was going on with your father, but I knew we were putting too much pressure on you at the resort these last few years," she explained. "It became a habit to rely on you. Whatever needs doing, Kendall will do it. And it took me far too long to realize what a burden we'd put on you. And how unhappy you were."

"It took me a long time too," Kendall admitted. She'd needed a chaos monster dog and a conflicted ski god to blast into her life.

"Will you be back?" her father asked gruffly, coming to stand closer but still not touching her.

Laurie went to his side, and Kendall glanced over to where Brody had been standing. He was still there, though he now looked uncertain if he was in the way. Kendall waved him closer. "Brody and I were thinking we might come back to Pine Hollow. Set up a company running adventure tours. We could offer our services to the guests at the resort, but I don't think I want to work there anymore. I think I might just want to be your daughter."

Her father nodded, but he was frowning at Brody, who had slipped his arm around Kendall's waist. "Are you two…?"

Kendall blinked, almost laughing. "Are you seriously the only person at the entire resort who didn't know we were dating? We literally ran away together."

"Well, you both left at the same time, but how was I to know…? How long has this been going on?"

Laurie patted his arm. "Don't worry, dear. I'll explain everything. But we should probably get back in there before Kevin wonders why his family abandoned his rehearsal dinner."

"Oh God, Kev," Kendall groaned, reminded of why they were actually here. "Yeah."

Her parents headed inside, but Brody tightened his arm slightly around Kendall's waist, and she glanced up at him. He waited until they were alone on the patio again to murmur, "You good?"

And then her stupid eyes were wet all over again as she nodded. "Thank you. For being here. And I promise, from now on, no more family drama."

"You know I don't actually mind the drama as much as you do. It keeps life interesting." He grinned. "Tomorrow I was going to dare you to start a feud with one of Kevin's new sisters-in-law. She was bragging about her plans to catch the bouquet, and I think we both know who's actually going to catch it."

Kendall smiled, shaking her head. "You're a bad influence, Brody James."

"Devil on the shoulder, at your service." He offered her his arm, and she took it. They started back toward the rehearsal dinner. "You know, you keep catching those flowers, I'm gonna start to think it's a sign."

"A sign I'm competitive?"

He hummed. "You ever thought about it? Getting married again?"

She looked up at him, arching one brow. "Are you asking?" she teased.

But he wasn't smiling. "I might be."

Kendall's jaw fell. "Brody. We've been together for like two seconds."

"And since you were seven. But yeah, I see your point. Wouldn't want to rush things."

"Don't go getting wedding fever on me. I already got married on a dare once."

"Yeah. But he wasn't me." They'd been strolling toward the private dining room and were almost there, but Brody seemed completely unaware of the sound of a toast being made drifting down the hallway. "I've skied on mountains all over the world, and yours was always my favorite. You know why?"

"Because we have the best runs?"

"Nope. Not even close. Because of you. Because you made me feel more alive. More daring. More myself. Because you made me want to be better. Even when we were kids. You were the reason I loved racing before I even knew why. And I want to spend my life trying to be a better man, for you. So I'm not daring you to marry me. I'm not even asking. I'm just tossing it out there as an idea. Something to think about." He stopped outside the doorway to the private dining room. "I'm crazy about you, Kendall Walsh. And I really like *us*."

"I like us too," she agreed. "And I will think about your very interesting proposal."

A cheer went up from the rehearsal dinner as the toast ended and Brody grinned. "Excellent. Now how can we mess with your brother?"

Kendall was laughing as she walked back into the rehearsal dinner. She wasn't quite ready to say yes out loud, but a life with Brody James sounded like a lot of fun.

They might crash and burn. There were no guarantees in life. It wouldn't be easy, and there would always be the risk that it wouldn't work out.

But it might.

Good things could happen too. And however it turned out, she was sure as hell going to enjoy the ride.

Epilogue

You have to admire the courage of this young man, fighting his way back from a knee injury that derailed his season two years ago to be number one in the world rankings going into tomorrow's trials—"

"*I admire the fight in him, but I don't think we can still call Brody James a 'young' man, which is why he's not even on my list of picks to make it to the Olympics this year. He just doesn't have that fire. He's had an epic season so far—but it's early and a lot of our real contenders weren't even at those competitions—*"

Kendall smacked the remote, shutting off the television with more force than necessary. "Assholes. What do they know?"

Brody came into the living room, carrying Banner like he was a monkey, with his paws draped over Brody's shoulders. "Why were you watching that?" he asked, his eyes glinting, amused as always by her grumpiness, which had only increased now that she was pregnant.

"What are you doing?" Kendall demanded. "If you pull something the night before the trials lugging that dog around—"

"I'm not that old," Brody grumbled as he carried Banner toward the bathroom. "He got into something. Smells like fish. I figured you didn't want his grubby paws all over your pretty floors."

The alpine skiing Olympic trials were in Stowe this year, only about an hour away, so Brody had elected to spend the night before at their place in Pine Hollow. They'd lived in a rental condo in Charlotte's complex for a while until the perfect place finally came on the market. A three-bedroom A-frame five minutes from the resort, with exposed rafters and hardwood floors that reminded them both so much of the old lodge they hadn't been able to resist.

"I can do that," Kendall insisted. "You should be resting."

"Sit," Brody ordered. "I've got this."

Kendall sat—glaring at her tiny bump of a stomach. She was barely showing. Mostly just throwing up and feeling like crap all the time. She was a little freaked out by the whole impending parenthood thing, but she kept reminding herself that it was a new adventure.

She glanced down at the tattoo on her left wrist. It read simply DARE. A match to the TRUTH that was on Brody's right wrist. They'd gotten them on their honeymoon in Mexico. Brody liked to tell people that his was a reminder to always be true to himself and hers was a reference to her business, Dare Me Adventures, but she was pretty sure most people didn't believe him.

The business had really taken off—thanks in part to the shirtless video Brody had filmed for her after she'd trounced him at ax throwing one night. They'd become a draw for daredevils but still got most of their business from guests at the resort who wanted to step a bit out of their comfort zone.

Kendall's favorite events had turned out to be the bachelor

and bachelorette parties—but that might be because she got to plan them with Laurie, who had taken over the events side of the resort business and made it thrive.

She reached for her phone, moving as little as possible lest she throw up her prenatal vitamins, and flicked through some messages.

"People are sending you good luck," she shouted to Brody over the sound of him wrestling with Banner in the tub. "They know you're in distractions lockdown and ignoring your phone, so they're all texting me."

She flipped through a few more messages. "Mags got another audition interview for *Cake-Off*," she called.

Banner bolted out of the bathroom, dragging a towel with him, and romped all over the room in his victory dance before throwing himself onto the rug and wriggling wildly on his back.

Brody emerged more slowly—all of his clothing soaked to the skin. "Good for her."

Kendall's lips twitched, but she refrained from commenting on his drenched appearance. "Hopefully the third time's the charm."

Brody stripped off his wet shirt, and Kendall shamelessly ogled him until he said, "I heard Mac is going out for it too."

She groaned. "I'm not sure if I should never tell Magda that, or if I should tell her right before her interview to fire her up. She would probably sneak into his place and murder him in his sleep if he got in and she didn't."

"You ever going to tell me why those two hate each other?"

"Not my story to tell. Ask Mags. Or Mac."

"I have. No dice."

Brody had become friends with the diner owner after he had joined George's poker group, though Brody hadn't been to a game in months, too focused on training. He had better work-life balance these days, but this year he seemed to want to win more than ever.

He returned from the bedroom in dry pajama pants and a T-shirt, flinging himself onto the couch beside her—which a still-damp Banner took as his cue to come over and try to crawl on top of both of them.

The wet dog smell had her gagging, and she had to run to the bathroom again. Brody followed and held her hair back, then sat on the bathroom floor with her as she rested her head against the cool tile wall.

"Truth or dare?"

She opened one eye, glaring at him. "Do I look like I'm in the mood for a dare right now?"

"Truth it is." He linked their hands together, lining up their tattoos. "Are you happy?"

"Right at this very instant?" she asked skeptically—since there was still a chance she was going to puke again, even though she'd *just* thrown up.

"Right this very instant," he confirmed.

"Are you?" she countered. "With all the pressure of compet-ing again?"

"Ecstatic. I just needed a new reason to want it." He looked at her meaningfully. "Your turn."

She glared at him. But she'd promised him truth. It had even been in their wedding vows. And he knew better than to ask if he didn't want an honest answer.

Was she happy?

She was pregnant, which scared the shit out of her. He was skiing tomorrow, which she'd discovered always tied her stom-ach in knots even when she wasn't gestating a human. She still worried about her work—though it was sort of a good worry now, because it was hers. Her dad still drove her nuts, but when they yelled at one another now, it felt different. Sort of cathartic. She was never going to ski competitively again, but she'd stopped looking back.

The future was scary as hell. She was petrified she was going to be a horrible mom. And equally scared she was going to lose who she was again, building her life around the tiny person and sacrificing the most daring part of her.

Her body kept coming up with new symptoms to make her miserable. Her back hurt constantly. And yet...

"Never been happier."

"Really?"

She gently tapped his tattoo. "Truth."

Kendall James wasn't a romantic. She didn't go in for the sappy feelings stuff. But as she sat on the bathroom floor, holding her husband's hand, she decided again that sometimes the best thing you could do was risk your heart.

"No risk, no reward," she murmured.

"Hmm?" Brody asked.

"Nothing. Just thinking about shoes."

DON'T MISS LIZZIE'S NEXT BOOK, COMING LATE 2024!

ACKNOWLEDGMENTS

Before I was born, my parents made the move from Hawaii to Alaska, and from bodysurfing to downhill skiing. They put me on my first pair of skis while I was still in preschool, and I never looked back. When I was small, my older sister would ski backward down the hill in front of me to teach me to snowplow, and when I got a little bigger, my brother was constantly daring me to go faster. Some of my strongest memories are of skiing at our local mountains, trying to squeeze in one last run before my lift ticket expired at the end of the day—and those who are familiar with the Alyeska ski resort in Girdwood, Alaska, may see some similarities to Kendall's resort. So a big thank-you goes to my entire family for skiing with me all those years, and inspiring much of this book.

As much as I love skiing, it can be a dangerous sport, and I also need to thank Michael Phelps and the *Weight of Gold* documentary on HBO, for shining a light on the mental health challenges facing elite athletes. Oskar's story is not based on any particular athlete, but I did draw on several of the stories included in that film.

I would also be remiss if I didn't thank the incredible team at Forever who made this book so much better and helped to launch it into the world: Junessa, Sabrina, Lori, Stacey, Joelle, Dana, Leah, and the rest of Team Forever. I am so fortunate to be able to work with you, and benefit from your awesomeness. Thanks also to my agent, Michelle Grajkowski, and her team at Three Seas.

Special thanks to my fabulous friends who read my early drafts and listened to me talk (ad nauseum) through plot holes and character arcs—Kim Law, Kris, Kali, and Leigh. And my mom, who remains determined to hold her position as my number-one fan—and who was remarkably forgiving when my golden retriever, Darby, dug a hole through the carpet in our dining room when I was a teen.

And finally, thanks to all the readers who have fallen in love with the Pine Hollow series. I hope you enjoyed returning to my little imaginary town—and yes, I promise, Mac and Magda are next.

ABOUT THE AUTHOR

As a lifelong dog-lover, **Lizzie Shane** is a sucker for books about pups dragging their humans into love. Born in Alaska to a pair of Hawaii transplants, she graduated from Northwestern University and began writing romance novels in an attempt to put a little more love into the world. An avid traveler, Lizzie has written her way through all fifty states and over fifty countries. Her books have been translated into seven languages, and her novel *Sweeter Than Chocolate* was adapted into a Hallmark Channel Original movie, but her favorite claim to fame is that she lost on *Jeopardy!*

Learn more at:
LizzieShane.com
Twitter @LizzieShaneAK
Facebook.com/LizzieShaneAuthor
Instagram @LizzieShaneAK